MIRRORS

KARL C. KLONTZ

To my former students in the
Master of Public Health (MPH)
degree program.

The most important failure was one of imagination.
Imagination is not a gift usually associated with bureaucracies.
It is therefore crucial to find a way of routinizing,
even bureaucratizing, the exercise of imagination.

—The 9-11 Commission Report.
Final Report of the National Commission
on Terrorist Attacks Upon the United States,
Official Government Edition

Prologue

THE LATE THOMAS "Tip" O'Neill, Speaker of the U.S. House of Representatives from 1977 to 1986, often reminded others that, "All politics is local." It was his father who uttered the words first —shortly after Tip O'Neill had lost a close race for a seat on the Cambridge, Massachusetts City Council, his first bid for political office. After the defeat, the aspiring politician acknowledged that he had spent too much time campaigning citywide without locking in votes from his own neighborhood first.

All politics is local. Had I known ...

Day 1. Late July ...

TWENTY CHICKEN PENS bristled in the sun on wooden stilts. I opened a door to one and extracted a chicken. Wrapping it with a towel to access the underside of a wing, I cleaned a vein with alcohol before drawing enough blood to run a test for antibodies to West Nile virus. I'd drawn blood from other flocks in like fashion every week since mosquito season began that summer in a program to detect West Nile virus in areas surrounding Washington, D.C. A positive test would mean chickens had been infected with the virus by mosquitoes, which, in turn, could infect humans, an event that would prompt health officials to alert the public.

As I compressed the vein following the blood draw, my cell phone rang.

"What is it, Francois?" I asked, annoyed with my supervisor from the Pan American Health Organization, or PAHO, in Washington, D.C. He had a penchant for interrupting chicken rounds.

"I've got a job for you."

"I have one."

"A *temporary* one," he countered. "They're calling it a 'detail.'"

"Who is?"

"CDC—the Centers for Disease Control and Prevention. They want you to do a stint in their Washington office."

"They don't have scientists there; that's an administrative office."

"Right, but they want you there."

"Why?"

"They wouldn't say. You need to call them immediately."

"Tell them I'm not available for a detail. The West Nile season is heating up."

"You don't have a choice because CDC feeds you."

He had a point. My job at PAHO was funded by CDC, the mission being to determine whether a protein I discovered might be tamed to serve as a mosquito killer. CDC funded the position at PAHO because West Nile virus had abruptly entered the United States for the first time in 1999 and was spreading through the Americas. It was a virus to be feared given its ability to infect the brain.

I sighed. "Give me the number."

He did. "It's a guy named Randy Flagstaff you need to talk to."

I got into the pickup and placed the call. Within moments, Flagstaff was on the line. "Can you get here in 30 minutes?" he asked. He gave me an address.

"No," I replied. "That's downtown D.C. and I'm an hour away."

"Drive fast."

"Listen, this isn't a good time—"

"You want to clear your name?"

"Of what?"

"You're a suspect in an attack on America. Ten people sick so far, including two dead. Your protein's the culprit."

A rooster crowed behind me. Although the sun was high, it felt like a new day dawning.

WHEN ASKED WHY I became a physician, I answer, "roadkill." Having grown up in rural Wisconsin, I was fascinated by dead animals encountered along country roads—opossums, beavers, dogs, cats, you name it—with their entrails splattered along asphalt. I often returned with knife and tweezers to dissect the remains, although foxes and raccoons were taboo given their propensity to be rabid. With each dissection, my interest in anatomy grew, prompting me to enter medicine. I chose human over veterinary medicine because of an ailment my mother had. After graduating from the University of Wisconsin, I went to medical school at the University of Nevada and spent the following decade in Las Vegas—four years in medical school, three in internal medicine residency, and three in a hematology fellowship.

Early in my hematology training, I evaluated a patient who sustained a leg wound in Madagascar. He was a graduate student at the University of Nevada in Reno who traveled to Africa to collect snakes for his PhD research. During an expedition to a remote region of Madagascar, he and a colleague were crossing a ravine on a bamboo bridge when the supports crumbled, hurtling them into a thicket of trees. My patient suffered a crushing blow to the thigh which required a splint to hike back to civilization. His colleague fared less well. Having lacerated his arm on a tree trunk, the colleague's wound bled profusely despite the application of a tourniquet. Within minutes, the skin surrounding the laceration turned purple from subcutaneous bleeding. The discoloration soon spread to his shoulder and torso. Before long, the young man, healthy before, bled from his nose, lips and gums. That was followed by vomiting of blood and hemorrhaging from his bowels. Within an hour, the man bled to death, lying in a bloody pool on the forest floor.

The grad student who survived noticed a piece of bark wedged into the lacerated arm of his dead colleague. Taking care not to touch the bark with bare hands, he extracted the wedge and located the tree from which the bark came. He then carefully removed a larger section to carry home. After receiving first aid in Madagascar, he hurried back to the U.S. where he was admitted to the University Medical Center in Las Vegas with a dangerously swollen thigh. The attending physician who admitted him asked me to evaluate the young man after hearing the story about the colleague who had bled to death after being lacerated by bark.

I met the grad student on the hospital ward. He pointed to the bark beside his bed. "That's what killed my colleague," he said. He insisted it contained a substance that caused intractable bleeding.

Intrigued, I asked if I could show the bark to researchers in the lab. Three months later, I proved the grad student to be right: The bark contained a previously undescribed protein that, when fed to mice, caused fatal bleeding. I named the protein "XK59"—"XK" for extreme killing, and "59" for the average number of minutes that elapsed before the mice exsanguinated. Later, near the end of my hematology fellowship, a pharmaceutical firm hired me as a consultant to explore whether XK59 might serve as a clot dissolver. The protein proved to be too hazardous to tame. However, CDC heard about the protein and, wondering whether a reconfigured version might kill mosquito larvae, offered me a job at PAHO. But now, two months into my new job, I was charged with turning XK59 into a weapon.

WASHINGTON, D.C. OFTEN fares better in recessions than other areas of the country because of money Congress pumps into the region. Consider the late 1920's when millions were appropriated to erect new government buildings in the city, funds that bolstered the local economy during the Depression. One building constructed during that era had the indiscreet name of "Federal Office Building 18"—or FOB-18. Although it was located near the National Archives and Department of Justice, it abutted a vacant lot once used by pimps and hookers at night.

As I popped out of the underground Metro station, I noticed a limestone building nearby that fit the description Flagstaff had given me for FOB-18, its columns and granite a cheap impression of the Acropolis, only instead of commanding a hillside, FOB-18 lurked within a depression, a pit that once belonged to Washington's swamps, which, of course, had been drained to rid the mosquitoes so bureaucrats could infest the place. If the building's depressed setting didn't humble it, neglect did: its façade was stained with pigeon droppings, its flagpole peeled like a bad case of sunburn, and the statue before it was sullied by an oxidative green veneer.

I reached the building after passing the International Spy Museum. A stone staircase brought me to the entrance where I was greeted by a blast of cool air. A guard stopped me as I stepped inside.

"Purpose of visit?" he asked.

"Summoned by Randy Flagstaff."

"That would be *Randolph* Flagstaff."

I didn't begrudge him. As a boy, I was teased about my last name. "Krispy-critter," friends would say, or "Krispix-crème." I vowed to respect others' names henceforth.

He took my PAHO badge. "Second ID, please."

I produced a driver's license.

"Nevada," he observed.

"Yes, I just moved here from Las Vegas."

"My sister lives in Phoenix," he announced.

Did he know Las Vegas was three hundred miles from Phoenix?

"Does she visit Las Vegas often?" I asked.

"No."

End of niceties.

He dialed a number. "Dr. Krispix to see you, sir." Then: "Fine, we'll send him through." He turned to a colleague. "Iris check."

I followed a second guard to a wall holding an aluminum box with a glowing purple eye.

"Look in," came the command.

I did, triggering a mechanical voice: "ID verified."

"Metal detector," my escort instructed.

I cleared it with ease.

"Take a seat."

The austere waiting area had only a few wooden chairs. A sign in large letters read, *CDC*, while below it, in smaller letters, *Centers for Disease Control and Prevention, Department of Health and Human Services*. Beyond the sign, a hallway split into two corridors.

I heard my name called. The voice was soft and velvety, incongruous with the gargantuan figure who owned it. "Randy Flagstaff," he said, extending a hand.

I shook the vast expanse of flesh. "Jason Krispix."

The behemoth smiled, revealing gaps between his teeth the size of doorways. Had he been an actor, he would've been the giant in *Jack and the Bean Stalk*, only he appeared to be good-natured. He had bulbous shoulders, bulging biceps, and tree-thick arms. His eyes were sunken, or perhaps it was just that his brows were massive. His skin, reddish brown, was pocked by what looked to have been a tough case of teenage acne. Despite his Mack truck size, however, he exhibited tenderness, the sort a gorilla might show in cradling a kitten. A pony tail flicked to the side as he waved me to follow him.

"I trust you'll make this short," I said. "I'm testing chickens these days."

He adjusted his Bolo tie. "I know."

He said nothing else, leading me down a hall as his cowboy boots clicked the floor.

"Tell me," I said, "how can this be CDC when the directory lists the Washington office as being on the mall?"

"It isn't CDC," he replied.

"But, that sign—"

"It's a cover."

"For what?"

"A top-secret agency."

I gulped. "Which one?"

"The United Network to Interdict Terrorism, or 'UNIT.'"

"Is it part of Homeland Security?" I asked.

He shook his head.

"National Security Agency?"

"Nope."

We rounded a corner and passed numberless offices. At the end of the hall, Flagstaff swiped a card to open a door. "Our psychologists have dubbed this place the 'Amygdala,'" he said, "because, like the part of the human brain called the amygdala, we deal with fear and aggression here."

The vast concentric space before us was clearly the dome I had seen while approaching the building from Metro, and it buzzed with the activity of a busy anthill, only here, humans scurried among aisles with blipping monitors.

"Yup, fear and aggression," Flagstaff repeated. "Welcome to your detail."

"THIS MUST BE Dr. Jason Krispix," a sliver of a man said as he wedged himself between Flagstaff and myself.

I dropped my eyes from a walkway overhead that transected the Amygdala.

"Dr. Glenn Bird," Flagstaff said, introducing me to the man. "Lead scientist for the UNIT. Like you, he's a physician."

Bird offered a dead-fish hand—cold and limp. A tuft of aging blond hair jiggled as we shook hands. He was in his mid-forties, I guessed, which made him a decade older than I, yet his complexion was youthful. He wore tasseled loafers, crisp khakis, and a golf shirt with a thin silk tie, a medley of business and leisure.

"We appreciate your time," Bird said. He opened a folder. "Seen this?"

"Of course, that's the paper I published on XK59 six months ago."

"Correct, in the *Journal of Pharmaceutical Metabolism*. Why did you publish it when you were advised not to?"

"Because the findings were significant."

Shortly before my article went to press, an official from the Department of Homeland Security who learned of the paper from one of the manuscript's reviewers called me to express concern that the protein might fall into hostile hands. He followed the call by sending me an official letter delivered by courier.

"They were trying to protect the homeland," Bird said.

"Censorship doesn't protect," I replied.

"Say what you will. The fact is XK59 has become a weapon, which makes you an accomplice to ten illnesses involving three deaths."

I turned to Flagstaff. "You mentioned two deaths."

"The number's growing."

"Who's behind this?" I asked.

"We hoped *you'd* tell us," Bird retorted.

"How would I know?"

"You pocketed a quarter million from selling a sample of XK59 to a pharmaceutical firm recently. What did they do with it?"

"They tried to develop it into a clot dissolver before they went bankrupt."

"They were a sham from the start. Their sole mission was to acquire XK59 to attack the homeland. The question is: Besides selling them XK59, how else did you help them poison the public?"

I turned to Flagstaff. "I don't have time for this."

"We need your help," he replied.

"As a *suspect*?"

"We'd like you to prove us wrong."

"Flagstaff is being polite," Bird said. "We were *ordered* to recruit you."

"By whom?"

"You'll find out shortly on Capitol Hill."

THE WALKWAY ABOVE the Amygdala was a tube made from see-through plastic and was connected to two spiral staircases on opposite sides of the rotunda.

"The 'crow's nest,' " Flagstaff explained, looking up. He stood with me now in Bird's absence.

"What's it for?"

"I'll show you." We climbed one of the spiral stairways and with each revolution a spoke-in-wheel array of aisles came into view below, each chockablock with computers and minions whose heads turned between monitors like metronome blades.

At the top of the stairway, I grasped a handrail and gazed about. Encircling the Amygdala was an enormous screen depicting a world map. Blipping lights flashed across it in menacing style.

"Each blip is an event of interest," Flagstaff explained. "Blue —cybersecurity; red—hostile incursions; green—bioterrorism." He swept an arm across the U.S. "Those green lights are XK59 poisonings."

The lights spanned the nation in what appeared to be random fashion.

"And what about them?" I asked, pointing to the staff below.

"Event monitors. Bird and I oversee them. We supplement them with experts like you as needed for short-term details."

I lifted my gaze and pointed to blue lights flashing along a border in eastern Europe. "And those?"

"Pro-Russia cyberattacks on the electric grid in Ukraine."

"And there?" I moved my arm to the southeast.

"The Caucusus, a region between the Caspian and Black Seas where an epidemic of brucellosis is raging—bioterror in nature."

I dug deep to recall my medical school lectures. "Brucellosis— an infection with the bacterium *Brucella abortus*... mostly afflicts animals but can sicken humans...produces fever, weakness, and fatigue; can be lethal if untreated."

He nodded. "More than a thousand humans sick in the Caucusus from sabotaged milk. It would have been easy for terrorists to acquire the pathogen because it's endemic in cows and goats there." He peered at me. "How long do you think it takes to fly from the Caucasus to the dairy state of Wisconsin where you grew up?"

"I'm not sure."

"Roughly fifteen hours, which means one could transport a suitcase of *Brucella abortus* from the outbreak zone to a major livestock region of our country in less than a day. If they released it in areas where there were unvaccinated cows, illnesses among the cows could lead to havoc." He paused. "Worse yet, if they managed to breach a dairy and contaminate pasteurized milk with the pathogen, we'd have an epidemic of the sort happening in the Caucasus. That's why we track these events: We want to know what could be heading our way before it arrives."

A narrative scrolled across the screen:

Additional XK59 illnesses in U.S.... "Two new lights," I stammered.

"Yup, the outbreak's growing."

LIKE A WEED, Glenn Bird popped up again, this time on the crow's nest. He straightened his tie with spindly fingers before pointing to the screen. "Check out Seattle," he said, tapping a keyboard on a rail.

New text appeared on the screen beside Seattle:

Byron Rudolf
36 years old
Software engineer
Became ill July 1st
Died July 2nd

"Our first fatality," Bird said. "He succumbed rapidly. Here's what happened."

More text:

Sore throat
Spitting up blood
Abrupt onset of fever

"A co-worker found Rudolf puking blood in the bathroom."

"Did he have a history of stomach ulcers or easy bleeding?" I asked.

"No, he was completely healthy."

"Was he taking any medications?"

"None."

Bird tapped the keyboard...

Rushed to hospital
Multiple blood transfusions
Admitted to intensive care

"They described him as a hole-ridden hose, blood oozing from everywhere—lips, gums, nose, ears, between webs of hands and feet. His skin became mottled before turning purple."

"Subcutaneous bleeding," I muttered. "What about his clotting system?"

"Depleted from all the holes XK59 punched into him."

"Was XK59 recovered from his body?"

"From muscles, skin, liver, kidneys, heart, brain... you name it. He was reduced to a pool of blood 18 hours after reaching the hospital."

"What led them to look for XK59?"

"We told them to test for it," Bird replied. "We work with select hospitals around the country to investigate unusual illnesses. It's a surveillance system designed to detect covert attacks on the homeland. After you published your paper, we added XK59 to the list of agents that cause bleeding."

"Rudolf became ill three weeks ago. Why didn't you call me earlier?"

"Five months ago, you pocketed a quarter million from the sale of XK59 and then used the funds to pay off gambling debts. Not the sort of guy we're inclined to recruit."

A CHINESE PROVERB states: *If you must gamble, decide upon three things at the start: the rules of the game, the stakes, and the quitting time.* I wish I had minded the last part before I started gambling; it would have prevented much pain.

I began gambling during the summer before my senior year in high school. My twenty-two-year old brother and I were on a road trip from Wisconsin to the west coast to visit colleges, not because I wanted to, but because my mother insisted I do so. My idea after graduating was to join the merchant marines rather than go to college. A ferry ride I took across Lake Michigan during middle school instilled in me a drive to breathe salty air, hopscotch ports, and ply sea lanes.

My mother was displeased when she learned of the plans. She summoned my brother at the start of summer before my senior year of high school and instructed him to take me cross-country on a college-visiting tour. Midway through the trip, before returning home, I cajoled my brother to add Los Angeles to our itinerary. When we arrived, I went to the port to inquire about seafaring jobs. I was informed that I would have to finish high school and then attend a marine academy before I would qualify to go to sea. Discouraged, I set off for home with my brother but we hit a snag at the Nevada line when we ran short on cash. Without credit cards, we limped into Las Vegas with fifty-five dollars to our name.

After camping in the sweltering heat, I approached my brother. "Let's gamble," I told him.

"With *what*?" he asked.

I asked for his wallet and took out a five dollar bill. "This is for calling mom if we need a ride home. The rest is for gambling."

He swore under his breath.

"Got another plan?" I asked.

He took the money and started off. "If I lose, it's your fault."

"Bet on black," I shouted, pointing to our pickup truck. "Hasn't missed a beat this trip."

An hour later, he returned with a hundred dollars.

"Go back and bet on red this time," I told him.

He disappeared, only to return with a wider grin than before. With two hundred dollars to our name, we checked into a motel, showered, and went to a seedy casino off the strip where a twenty-dollar bribe bought me a seat beside my brother at a blackjack table. By dusk, we quadrupled our bounty. After dinner and a sweet night's sleep, we departed for Wisconsin without telling my mother what happened. The Las Vegas stay played a large role in my decision to return years later to attend medical school there.

In the meantime, gambling lured me. During my senior year in high school, I formed a poker circle and bet on sports. Every time I rolled the dice or drew a card, I felt a rush of adrenalin. Nothing rivaled it—not music, hobbies, or girls. Winning was synonymous with success. My esteem soared, as did my cash holdings, which brought relief from the austerity my father foisted upon us after leaving the family for a younger woman, one who, as he put it, had a *real* heart. I never knew what he meant by that until my mother told me years later that *her* heart was failing from an auto-immune ailment. That explained the difficulty she had climbing stairs or walking distances.

My mother was aware of the gambling I did. While she disapproved of it, economic necessities in a single-parent household with a balance sheet tilting more toward debt than savings has a way of inducing tolerance. Even with gambling earnings, food ran short at times. At one point before I started gambling—I was fifteen at the time and bowlegged—a rumor spread that I had rickets from vitamin D deficiency. It wasn't a nutritional deficiency that caused my legs to bow so much as the hours I spent on an ancient John Deere tractor, a vehicle with a metal seat so wide it strained the muscles in my thighs. One day, a social worker appeared at our door to check on me. After eyeing our sparse living quarters and inspecting the barren kitchen cabinets, she announced she was taking me to a foster home. My mother emerged from the shadows with a shotgun aimed at the social worker and warned the lady that if she laid a hand on me she'd pull the trigger. It was the last we heard of foster homes.

With the merchant marines no longer an immediate career option, I entered the University of Wisconsin in Madison where, to my surprise, I enjoyed studying. My years of roadside dissections led me to major in biology, and having learned of my mother's auto-immune disease, I decided to apply to medical school.

On a trip home to visit her during my first year of medical school in Las Vegas, I found her breathing from an oxygen tank with a plastic tube around her head that looked like a drooping halo. She had little hope of getting a heart transplant because of her age and her failing bone marrow. Six months later, she died. I thought about dropping out of school to tend the farm but I knew she would have disapproved of the plan, particularly since my brother stepped in to run the land. Instead, I pledged to honor her by becoming a hematologist, *my* way of challenging the anemia that took her life.

The pledge couldn't ward off depression, particularly during the third year of medical school as classmates dispersed to different hospitals to complete clinical rotations with seemingly endless hours. The diaspora curtailed the gathering I coveted most, Friday night poker games. I returned to an empty apartment at the start of each weekend, turning to the city's gambling sites for solace. I played baccarat, keno, and slots, and while lady luck accompanied me for a while, mid-way through my first year of residency, a losing streak set in. During my residency and fellowship years, my entire salary went to pay off debts. I opened a line of credit but soon exhausted it, turning next to revolving credit card accounts. By the start of my hematology fellowship, I was a quarter million in the hole. I began trading options, futures, and commodities. Between seeing patients, I tracked the price of pork bellies, coffee beans, and sugar. For a while, luck returned, but then I got cocky and traded without doing the required research. The debt deepened. Collection agencies began calling. The Repo man took my car, but then XK59 bailed me out.

Or so I thought. Standing on the walkway over the Amygdala, I realized that instead of being my salvation, the protein had turned me into a suspect for a mass poisoning event.

GLENN BIRD WAVED a hand before me to get my attention. "We need to talk about the firm you sold XK59 to. It was called *Natow Pharmaceuticals*, right?"

"Yes…in New Orleans."

"And you consulted for them?"

"Yes, to help them try to turn XK59 into a clot-dissolving drug."

"Didn't the medical center in Las Vegas hold a patent on the protein?"

"Initially, but they allowed me to acquire it because they concluded the protein was too hazardous."

"Did you work on-site at *Natow*?"

"No, electronically only."

"So you never visited their office?"

"Didn't need to; a computer and a phone did the job."

Every week for several months, I conversed with the CEO, a hematologist who led the company. I met him initially when he approached me after I presented a paper on XK59 at a conference in Singapore shortly before my paper was published. Over coffee, he convinced me that *Natow* had a future in producing drugs to treat blood disorders. After learning I owned the patent for XK59, he offered me a consulting position and, later, paid me a quarter million for a gram of XK59. I was surprised two months later to receive a call from him saying the firm had gone bankrupt. I had hoped to delve into the matter further but was in the midst of getting married, completing my fellowship, and moving to Maryland. When I finally called him, I got a recording stating *Natow* had shuttered.

Bird turned to Flagstaff. "Alright, let's do it."

Flagstaff placed a palm on my head and pressed on it.

"What are you doing?" I protested.

"On your knees," he ordered.

"Why?"

"Do it."

I buckled onto the walkway above the Amygdala.

"Repeat after me," Flagstaff commanded. *"Distamus ab aliis."*

"What the hell's that?"

He pressed harder.

"Distamus ab aliis," I cried.

"It's Latin for, *We stand apart*. Repeat it."

I did.

"Now: *Proprius orbis*."

I obeyed.

"A world unto our own," he translated. "Repeat both."

I did my best, accent flawed.

"Again," Bird insisted.

Slow improvement.

"Good enough," Flagstaff said, helping me up. "Welcome to the UNIT."

"I didn't ask to join."

"Too bad," Bird said. "You're here until we solve the XK59 affair."

"And if I refuse?"

His face hardened. "Wanna end up in a dumpster like the CEO of *Natow*? Someone lodged a bullet in his head."

I froze. Two days earlier, my wife informed me that a car had followed her while she strolled through our neighborhood, departing only after she glared at its tinted windshield. I assured her it had been innocent.

Flagstaff swished his pony tail. "You're safer with us than at your job until we figure out what's going on. We'll assign a security detail to your house."

"What do you want from me?"

"Tell us who killed the CEO of *Natow*," Bird said.

"I don't know! This is the first I've heard of his death."

"The place was torched, so we know little more," Bird added.

"What about bank statements, tax returns, employee records?" I asked.

"What remains is unrevealing," Bird replied, his eyes narrowed. "But we think we know who's behind the XK59 poisonings —white-supremacists. Spell *Natow* backwards."

I did.

"That's right: *Wotan*. Heard of it?" he asked.

"No."

"Acronym for *W*ill *o*f *t*he *A*ryan *N*ation—a group that espouses white nationalism and white separatism. We've been hearing more from them as WAFTA heats up."

"WAFTA," I repeated. "The trade bill." For the past year, it had commanded headlines and triggered protests across the nation.

"Yes, the World-Around Free Trade Agreement," Bird acknowledged. "It's been debated heatedly in Congress and globally for over a year now. It calls for a total elimination of tariffs on imported goods around the world, no nation excluded. It's due for a vote on Capitol Hill any day now."

"Right," Flagstaff continued, "and it has splintered both business and labor into multiple shards. Supporters of WAFTA tout eighteenth century Scottish economist, Adam Smith, who famously argued that *the invisible hand of the market* will fuel economic resurgence. On the other hand, opponents decry the bill as a devious strategy to lower wages in order to produce less expensive goods that will compete more effectively in international trade."

"What's this got to do with *Natow Pharmaceuticals*?" I asked.

"Your CEO friend had ties to white supremacist groups," Bird said. "But one thing set him apart from his brethren: he supported the elimination of tariffs on pharmaceutical products so that the medicines he planned to manufacture could gain easy access to other nations. He paid for that view with his life. We think *Wotan* supremacists killed him for straying from their tenets."

"Why would white supremacists object to the elimination of tariffs?" I asked.

"Because they're convinced once tariffs are eliminated, the next step will be to open borders to unfettered immigration. They're convinced the ultimate goal is to make borders more porous to stimulate economic growth."

"Don't forget," Flagstaff interjected, "we've got home-grown terrorists in the U.S. The bombing of the Alfred P. Murrah Federal Building in Oklahoma City in 1995 proved that. So did the shootings by an avowed white supremacist in 2015 of nine African-Americans at a church in Charleston, South Carolina. While we focus on extremists linked to the Middle East, with the ascent of WAFTA, splinter groups with strictly domestic agendas have become more belligerent here. You've heard their threats: commandeer national parks; eschew taxes; conduct commerce by barter. These folks are armed, too, and prepared to defend the lands they usurp. They've threatened to unleash attacks on the homeland should WAFTA pass."

"So," Bird added, "the XK59 poisonings may be the beginning of a frontal assault. All hell could break loose if WAFTA prevails."

GLENN BIRD GLANCED at his watch. "Time to go," he said. As he led the way to Amygdala floor, he cautioned me: "Your work here is to remain strictly confidential. You'll say nothing about it to your colleagues at PAHO."

"But they'll ask about my absence."

"Tell them you're on temporary duty with CDC."

"Doing what?"

"Working on policy issues pertaining to anemia from lead poisoning. Embellish it if you wish; you're a hematologist." At the bottom of the stairs, he handed me an ID. "Welcome to the CDC."

I examined it. "Does CDC know they're being used as a front?"

"The key folks, yes."

"Am I in their directory?"

"Yes."

"As what?"

"A temporary employee based in the Washington office."

"And if someone calls me?"

"A recording will instruct them to leave a message."

We entered an office along the circumference of the Amygdala where Bird introduced me to a man with café au lait skin named Ricardo Muñoz.

"Dr. Krees-peeks, nice to meet you," Muñoz said.

"Muñoz is an infectious disease physician who truly works for CDC," Flagstaff explained. "We recruited him a week ago to assist with XK59."

I frowned. "Infectious diseases?"

"You'll see why shortly," Bird said. Another glance at his watch. "On to Capitol Hill."

We departed the Amygdala for an underground garage where Bird took the wheel of an official vehicle. A guard waved us through the gate.

In front, Muñoz pivoted. "From your article in the *Journal of Pharmaceutical Metabolism*, remind me what the minimum dose of XK59 was that killed your mice."

"Five one-hundredths of a microgram," I replied. "If you divide a small grain of sand into a hundred sections and weigh a single section, that's about how much five one-hundredths of a microgram is."

Muñoz extracted a notepad. "And what was the average weight of the mice?"

"About 25 grams."

He scribbled something before fingering a calculator. "Which means a 155-pound human weighs roughly 2,800-times more than a mouse. If humans and mice react similarly to XK59, it would take about 140 micrograms of the protein to kill a person."

"Yes," I agreed. I was familiar with the calculations for I'd done them repeatedly. "One hundred forty micrograms is about how much three eye lashes weigh. That ranks XK59 in the number two spot behind botulinum toxin as the most lethal protein known."

Beside me in the back seat, Flagstaff said, "Dr. Muñoz reviewed the victims' medical records."

"What about autopsy results for the Seattle victim?" I asked. "Did you review them?"

"Yes, the findings were consistent with what you reported for mice: bleeding all the way from the pharynx to the anus and in internal organs as well. At the microscopic level, they found ruptured cell-to-cell junctions, especially those lining blood vessels."

"*Pac-Man* effect," I muttered, alluding to the V-shaped jaws each XK59 molecule possessed. As it moved, the jaws opened and closed to splice its preferred targets, the fibrous bands, or "tight junctions," that connect cells. In its aftermath, tissues turned into bloody bogs.

"What *stops* the bleeding?" Flagstaff asked.

"Antibodies," I replied. "In my studies of mice, rodents given sub-lethal doses of XK59 produced antibodies that neutralized XK59, but it took several days for the antibody response to occur."

In the mirror, I saw Bird's eyes round into angry balls. "You sold the extremists quite a weapon, Krispix! Good luck explaining that to the Task Force."

"Task Force?" I repeated.

"Yes, a secret forum of Congressmen from the House Select Committee on Homeland Security. We report to them."

"*Congress* is your boss?"

"Yup."

"That's unusual, isn't it, having Congress direct an intelligence unit?"

"It was designed that way to keep Washington's Kudzu bureaucracy from consuming us."

"Has it worked?"

"So far, yes, but XK59 has the potential to unveil our secrecy."

Outside, we had reached the base of Capitol Hill where police had cordoned off a raucous crowd protesting WAFTA. On both sides—protestors and police—tempers flared, a volatile mix that seemed poised to explode at any point.

THE RAYBURN HOUSE Office Building was built in 1965 for the House of Representatives. Located across the street from the Capitol, it straddles the south side of Independence Avenue. I'd seen the building previously on a visit to the Library of Congress but never had reason to enter it.

We paused at a guard station where a sentry checked Bird's ID. He waved us to a subterranean garage from which we rode an elevator to a third floor conference room. Three men and a woman had assembled at a table leaving four chairs free. A bare wall glowed blue from the lamp of an overhead projector while, sitting just beyond the blue and apart from the table, a diminutive man slunk in a chair.

Silence fell over the room as we entered.

"Gentlemen," a burly man at the head of the table called in a gravelly voice steeped in a southern accent. He attempted to stand but his paunch struck the table, sending him back. "Please take your seats so we can begin."

Bird lifted a deferential hand toward the man as he addressed me. "Dr. Krispix, please meet The Honorable Homer McCloskey, Chairman of the Task Force that oversees the UNIT."

"Ah, Jason Krispix," McCloskey bellowed. "We appreciate you taking time from PAHO to work with us."

"Yes sir," I said, observing discordance between his welcome and the cold eyes that bore in on me. Had I been in court, I would have been the defendant meeting the prosecutor.

We took our seats.

"I wish these were better times," McCloskey continued, "but we play the cards as they're dealt." He pivoted. "Dr. Moon-Oz, your report, please."

Muñoz placed his hands on a laptop, unfazed by the mispronunciation of his name, but before he could speak, a lanky figure leaned forward onto the table and asked, "No introductions?" His voice undulated through phlegm.

"My apologies," McCloskey quipped. Although his tone was deferential, he glared at the lanky man. "Go ahead, Pete, start us off."

"Congressman Peter Shaker," the man gurgled through more phlegm. "Eighth district, Virginia—serving the suburbs just across the Potomac River from us." He slumped to the point where his graying goatee swiped the table. An arched nose protruded between sunken eyes the color of alpine lakes.

I nodded obligingly.

McCloskey shifted his glare to the man beside Shaker, making me wonder whether the Chairman of the Task Force was irascible by nature or simply having a bad day.

"Nick Kosta, thirtieth district, Texas," the man said, his voice little more than a whisper. He had a pleasing quality—suave, gentile, urbane—yet his cheeks were hollow, skin sallow, eyes haggard. He was languid, all but his moustache, a silver sliver that quivered anxiously.

"The final introduction is mine to make," McCloskey said, his face finally brightening. He motioned to the sole woman. "This is Dr. Sigrid Bjornstad, a psychiatrist from the International Court of Justice in The Hague, Netherlands. We recruited her for her expertise in profiling psychopaths. After Dr. Moon-Oz speaks, she'll discuss the mysterious messages the XK59 victims received after they fell ill."

Bjornstad was all vertical lines—sleek, tall, and poised. She had long blonde hair that spilled over her shoulders in the style of the Swiss girl portrayed on chocolate bars who stands in a dirndl before a chalet and snow-capped mountains. I expected her to break into *Sixteen going on Seventeen* or *Do Re Mi*, but she sat stone-faced with nary a twitch.

McCloskey held his smile for Bjornstad well after she nodded diplomatically. Rotating, he said, "You'll have to forgive the absence of the remaining Task Force members. With the WAFTA vote approaching quickly, a number of them are double-or triple-booked." His eyes tightened. "Dr. Bird, I trust you underscored the need for the strictest secrecy here."

Bird nodded.

"Very well, Dr. Mooz-Oz, the floor's yours."

From the wall, a soft "ahem."

McCloskey rolled his eyes. "Oh, almost forgot you, didn't I, Paul? Are you there still?" He looked over his shoulder.

The diminutive figure squeaked, "Aye, sir."

"Speak up, my friend!"

The man stood. "Paul DeTrigger, Task Force assistant."

"That's my boy," McCloskey chortled. "Keeps the trains runnin' here."

It struck me then: I'd heard McCloskey's warbling drawl on Sunday talk shows among policy wonks, journalists, and politicos. He was a wizen Representative who floated trial balloons for the Administration, a man who staunchly defended its policies and took barbs flung at it. He was an ideal front man because his down-home style disarmed critics: an attack on "Gramps McClosker" was an assault on America's seniors, and few ventured to launch such attacks.

I studied him closely. His hair was parted in the middle, creating two arched tufts that jiggled when he moved. Without makeup, he revealed more wrinkles than on television, although his eyes were truer blue than the camera made them to be. With each syllable he uttered, his bushy white eyebrows sailed up and down like horses on a carousel. I could see now how he'd held his seat in Congress for forty years: He was a marquis of middle-America, a man who gracefully accepted the foibles of aging—stooped back, knotted hands, skin thinned from years of sun—without succumbing to them. It would have taken a mighty foe to unseat him, one with an invincible war chest of the sort yet to amass in his New Orleans district.

"Well, then, Dr. Moon-Oz," he said. "Without further ado, I ask you to take a moment to summarize your professional background for my colleagues."

"A pleasure, sir," Muñoz said. "I was born and raised in Peru but came to the United States after medical school to train in internal medicine and infectious diseases at the Massachusetts General Hospital in Boston. Following that, I assumed the job I hold now at the Centers for Disease Control and Prevention in Atlanta. My work there focuses on dengue virus, a pathogen transmitted by mosquitoes that causes, among other things, a bleeding disorder called dengue hemorrhagic fever or dengue shock syndrome that shares similarities with the illnesses we're seeing with XK59."

"Which is why we recruited Dr. Moon-Oz in the first place," McCloskey interjected. "Some initially thought dengue virus might be responsible for the illnesses."

"Not all of us," Congressman Peter Shaker objected. He looked at McCloskey with defiance. "It would be most unusual for dengue virus, transmitted as it is by mosquitoes, to strike simultaneously in various regions of the U.S. given its virtual absence from our country for decades."

Flagstaff whispered into my ear: "Shaker's a physician, too. He practiced for decades before coming to Congress."

"A valid point," Muñoz relinquished, "but with global warming we may see more domestically-acquired mosquito-borne infections." He pointed to me. "Dr. Krispix can attest to that. The virus he's working with, West Nile, abruptly entered the U.S. in 1999 and has been spreading throughout the Americas since."

Bird, disquieted it seemed for being excluded from a doctor-to-doctor exchange, added: "So, before we discovered XK59 in the victims, we considered a wide array of diagnoses. That's why we tested the victims for more than forty viruses known to produce fever and bleeding." He nodded at Muñoz, who, taking the cue, started his slide show.

Viruses that cause fever and bleeding

Bunyamwera	Junin	Ngari
Crimean-Congo	Kyasanur Forest	Omsk
Dengue	Lassa Fever	Rift Valley
Ebola	Machupo	Yellow Fever
Hantaan	Marburg	

"This is just a partial list of viruses we checked the victims for," Muñoz noted. "But none were present, including dengue." He turned to me. "West Nile's not listed because it doesn't cause bleeding."

"Which leads us to XK59," Bird said, moving Muñoz along.

"Yes," Muñoz agreed, displaying a look of irritation for being prodded. "So, let's define what I mean by a 'case of XK59 poisoning.'"

He advanced the slide.

"As you can see, it's any person in the U.S. who, beginning as early as three weeks ago, experienced abrupt bleeding and exhibited XK59 in one or more tissue specimens."

"Did you quantify the level of XK59 in the victims?" I asked.

"That's under way at—"

"—our lab," Bird spurted. "We should have the results shortly."
Another slide...

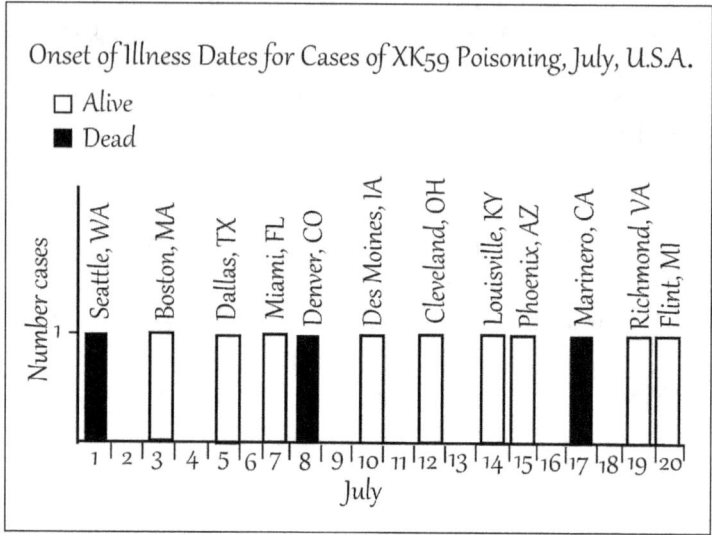

"This is what epidemiologists call an 'epidemic curve,'" Muñoz
explained. "It plots the cases by date of onset of illness, location,
and whether they survived or died. As you can see, there are twelve
victims we know about so far from around the country, all hospitalized. Three have died. The latest fell ill a little more than a week
ago on July 20th."

I flinched at the location of the most recent fatal case: *Marinero, CA.*

Congressman Kosta stirred. "Had the victims gathered at a
common site any time—at a conference, airplane, or wedding, for
example?"

"No," Muñoz replied, "which leads me to ask Dr. Krispix
something: Is it conceivable the protein could spread through the
air?"

My eyes held fast on the name, *Marinero, CA*. "Airborne transmission?" I asked, finally prying them away. "I doubt it because
I found that ultraviolet light disrupts the protein and, besides, if

airborne transmission accounted for the cases, we'd probably have seen far more illnesses by now."

"What about water?"

"Unlikely because chlorine denatures XK59."

Muñoz tapped the keyboard...

Demographic features of XK59 cases	
Feature	Number of cases (n=12)
Gender	
Male	7
Female	5
Age (years)	
< 20	0
20 − 50	9
> 50	3
Race/Ethnicity	
White/non-Hispanic	6
White/Hispanic	2
Black	2
Asian	2

"As you see, both males and females of varying races and ethnicities have become ill."

Clinical features of XK59 cases

Time to onset of symptoms (hours)	Clinical features
< 1	Sore throat, spitting up blood
2 – 5	Fever, chills
6 – 8	Bloody vomit, diarrhea, and urine
	Bleeding gums, nose, ears, eyes, and webs of hands, feet
9 – 12	Shock

"Here we see the nature of the illness that developed after exposure to XK59 and the timing of onset of symptoms," Muñoz said. "You can appreciate why, initially, we looked for viruses that cause fever and bleeding."

"The first column implies you knew when each victim was exposed to XK59," Shaker objected. "How could you know that?"

"You'll see momentarily," Muñoz replied. "For now, please observe that all victims had fever, most in the 105° Fahrenheit range."

"Which is curious," I said, "because none of my mice exhibited fever."

"I was going to ask you about that," Muñoz responded. "You monitored their temperatures?"

"Very closely."

"But, Dr. Krispix," McCloskey intervened, "mice and men aren't *mirror* images, are they?"

"With regard to the development of fever, they may be," I postulated.

Shaker nudged slightly to one side. Each move seemed to be metered and difficult, as if dictated by gears with teeth locked in arthritic rust. "But your mice may have died from bleeding before they had a chance to develop fever," he suggested.

Muñoz stepped closer to the table. "I believe the question of fever will be answered in the next slide."

Laboratory results, XK59 cases

- Anemia
- Elevated white blood cell count
- Presence of XK59 in blood, tissues
- 2 pathogens in blood, feces:
  - *Vibrio parahaemolyticus*
  - *Aeromonas hydrophila*

"From a lab standpoint," Muñoz continued, "we've seen anemia and elevated white blood cell counts in all victims along with the presence of XK59 in blood and tissues." Turning more sober, he added: "And two bacteria—*Vibrio parahaemolyticus* and *Aeromonas hydrophila*—present in blood and feces."

"In *all* victims?" Shaker volleyed.

"Yes."

"That's incredible!" he gasped.

"But it may explain one of the findings," I said. "The presence of the two bacteria in the blood most likely caused fever in the victims."

"Hold on!" Kosta protested. "Not everyone here is a microbiologist. What's the significance of the bacteria?"

"Blood is normally sterile," Muñoz explained, "meaning bacteria should be absent. The presence of these particular bacteria suggests a connection between the victims and the sea where both microbes reside. You'll see that connection shortly when I identify the exposure that probably caused the XK59 poisonings."

"*Vibrio*," Kosta said, holding a hand up unsteadily. "It causes cholera, right?"

Muñoz propped a palm under his chin as if to reckon how much detail to divulge. "You're thinking of *Vibrio cholerae*, one of the various species in the genus, *Vibrio*. What we're talking about here is a cousin called *Vibrio parahaemolyticus* that also causes diarrhea and, like *Vibrio cholerae*, resides naturally in the sea."

"Yes, and we've had several outbreaks of illness in the United States recently due to *Vibrio parahaemolyticus*," Shaker volunteered, "ones following the ingestion of raw oysters." He raised a hand as if to reserve his speaker status while he pondered something. "And if I'm not mistaken, some patients in these outbreaks experienced bloody diarrhea."

"Correct," Muñoz replied. "Unlike *Vibrio cholerae*, which causes exclusively watery diarrhea, infection with *Vibrio parahaemolyticus* can cause bloody or non-bloody diarrhea. Recent rises in sea temperature may have allowed *Vibrio parahaemolyticus* to multiply to unprecedented levels, and since oysters are filter feeders that concentrate bacteria in their guts, people who eat them raw can become infected." He paused. "However, it's unusual for *Vibrio parahaemolyticus* to enter the bloodstream." He pointed to the slide. "Yet here we see *all* victims had that pathogen in their blood."

"With XK59 slicing and dicing blood vessels in the gut and elsewhere, I'm not surprised the bacteria entered their blood," I said.

"And the second organism?" Kosta asked, sliding a pale hand forward along the table.

Muñoz approached him tenderly.

"Yes, *Aeromonas hydrophila*." Muñoz paced along the side of the table in professorial style. "Like *Vibrio parahaemolyticus*, this bacterium is a denizen of the sea, but debate exists as to its ability to cause diarrhea in humans. If you search the literature, you will find reports that describe gastrointestinal symptoms linked to this organism in persons who consumed raw oysters."

"Hold on!" McCloskey bellowed. "Are you saying *oysters* caused the XK59 poisonings?" He seemed affronted by the notion.

Muñoz donned a coy look. "To answer that question, we need to discuss a tool epidemiologists often use to study illness outbreaks. It's called a 'case-control study.' It compares exposures among persons with the disease of interest—'cases'—to others without the disease, or 'controls.' The goal of case-control studies is to identify one or more exposures reported more commonly among ill than well persons and thereby identify a likely cause of illness. During the past week, I conducted such a study by interviewing the twelve cases or their next of kin along with a group of persons without XK59 poisoning. I just completed the analysis today."

"Who were the controls?" Shaker asked.

"Individuals in neighborhoods where the cases resided. I identified two controls for each case."

Whispering into my ear, Flagstaff said, "He used his CDC affiliation, saying nothing about the UNIT."

The next slide showed the dozen cases and 24 controls to be similar in age, race, ethnicity, education level, recent travel history, and presence of underlying medical conditions.

"What I did next was get a diet history from cases and controls," Muñoz continued. "I asked cases what they ate during the week before they fell ill and controls what they ate during the week before the interview. To refresh memories, I had subjects consult a calendar. Here's what I found."

Food histories, cases and controls, XK59 study

Food	Cases (n=12)	Controls (n=24)	Different?
Salads	75%	88%	No
Chicken	50%	54%	No
Beef	88%	83%	No
Dairy	74%	71%	No
Seafood	92%	21%	Yes**

"As you can see from the asterisks, the only statistically significant difference was cases were more likely than controls to have eaten seafood." He scanned the room. "Are we together?"

Heads nodded with the lone exception of McCloskey who sat stoically with a look of defiance.

"Seafood is a large category," he said. "Did you narrow it down?"

Muñoz advanced the slide.

Seafood consumption, cases and controls, XK59 study			
Seafood	Cases (n=12)	Controls (n=24)	Different?
Finfish	58%	63%	No
Raw oysters	8%	4%	No
Lobster	0%	0%	No
Shrimp	92%	17%	Yes**
Mussels	8%	4%	No
Clams	16%	8%	No

"*Shrimp?*" McCloskey erupted. "Are you saying *shrimp* caused the XK59 poisonings?" He raked his eyes over Muñoz as if the Peruvian were a traitor for maligning a major seafood product harvested from his home state of Louisiana.

Muñoz, feeling the heat, deferred to Bird.

"Indeed, sir," Bird said, his voice subdued. "We obtained a sample of leftover shrimp from one of the victims and it yielded *Vibrio parahaemolyticus*, *Aeromonas hydrophila*, and XK59."

"Was the shrimp cooked that you tested?" I asked, incredulous that XK59 was present.

"No, it was raw. It was a portion the victim had refrigerated before barbecuing the rest."

"But cooking should have killed the bacteria," Shaker insisted.

"And denatured XK59," I added. "The protein is heat-sensitive."

"That's the problem," Muñoz riposted. "The victim didn't barbecue the shrimp thoroughly. Which raises a key point: All of the victims ate shrimp that was outright raw—at sushi bars, for example—or only partially cooked."

"How much XK59 was in the shrimp you tested?" I asked Bird.

"The results are pending."

Kosta: "I don't understand how the shrimp became tainted with XK59 in the first place."

"Nor do we," Muñoz replied. "As for the bacteria, both were probably present in the shrimp to begin with since they're marine organisms."

Shaker sighed aloud. "The public needs to know what's happening." He addressed McCloskey. "And your shrimpers in Louisiana are gonna take a hit."

"I know it, goddammit!" McCloskey shouted. "But they're hardy folks. They've weathered hurricanes, oil spills, recessions, and competition from imported shrimp; they'll survive this crisis, too." He glowered at the slide before his expression changed. "Hang on! Am I reading things correctly? It says 92% of the cases ate shrimp. Was there one case who didn't eat shrimp?"

"One didn't," Muñoz confirmed.

"How'd he get poisoned?"

"I don't know, but his parents insist he never ate shrimp because he was allergic to it."

"Who was the patient?" I asked, heart racing.

"The California victim, a young man from Marinero."

Pain seared my abdomen.

"Could he have eaten shrimp accidentally while dining out?" Kosta asked.

"He rarely ate out. His food allergies led him to prepare most of what he ate."

"So if it wasn't shrimp that poisoned him, what did?" McCloskey repeated.

Muñoz shook his head. "Again, I don't know. He's what we epidemiologists call an 'outlier'—a case distinct from the others.

Such cases often provide critical clues to unsolved mysteries, so we need to interview his folks in greater detail."

"Where are they?" I asked, voice cracking.

"Up the coast from Marinero, in Half Moon Bay."

I felt sick to my stomach.

"And what about the shrimp the victims ate?" Shaker asked. "Did it come from a single source?"

"As far as we know," Bird replied. "All of it came from an aquaculture firm in Ecuador. Muñoz and Krispix will be going there shortly."

I glared at Bird. "I *can't* go! My wife's due date is in six days!"

EVE WAS A flight attendant for Australia's *Qantas* airlines when I met her. Our encounter occurred at the end of my first year of hematology fellowship on a flight across the Pacific after I attended a research forum in Sydney. Midway through the flight to Los Angeles, we hit a patch of turbulence. Serving drinks at the time, Eve stooped and clutched the armrest beside me.

Ill at ease, I closed my eyes and gritted. I felt a hand grasp one of mine. It belonged to Eve, and she assured me in her tender Aussie voice that all would be well. Shortly, with the return of calm, she stood and offered me a drink.

"You're cool under pressure," I told her.

She smiled. "That was nothing."

She moved up the aisle but as she traversed the opposite lane with dinner trays, our eyes locked. She turned abruptly and returned aft where she conversed with a colleague before returning to my side. "Recovered?" she asked.

"Almost."

She glanced at a medical journal I held. "Are you a doctor?"

"Yes, a hematologist."

"Where do you live?"

"Las Vegas."

She moved on, but after dinner, while I stretched near the galley, she approached me.

"Your hands," she said. "May I see them again?"

I lifted them.

She caressed both. "As I thought: You should have become a surgeon; they hold healing powers."

She left to answer a call button, and I saw little of her the rest of the flight as she worked the forward cabin. Upon deplaning, I was excited to see her beside the exit. I asked her to step aside. "Does *Qantas* fly to Las Vegas?"

"No, Los Angeles is the closest we get."

"Fine, then will you have dinner with me the next time you're in Los Angeles? I'll meet you here."

She blushed but said nothing.

"Here, take my card," I said. "Think about it."

I joined the throng and left, but halfway up the walkway, I turned to catch her wave.

Two weeks later, we dined in Malibu. She told me that she, like I, had grown up in the country—in her case, on a horse ranch outside Brisbane—and while I had driven a tractor, she rode horses along the hills that rimmed the ranch. After several months of meeting in Los Angeles every other week, I visited her in Australia where we rode horses and drove along the Gold and Sunshine coasts east of Brisbane to visit her favorite surfing spots. I reciprocated by escorting her through national parks near Nevada—Zion, Grand Canyon, and Death Valley. Shortly after starting the final year of my hematology fellowship, I received a call from her saying she was pregnant. Rather than wait for her next trip to Los Angeles, I hopped a flight to Australia to see her.

"Yes," she said at her apartment in Sydney when I offered her a ring. "After holding your hands on the plane the day I met you, I never wanted to let them go."

THE AROMA OF fresh-brewed coffee filled the air, a fragrance that normally stirred my hunger, but food was the last thing I craved. In the corner of the room, Paul DeTrigger scurried about preparing sandwiches and beverages.

"Let's take a five-minute break before Dr. Bjornstad speaks," McCloskey announced from the head of the table.

Chairs pushed back. I went to Glenn Bird. "I'm serious, I can't travel," I whispered.

"I understand your dilemma, Krispix, but we need you to go to Ecuador."

"But this is our first child; I gotta be here!"

"We've got people *dying* from XK59."

"I understand, but it's not just a baby we're dealing with. Eve recently discovered a breast mass as well."

"I'm sorry, but there are surgeons who can help her while you help your country."

"Screw you, Bird!"

I turned to leave, but he grasped my arm.

"Watch it!" he murmured. "I can make your life hell."

"You already have."

"*Real* hell—so bad you'd wish you weren't alive." He drilled his eyes into mine. "Does Eve know about the back-taxes you owe the IRS for gambling profits?"

From the food table, McCloskey turned an eye on us.

I withdrew from Bird's grasp. "I hold no secrets from Eve."

"A happy couple." He left for a bite to eat.

McCloskey, seated with a beer now, summoned us. As we sat, Sigrid Bjornstad remained standing at one end of the table, tall and sleek with a feline face that tapered from temples to jaw. Her eyes were icy cold, as if dug from a glacier with a melon scooper. In high school, we called girls with snow-white hair like hers "Scandinavian blondes."

"We're fortunate to have Dr. Bjornstad here," McCloskey began. "As a former member of Sweden's downhill ski team, she became interested in the psyche as she noticed teammates deal with fear differently. After medical school, she completed a residency in psychiatry and then practiced for years before taking a post at the International Court of Justice in The Hague. She specializes in evaluating war criminals—dictators, terrorists, warlords. There's no one more qualified to profile the mastermind of the XK59 poisonings than she." He raised a hand. "Dr. Bjornstad, the floor's yours."

She smiled wanly. "Mr. Chairman, members of the Task Force, and staff from the United Network to Interdict Terrorism, I begin with the premise that shrimp was deliberately poisoned with XK59. I say this because of the messages the victims received after they fell ill from XK59 poisoning. I'll refer to these messages as 'missives,' and as you'll see shortly, they're little more than truncated, perplexing clauses. To understand who might commit a crime of this sort, we'll review the messages he mailed to seven of the victims after they fell ill from XK59."

"You're assuming the perpetrator is a male," Kosta observed.

"Indeed, I believe he is someone like Ted Kaczynski—the so-called Unabomber who sent explosives to 16 victims from the late seventies to the early nineties, a man who mailed letters to many of his victims and demanded that a major newspaper print his 35,000-word paper dubbed the *Unabomber Manifesto*. He got his way, but it cost him his cover because his younger brother recognized the writings and notified authorities. Kaczynski was apprehended shortly after that."

She presented a slide. "So, the first missive …"

… your father's cruelty.

"Sent to the software engineer in Seattle," she added. "Any thoughts as to what it means?"

I shuddered.

"*You're* the expert," Shaker scoffed.

"God, Pete, don't be a churl," McCloskey snapped. He held a look of anger for Shaker even as Bjornstad resumed speaking.

"That's alright, Mr. Chairman," the psychiatrist purred. "The Congressman is right: You're paying for my expertise, and I could simply tell you what I think, but I prefer an interactive approach."

"I agree we're dealing with a male," Kosta said. "I can't see a woman poisoning people willy-nilly."

"Can you envision a woman drowning her kids in a bathtub?" DeTrigger asked, his tone animated as he folded a table cloth. "That's happened, you realize!" Immediately, he blushed.

"Paul!" McCloskey lashed out. "Did someone ask you to speak?"

The aide retreated.

Kosta, inclined to indulge DeTrigger but unwilling to expend the effort to look at him, said: "I see your point, Paul, but drowning kids in a bathtub is a domestic affair. Here, we're dealing with random strikes on society, the sort of thing loner males do."

"But speak to the slide," Bjornstad insisted. "What do the words tell us?"

Glenn Bird read the words aloud, "… *your father's cruelty.* The guy was probably abused as a child."

"By his father?" Bjornstad asked.

"Or another male."

Bjornstad advanced the slide.

… of the lovely cheeks,

Beneath the table, I clenched each knee with all my might.

"Bird's onto something," Flagstaff proffered. "The perpetrator may have been sexually abused."

"Why do you say that?" Bjornstad asked.

" 'Cheeks,' " Flagstaff replied. "As in buttocks."

"A former altar boy!" Paul DeTrigger squeaked, coffee pot in-hand.

McCloskey: "We'll handle this, Paul!"

DeTrigger left the room carrying a bag in each hand stacked with supplies.

"Good riddance," McCloskey grumbled. To Bjornstad: "Please …"

She tapped the laptop …

But she, surrendering to …
But she, surrendering to …

"Why the duplication?" Kosta asked.

"Because, two victims received identical missives."

"So much for the male theory," Kosta lamented.

"Hold the thought," Bjornstad advised. "Let's review the next missive."

... *Power and Strength,*

"I can understand that one," Bird said. "Someone who had been abused would attribute power and strength to the abuser."

"And then unleash his anger on society?" Bjornstad proposed.

"*Plleaseeee,*" Shaker objected. "You're making it sound so simple."

Bjornstad pressed ahead. "And the final missives ...

... *not that rich chimaera.*
... *who lives under the earth,*

The room fell silent.

"*Chimaera,*" Bjornstad said. "Note the spelling with 'ae' instead of just 'e', an older version of the word, it seems." She paused. "And as we all know, a chimera is a mythological, fire-breathing monster commonly represented with a lion's head, a goat's body, and a serpent's tail. In my view, the most telling missive because it opens a door to the perpetrator's mind, an angry, hideous zone of conflicting emotions. As the chimera of Greek lore was known to breathe fire, so our man exhales fiery flames."

"You presented six missives, one sent to two victims," Shaker noted. "Did the remaining victims not receive any?"

"As of yet, no. So, I ask you to dwell on what you've seen so that we can discuss them later in more detail." She took a seat.

Shaker's expression suggested he had many questions. He launched one: "How could the perpetrator have identified the victims so readily?"

"Care to comment, Dr. Bird?" McCloskey asked.

"We're dealing with a techie," Bird replied, "a wizard who planted microchips in shrimp soft enough to go undetected yet sophisticated enough to transmit GPS signals upon contact with blood in the intestinal tract. We found the chips in leftover shrimp."

Shaker raised his brows. "That seems far-fetched."

"A lot of things about this outbreak seem far-fetched, but they are what they are."

"And the missives," Shaker continued, "how were they sent?"

"By U.S. mail addressed to *Current Resident* at the sites specified by GPS."

McCloskey stirred. "Alright folks, the Task Force needs to huddle at this point." He eyed Bird. "If you'll give us a few moments …"

Bird led us out of the room at which point I approached Muñoz immediately. "Can I see that epidemic curve you displayed?"

He handed me a printed copy of the slide. I zeroed in on the name *Marinero, CA* above the solid bar indicating a death. "This was the one you called the 'outlier,' the one who didn't eat shrimp?"

"Right," Muñoz replied.

"Did he get a missive?"

"Yes—…*who lives under the earth*,"

My heart heaved.

"How old was he?"

"Thirty-three."

"What did he do for a living?"

"He ran a surf shop."

A stabbing pain pierced my belly.

"Was his name Danny Rogers?"

Muñoz glared at Bird. "Did you tell him? The names were to remain confidential!"

"I didn't reveal any names!" Bird parried.

The hallway closed in on me. Turning, I raced down the corridor but stopped abruptly to vomit. I watched the contents ooze along a wall beside me. Slumping to the floor, I sobbed, "God! Why *Danny*?"

AS A CHILD, six months is an eternity to keep a secret, but that's how long I sequestered mine, hoping it would dissolve like a toxic granule. Even after sharing it with Danny Rogers, the memory haunted me for years and caused me to shun storage areas.

Shame kept me from divulging the torment to my mother and brother, and I had no father in whom to confide because he had abandoned us. That left Danny Rogers as my sole counselor, and it was he who implored me to tell our sixth grade teacher what had happened, the very woman who sent me on the ill-fated mission.

At the time, although I ranked as an average student, I held the honor of being my teacher's go-to guy when it came to computer-related tasks. Among my jobs was setting up projectors for class presentations. The skills earned me the right to slip out periodically to help other teachers with their technical needs as well. It was a privilege I coveted.

So it was with the usual pride I felt one morning when my teacher asked me to retrieve a replacement light bulb for a projector. It meant journeying to an expansive stock room in the school's basement, and to get there, I took a remote stairway that led to a long, dark hallway that opened into a cavernous space. It was dank and dimly lit with fluorescent bulbs sputtering intermittently.

I went to the shelf where light bulbs were stored. At the very back of it, behind an extension cord, I found the replacement bulb I sought. I retrieved it and started for the exit but was forced to stop short on account of a figure who blocked the way. She was a teacher's aide, a woman in her forties with a bouffant hairdo who roamed from class-to-class supposedly to help, although none of us thought she was of any use. The only reason she got the job was because her husband was a city council member, a wealthy man who owned one of the largest dairies in Wisconsin. Rumor had it she was infertile, so to get her fix of kids, she worked as a teacher's aide.

I tried to side-step her, but she mirrored my moves.

"I need your help," she said. "There's a box of pencils on a shelf back there I can't reach. I want you to get it for me."

"Where?" I asked.

She pointed over my shoulder and motioned for me to walk. As I did so, she followed closely. She stopped me deep inside the room before a shelf with art supplies. Pointing to a waist-high shelf, she said, "Back there. See it?"

I stooped to find the box she spoke of. It was wedged between the back wall and a tray of small paint cans. I leaned forward with my chest resting on a ream of construction paper, but as I stretched for the box, I felt a hand slide into my shorts and caress my buttocks. A thick scent of perfume wafted into the air between the shelves.

For a moment, I froze before calling out, "No!" I tried to back up but couldn't because she pressed against me. My head struck the shelf above.

"Get off me!" I wailed.

She removed her hand. "Fine, come out."

I extracted myself and faced her, trembling.

"You needn't be afraid," she said. She rubbed her cheek against the side of my face. Parting her lips, she licked my ear. Her breathing became labored, and as she reached to unbutton my shorts, I pushed her aside and ran from the room. From behind, I heard her call: "Wait! My pencils!"

"GET UP, KRISPIX," Bird said. "This is a public space."

As I rose from the floor, I saw the contents of my stomach had coalesced into a fetid pool.

"Clean it," Bird ordered. "You'll find paper towels down there." He pointed to a restroom.

"No," Flagstaff countered. "We need to talk." He led us to an empty room where he closed the door. "What was that about?" he asked.

"They're playing with my mind," I uttered.

"Who is?"

"The author of those missives." I sank into a chair. "They were directed at *me*." I voiced the first one: "*…your father's cruelty. My* father abandoned me when I was young."

"That's true for a lot of kids," Bird said. "What makes you feel targeted?"

"*…of the lovely cheeks,…*," I added. Haltingly, I relayed the story about the teacher's aide.

"God, Krispix," Flagstaff whispered.

"*But she, surrendering to…*," I continued. "It refers to my sixth-grade teacher who was fired after telling authorities about what the teacher's aide had done."

"But why did two victims receive that missive?" Bird asked, cold calculus in his eyes.

"I don't know."

"Who fired your teacher?" Flagstaff asked.

"The school board—by order of the city council. The aide's husband was a council member."

Flagstaff tapped my back. "You did the right thing to tell your teacher what happened."

"Only because Danny Rogers told me to." I paused, and then added: "As soon as I saw the name *Marinero, CA* on Muñoz's slide, I became worried Danny was the victim. It's a tiny place, and I knew Danny lived there. The bit about the shrimp allergy convinced me beyond any doubt it *had* to be Danny. I saw him have an allergic reaction once after he ate shrimp accidentally at a buffet. He stopped breathing. It took adrenaline injected by the paramedics to revive him."

I looked out a window facing the Capitol. "...*who lives under the earth*," I sputtered. "That was the final straw: Danny's cabin lies within a hill."

For a moment, I recalled how Danny would push his glasses up his nose, lenses as thick as Coke bottles that made his eyes look like harvest moons.

Bird consulted his notes. "What about … *Power and Strength*," he asked.

I shrugged. "The aide's husband? He was a powerful man in town."

"When did Rogers leave Wisconsin for California?"

"After eleventh grade."

"And you kept in touch?"

"Religiously."

During college, I flew to California every year to visit him in Santa Cruz. On one trip, he took me up the coast to show me Marinero. It was little more than a cluster of artichoke farms. He told me he wanted to move there after graduating from the University of California, Santa Cruz, which he did, although because so few people lived in Marinero, he opened his surf shop in Half Moon Bay further up the coast. Waves were his temples.

Bird glanced at his watch. "We gotta go."

I remained seated. "I'm not going to Ecuador," I said.

"Agreed," he replied.

I looked up at him.

"You're going to California instead. You need to find out how Danny Rogers got poisoned."

EVE SAT IN a chaise longue with a hand on her belly and a pillow behind her back. "Jason, I'm glad you're back!" she said worriedly.

I sat beside her.

"I just got off the phone with Randy Flagstaff," she said. "He told me about your detail and what's happening with XK59. All hush-hush, I understand, but he said it was important that I knew." She squeezed my hand. "It's terrible!"

"Did he tell you I need to go to California?"

"Yes."

"And why I need to go?"

"No, just that it was in the line of duty."

I shook my head. "It's not good, Eve. Not good at all."

She ran a hand along my cheek. "What is it?"

"Danny Rogers died from XK59 poisoning. I need to find out how it happened."

"Danny!" she gasped, covering her mouth.

I had spoken of Danny often with Eve and had even taken her to Half Moon Bay to have lunch with Danny and his parents. Initially, we invited him to be a groomsman at our wedding before we decided to forgo the ceremony for a civil marriage.

"I'm going to talk to his parents in California," I said.

"*Danny*..." she muttered. She looked about the room as if whatever or whoever had killed Danny could be lurking in our midst. "I don't like this, Jason."

"There's more," I said, nestling closer. I told her about the missives and how I believed they targeted me somehow.

"Okay, that's it!" she cried. "We need protection."

"We've got it. Flagstaff assigned a security team to us. You'll see a black SUV about whenever you leave the house."

I placed a hand on her belly. "What happened at the obstetrician's today?"

She seemed reluctant to switch topics. "The baby's fine."

"And you?"

She turned toward the window. "I'm frightened."

I held her tightly. "Remember what we said: One step at a time: baby, then breast mass." I cleared her hair from her tears. "It's probably nothing more than a cyst or a blocked gland."

She lifted her eyes to me. "With my mother's history?"

Eve's mother died a decade earlier of breast cancer at the age of forty-one. Eve was seventeen at the time. After giving it wrenching thought, Eve underwent genetic testing in Australia during college to see if she carried breast cancer genes. The results were ominous: She harbored the *BRCA1* gene, a finding that gave her almost a 60% lifetime risk of developing breast cancer and an elevated risk of experiencing ovarian cancer as well. She shared the news with me after several dates, saying she was torn about whether to have her ovaries and breasts removed to reduce the risks of cancer. I already knew I wanted to marry her; what she told me made me want to have children sooner than later.

"Did they ultrasound the breast today?" I asked.

"Yes, no change from last week, which means we still don't know what's going on."

"What about antibiotics? Do they want you to continue them in case there's an infection?"

"For now, yes, but a mammogram's out of the question until I give birth. They're considering doing a biopsy after the birth as well."

I stood and leaned against the window. In the distance, thunder rumbled in a blackening sky. I pressed the numbers on my phone.

"Who are you calling?" Eve asked.

"The airlines. I want to get California over before you deliver."

Day 2.

THE TEMPERATURE IN San Francisco was forty degrees below the swelter of the east coast. Fog swirled about the elevated tram leading from the airport terminal to the rental car center, blurring the lights of taxiing airplanes.

It was just after midnight. Before leaving Dulles Airport, I called Danny Rogers' parents to ask if I could see them urgently. It was Danny's mother who answered the phone. My stomach knotted as I informed her that XK59 had killed her son and that I had been recruited by the CDC to determine how the poisoning had occurred. Stoically, she agreed to meet for an interview, but because she felt she would be too emotional to do so at her house, she suggested we meet at a park along the coast south of Half Moon Bay where Danny often surfed.

After picking up a car, I drove to a hotel south of San Francisco. In the sleepless hours that passed, I stared at the ceiling. At 3 a.m., hours before my alarm was set to ring, I checked out and began driving toward the coast knowing I'd reach my interview spot long before Danny's parents were due to arrive. I drove slowly, allowing GPS to lead me along Highway 101 south, but as I traveled, I flicked on the light and filed through my wallet for a slip of paper. It prompted me to reprogram the GPS with the address to Danny's house in Marinero. Although Danny had invited me repeatedly to visit him there, I'd never done so because of scheduling issues. The time had come to pay that visit now.

I left the freeway and began climbing the coastal hills. Moonlight pierced the fog in silver daggers only to be stanched by a thick blanket at the summit. My headlights became useless as their beams shattered into a thousand rays. I slowed to a crawl and hugged the middle of the road for fear of careening into a canyon.

The hairpin bends eased to gentler curves that wound through fields of artichoke, garlic and evergreens destined for Christmas stands. At one point, I picked up speed and sailed into a dip that sent my stomach to the floor. After gliding over a knoll and passing more farms, I came to a junction with Highway 1, the famous strip that ribbons the Pacific.

I stopped to ponder my decision to visit Danny's home. It meant traveling south rather than north which would take me away from the interview spot. Tepidly, I turned south and passed a desolate stretch of bluffs. Five miles beyond the junction, I came to a wind-blown sign reading *Marinero* that led me to a narrow road heading away from the ocean. It scaled a hill before dropping into a valley where I came to a tackle shop, withering church, and convenience store.

After turning onto a gravel lane, a shower of stones pelted the underside of my chassis. I followed the lane up a hill, passing a meadow with cows huddled in a lifeless form that reminded me of peat piled in Irish bogs. An orchard appeared on my right, its trees laden with green persimmons. After a series of bends, the lane ended before a log cabin where a pickup truck sat in front, its tags reading *Surf'sUp*. Beyond it, off to the side across a grassy patch, the blades of a wind turbine turned in the swirling fog.

I parked the car and followed a path between surfboards standing on end among bonsai trees. It brought me to a cabin embedded in a hill such that the roof consisted of grasses and bushes. Only the front was exposed to the world, and I approached it cautiously, peering through a window into the dark interior. Seeing no sign of life, I placed a hand on the door knob but stopped short when a loud whirring startled me. I wheeled about to find the windmill moaning in a stiffening wind.

I turned the knob but the door was locked. Returning to the window, I checked to see if it might open, but it didn't. Picking a stone from the garden, I smashed the glass and slipped an arm through the gap. With a turn of a lever, I lifted the frame and climbed in. A flick of a switch brought a lonely bulb to life that illuminated a single room partitioned into four zones: a sitting space with lounge chair, desk, and wood stove; a kitchen and small table; a bed and dresser; and a work shop with a surfboard propped on a stand.

It was a mahogany roll-top desk with sliding door that caught my eye. I approached it and lifted a photograph of Danny riding a wave. He was crouched and had his arms perfectly balanced within a curl, a misty mane rising from the breaking water. He looked to be at total peace, reverent even, as if entering a holy place. Amidst tons of crashing sea, he'd found his temple.

I set the photo down to focus on a letter in Danny's handwriting beside which lay an envelope addressed to me. Inclined to pen more than keyboard, he often sent letters by snail mail, and because I knew he enjoyed receiving letters in turn, I reciprocated the favor. I began reading the letter…

> *Dear Jason,*
>
> *I've been meaning to write for a while, but things have been busy. Wanted to tell you about something weird that happened about a month ago. Someone broke into my cabin. A strange thing given we have no crime here. Even stranger was they took your letters… nothing else… no cash, no tools … only your letters.*
>
> *Go figure.*

I dropped the sheet and ran to the car. Jumping in, I gunned the engine and sped away, leaving the persimmons, cows, and meadow in a blur. At Highway 1, I turned north and glanced into my mirror with terror, sure someone was after me. Why else would they have taken my letters from Danny's cabin? Not only that, but shortly after moving to Bethesda, a set of my diaries in which I'd recorded, among other things, my long friendship with Danny had vanished from my home. Now, having read Danny's final letter, I had no doubt I'd been robbed. As in Danny's case, the perpetrator had stolen only written materials; everything else was left intact. My diaries, it now occurred to me, had marked Danny as a target.

But two questions haunted me: Who was the perpetrator, and why was he after me?

WITH JUST OVER two hours remaining before I was due to meet Danny's parents, I drove to the rendezvous site, a place called Bean Hollow State Park located along the coast north of Marinero. According to the map, Half Moon Bay was another forty-five minutes north of Bean Hollow, which meant Danny drove over an hour each day to tend to his surf shop. In one of his letters, he told me how much he enjoyed the drive because it took him along the coast the entire way. As he drove, he lowered his window to take in the cold air and watch swells roll in from the Pacific.

I opened a window in memory of my friend. The wind slapped me like a cold, wet towel, as if scolding me for not being Danny Rogers who it normally greeted each day. With penitence, I followed the undulating asphalt past deserted bays until a sign appeared for Bean Hollow State Park. I turned into a vacant parking lot and took a space facing the sea. A yard before me was a four- to six-foot drop-off that led to a long arc of sand that stretched in both directions. At one end, a shadowy hill tapered to the ocean while at the other, a promontory jutted into the sea. Enclosed by the arc was a bay, its inner waters calm, but beyond the inlet, massive rollers formed from an abrupt rise of the seabed. Through the receding fog, jets of white water surged into the bay. I shuddered at the thought of Danny riding those waves.

I stepped out of the car. Below, strewn across the sand, were remnants of kelp, their gas bladders resembling rubber balls the sea had rolled ashore. I envisioned Danny jogging across the sand, tossing his surfboard into the water, and paddling to the rollers. I felt my body rise and fall with the swells, each growing larger than the previous. Having taken a surfing lesson from Eve in Australia, I imagined catching a wave and riding it with Danny beside me, the two of us laughing with joy. A gust then whipped across the sand and sent me back into the car.

Shivering, I locked the doors and turned on the motor. With a stream of warm air blowing at me, I soon fell asleep. The next thing I knew, a tapping awoke me. I bolted forward and turned the ignition. It made a grinding sound from the idling engine. Looking out the window, I saw two faces peering in at me. I turned the engine off and got out of the car.

Only a year had passed since Eve and I had lunched with Danny's parents in Half Moon Bay, yet the furrows on their faces now suggested decades had passed. It was such a contrast from how they looked a year earlier, and even more so from the day they left

Wisconsin to move to California. After living in Wisconsin all their lives, they were ready for a change—ready to leave a community they felt had never truly accepted a lesbian couple for adopting a son. Half Moon Bay, on the other hand, offered a freer way of life, just as California had done for millions of pilgrims before them. Both Kristine Rogers and her partner, Emma, had found jobs there. They were eager to move on.

Kristine took me in her arms. In Wisconsin, she had treated me like a second son, although I never felt I deserved such. She said I was a saint for treating Danny as kindly as I did, but I would have it no other way for he was a soul mate as much as a friend. While others teased him for being clumsy and for a stutter he struggled with, I found peace in his presence. We spent hours together after school each day, and he was the only one who helped me dissect road kill.

I turned to Emma and embraced her, but it was a hug less engaging than the one with Kristine. If Kristine exuded spring and summer, Emma embodied fall and winter. Years earlier, while visiting their home during an early Wisconsin snowfall, Danny and I went outside to play. Big, wet flakes dropped like soggy corn chips. At the time, Danny had a cold and was dragging. As we put on our coats, Kristine called to Danny to bundle up so that he wouldn't get sicker whereas Emma followed with a command: "Shovel the walk while you're out there." The forecast called for less than an inch to fall.

Presently, Emma asked: "When did you get here?"

"A while ago," I replied. I said nothing of the visit to Danny's cabin.

Kristine turned from me. Her shoulders undulated from sobs. I put my arm around her. "I'm sorry about what happened."

"You can't imagine what it means to lose Danny," Emma said. I groaned.

Emma again: "Why did they kill him with your protein?"

It wasn't *my* protein, I wanted to tell her. Discovery didn't convey ownership, for if it did, oxygen belonged to Carl Wilhelm Scheele and Joseph Priestley, two inquisitive thinkers from the eighteenth century.

"I don't know," I replied. I wanted to tell them that I, too, felt targeted but referring to myself would only demean Danny.

"When Dr. Muñoz spoke to us by telephone last week," Kristine said, "he told us the FBI was involved in the investigation."

"Yes," I said, towing the party line.

"What have you learned from them?"

"Only that the investigation is ongoing."

"So, we *wait*?" Kristine asked.

"Not me!" Emma proclaimed. She went to the beach.

"Where are you going?" Kristine called.

"Where Danny went! Are you coming?"

I followed Kristine to the sand where I removed my shoes and socks. The retreating fog formed a silver bank now across the Pacific, allowing dawn to arrive with dignity. I savored the shifting tide of day as hints of warmth crept into the air.

"Follow me," Emma said.

As we set out, I found myself sandwiched between the two women, our shoulders bumping every few steps.

"Did we ever tell you how we adopted Danny?" Emma asked.

"No," I said, grateful for her olive branch.

"We approached a number of agencies," she began, synchronizing her steps with mine. "Many refused to deal with us because we weren't a traditional couple. Remember, that was a different time." Her face brightened. "Then, one day, a colleague at work told me about an orphanage that had just accepted a five-year-old boy whose parents had died in a car crash. He was unusual in that he'd been sheltered at home with practically no social contact—no daycare, no play groups, no classes for tots. His mother and father were farmers who largely shunned the outside world. They avoided doctors, in particular, and refrained from getting their son vaccinated and having his cleft palate repaired. My colleague asked whether Kristine and I would consider adopting the boy." She beamed. "You know the answer!"

"He was such a fine boy!" Kristine chimed. "Precious smile—even *with* the cleft palate."

"The truth is, he adopted us," Emma said. "He swept us into his heart where we blossomed as parents, and he never judged us."

She jumped ahead to face me squarely, stopping in my path. "Do you know what I mean about the non-judgmental part?"

"I do," I replied. "I suspect it stemmed from your unconditional love for him."

Emma released me to walk again.

"Danny told us *you'll* be a father soon," Kristine said, her first smile since we'd hugged.

I wondered how she could muster joy when she'd just lost her own child.

"Yes," I replied in hollow affirmation. I looked about, eager to change the subject.

Emma splayed her arms. "This was Danny's getaway." She took my hand and led me to a sandstone wall where, over the years, storms had etched designs into its slope.

"Danny adored these," Emma said, fingering a groove that outlined what I imagined to be a horse-drawn chariot.

"And these," Kristine added, holding a piece of driftwood. She ran her fingers across it.

"You remember Danny's hair," Kristine laughed, "so frizzy in the moist ocean air." She dropped to her knees, smoothed a patch of sand, and sketched a head with spirals atop it. " 'Brillo-boy'—that's what we called him at the beach."

We walked to the promontory where the ebbing sea had left a series of tide pools, many rimmed by pinkish-green algae. In one, I saw a sculpin fish dart away. Further out, sea palms stood like miniature trees brazenly daring the waves to douse them.

"He felt restored here," Emma said. "This beach invigorated him."

I could see why: In the Pacific's throbbing blue was an oceanic heart, its pulse reaching the shore in swells.

"Come," Emma said. "Let's go to the other end."

We retraced our steps past the parking lot before continuing to the hill along the southern end of the bay. A path through a carpet of ice plants brought us to the summit which afforded a view of swells morphing into thunderous waves that crashed below, each striking the seabed with sufficient force to shake the ground. In the surge of white water that followed each wave, a roar ensued as loud as a passing train.

"This is where Danny came to work out his problems," Emma said. "Relationships and the like."

A year earlier, Danny told me he had proposed to a woman, a joyous event for a man with a self-professed slow-start on the dating scene. A letter inked shortly after that delivered the crushing news that his fiancée had been unfaithful; marriage no more.

After watching the sea, we returned to the parking lot where we sat at a picnic table beside the cars. Above, the last of the mist had peeled away to leave a blazing blue sky.

"Danny's illness was horrific," Kristine said, clenching her hands. "Intractable pain, vomiting, and bleeding. He drowned in blood." She beseeched me with penetrating eyes. "Dr. Muñoz asked repeatedly if he could have eaten shrimp, but *you* know Danny: it was impossible." She paused, then: "I think it was a drink that poisoned him."

I raised my brows.

Emma explained. "A juice he drank every morning while commuting to his surf shop in Half Moon Bay. Just before dying, he told us he thought it was the drink that sickened him. It hadn't tasted right. He saved the bottle with the remnants and asked us to pick it up from his cabin."

My heart skipped. "Do you have it?"

Emma went to the car and returned with a paper bag, wrinkled and twisted at the top. She extracted a half-filled bottle containing an orange fluid and handed it to me.

"Did you tell Dr. Muñoz about this?" I asked.

"Yes, but he made little of it. He was convinced Danny ate shrimp without knowing it."

I studied the label...

Electric Jolt
Electrolyte Replacement Fluid for Serious Athletes
♥
Made with Minerals from the Sea.

In small print below a picture of a flexed arm with magnificent biceps was the manufacturer's name: *BioVironics Pharmaceuticals and Neutraceuticals, Germantown, Maryland.*

"May I keep this?" I asked.

Emma nodded.

Germantown, Maryland. I knew the name well. The day before, I was on the outskirts of Germantown when I received the summons from my supervisor at PAHO to call Randy Flagstaff.

I wondered now whether the town might bring other un-pleasantries in the form of this juice called *Electric Jolt.*

COMPARED TO PRIVATE colleges, the University of Wisconsin in Madison was a bargain, although I couldn't have gone there had it not been for work-study. My mother had exhausted her savings to pay for my brother's education so when it came my time to go to college I had to work my way through bussing dishes, guiding tours, and shelving books. My least favorite task was manning the all-night reading room during exam week. The work was as menial—checking out reserve readings and performing clean-up duties—as it was disruptive of the circadian rhythm. Every hour, I toured the room to keep awake, passing insomniacs and last-minute crammers who hovered over books with bottles of caffeinated tablets beside them. Dawn never came soon enough.

I thought of that job as I flew back to Washington, D.C. after leaving Kristine and Emma. I had driven to the airport directly from Bean Hollow State Park to catch a flight standby, but because the only seats that remained were middle ones, I was sandwiched between two hefty men. In the meantime, behind me, a gaggle of cheerleaders traveling to a competition prevented me from napping. To pass time, I reviewed the slides Muñoz and Bjornstad had presented on Capitol Hill, disturbed still by what I believed were missives personalized to my life.

After deplaning, I placed a call to someone I thought might help explain the elusive missives. Two features convinced me they came from a published source: the precise punctuation—as in the use of commas in *But she, surrendering to …,* and *… he lived under the earth,*—and, as Bjornstad had noted, the spelling of *chimaera* in the missive, *… not that rich chimaera.* In my unabridged dictionary at home, the spelling of "chimaera" was listed as an older, less employed version for "chimera," making me think the missive had been lifted from a dated work.

I listened now as my phone rang.

"Squills," a voice answered.

Lawrence P. Squills was a professor of English at the University of Wisconsin. During my sophomore year, I took a course in nineteenth century literature that he taught, a decision I came to regret. Tall and gaunt, he came to class each day with a stack of books under one arm and a pipe dangling from his mouth. He peppered students with questions and searched for those who hadn't done the readings. When he found his target, he was merciless. For that reason, I did my homework assiduously although it spared me little pain because he discovered one of my innermost angsts: reading aloud. It was a phobia I developed in middle school when a teacher had me read a sonnet aloud before the class. The wires in my brain somehow crossed to produce an anxiety short-circuit. I panted as my heart raced and beads of sweat dripped down my face. I felt like I'd been asked to read a novel rather than fourteen lines. Three-quarters into it, I made the mistake of looking up. A sea of faces gawked at my discomfort.

Thereafter, I did what I could to avoid reading before others: I feigned sore throats, laryngitis, dental problems—*anything* to keep from reading aloud. Professor Squills, having discovered the pathology, insisted I read at almost every class thereafter. When I tried to drop out of the course, he called me to his office.

"I won't sign it," he announced, waving the drop form.

"Why not?"

"Because, you need to face your fear, and I'll help you do it."

"Which fear?" I asked.

He smiled. "You have more than one?"

"Look, I want to drop the class because I need credits elsewhere to apply to medical school."

"Anton Chekhov and W. Somerset Maugham became doctors, but they found time for literature. Can't you?"

"Fine, give me hell," I said. I left his office empty-handed.

In class, he continued to call on me to read, although he did so with a different tack: He assigned only a few lines each time and praised me after I finished reading them, not in a way that made me feel like a teacher's pet, but with a crisp "Yup" or "Great." Slowly, *painfully*, the burden eased but not entirely.

"Congratulations, you stuck it out," he told me after the course ended.

I thanked him.

We met periodically thereafter in his book-lined office. During one visit, he told me we shared an experience.

"Which?" I asked.

"My father left me, too. That's when I turned to books. I found refuge in them."

At graduation ceremonies, I introduced him to my mother. It was the last time I saw him, but in the years that followed, we kept in touch through Christmas cards.

I greeted him now on the phone.

"Are you calling from a conference?" he asked. "I hear voices in the background."

"I'm at an airport."

I told him about the outbreak and my CDC affiliation.

"Missives?" he asked.

I read each aloud.

"Yes," he said, "I think I know their source, but let me check something first. May I call you back?"

"Will five minutes do?" I asked.

"*Five minutes?*"

I told him I had always wanted to see what it'd feel like to assign a professor a deadline.

WITH THE THREE-HOUR time change between coasts, it was 10 p.m. when I arrived home. I found Eve in the bedroom unfolding a Batik maternity dress she purchased six months earlier in Indonesia shortly after learning she was pregnant. She traveled to Indonesia after quitting her job at *Qantas* to volunteer at a shelter for battered women, a cause she held dear. With plans to move to the U.S. after that to prepare for marriage, she felt it was her last available window to volunteer.

She set the dress down as I walked into the room.

"Did they feed you?" she asked as we hugged.

"Nothing," I replied.

She shook her head. "They treat people like cattle now. How about we go out for a bite?"

We stepped into a hot, heavy night. Beads formed across Eve's forehead as we walked, and we stopped periodically to allow her to catch her breath. Eventually, we came to a small grill, and she sighed with relief in the cool air.

"Last night was a bear," she said. "The baby kept poking me in the ribs with its feet."

"Did you nap today?"

"Briefly … until the doctor called."

I sat straighter. "What did he say?"

She dabbed her mouth, her large brown eyes peering over the napkin. "He wanted to schedule a Caesarian-section so a surgeon could biopsy the breast mass at delivery."

"Great idea."

She frowned. "You know how I feel about Caesarians. I told him I wanted to deliver naturally."

"What did he say?"

"He relented, but reluctantly. He didn't want to delay the biopsy."

"Nor do I."

She took my hand. "Step-by-step, Jason."

When it came to health care, Eve was less main stream than I. After learning she harbored the *BRAC1* gene that placed her at increased risk for breast and ovarian cancer, she turned to Ayurvedic medicine, Buddhism, and Zen philosophy. She began meditating regularly.

"There's more travel ahead," I warned her. While riding home from the airport, Bird called to insist I go to Ecuador with Muñoz.

"Yes, I heard. Randy Flagstaff dropped by today." She reached into her purse and extracted a small package. "He left this for you."

Inside were a cell phone, passport, and business cards with the inscription:

> *Oscar Fields*
> *Sales Manager*
> *Omega-3-Seafood*
> *Frederick, Maryland*

"Your identity," she explained.

"Seafood?" I mumbled.

"You're traveling as a prospective buyer."

I found it odd to see my photo in a passport paired with the name *Oscar Fields* and a birth place of Iowa.

Eve took the passport and set it down. "Are you ready to talk about your trip to California?"

I hesitated.

"I visited Danny's house," I said after a while. "I found a letter he was writing to me in which he said someone had broken into his home and took the letters I'd written him."

"Why would they do that?"

I shook my head and told her about the rest of the trip.

After eating, we walked home along empty streets, although with traffic almost absent, the black SUV that trailed us was hard to miss. At least Flagstaff was true to his word: a security detail had been assigned.

THE NEW CELL phone rang as we stepped inside.

"Good, you got the packet," Flagstaff said. "You leave tomorrow first thing, which is just as well because the XK59 story will break then. The Task Force thought it was time to inform the public." He paused. "In the meantime, do you know someone named Charles E. Oxford, PhD?"

"No, why?"

"Because, our security team saw a young woman leave his business card on your door mat. You've never heard of his company—

BioVironics Pharmaceuticals and Neutraceuticals?"

My heart skipped. "Up the road, in Germantown?"

"You know it, then."

"I learned about it in California." I told him about the bottled drink Danny's parents had given me.

"Stay put. I'll have someone from the lab come get it immediately."

Forty minutes later, a man in a natty suit with boyish good looks appeared at the door. "*Distamus ab aliis.*"

"*Proprius orbis,*" I replied with scorn.

He extended his hand. "Alistair Brubeck, director of the UNIT lab. I've come for the bottled drink."

I gave it to him.

"What about the results on levels of XK59 in the victims?" I asked. "Have you got them?"

"Not yet." He started down the steps. "But I'll call you with them soon."

He raced away in a chauffeured car.

Day 3.

"MR. FIELDS, YOUR passport," a voice beckoned as I stared at a departure screen at Dulles International Airport.

"Mr. Fields!" the voice repeated.

I shifted my eyes to the counter.

"I'm sorry." I handed the airline agent my passport.

He took my suitcase in exchange for a boarding pass, and after clearing security, I rode a shuttle to the gate where I received a call from Alistair Brubeck.

"Can you talk?" he asked.

I glanced about. With an hour remaining before my flight's departure, the gate was sparsely populated.

"Yes," I said.

"I've got the results you requested—levels of XK59 in the victim who died in Seattle and in leftover shrimp recovered from his refrigerator."

"Let's hear them," I replied.

"It's odd, but the levels in the shrimp were far lower than those in the victim. We triple-checked them."

"Give me the values."

Papers rustled.

"In the shrimp, there was one *microgram* of XK59 per kilogram of tissue, which is equivalent to 1 part per *billion*, whereas in the victim, there was one *milligram* of XK59 per kilogram, or 1 part per *million*. That's a thousand-fold higher concentration in the victim."

"One part per million in the victim," I repeated. "That's the same level of XK59 I found in the mice that bled to death, only to produce that level, I had to feed the rodents chow that contained 10 parts per million of XK59."

"Sounds like one part per million of XK59 in tissue causes fatal bleeding," Brubeck observed.

"Yes, but it's baffling that the concentration of XK59 in the shrimp was so low. For the victim to have accumulated a level a thousand-fold greater than that present in the shrimp, he would have had to eat an inconceivably large amount of shrimp."

"The results are what they are," Brubeck said.

I recalled a colleague who used to help students visualize the difference between one part per *million* of something versus one part per *billion*. One part per million would be one particle of a substance for every 999,999 other particles, whereas one part per billion would be one particle for every 999,999,999 other particles. He suggested students think about wheat being loaded into shipping containers. If a full container carried 100 tons of wheat, then one would have to add a half-cup of sugar to the container to create a mixture of 1 part per million. By contrast, to create a mixture of 1 part per *billion*, one would have to mix a single *teaspoon* of sugar in 45 containers of wheat.

"Perhaps something other than shrimp contributed to the higher levels in the victim," I proposed.

"Like what?"

"I don't know, but let's see what results come from the drink I brought from California."

Just then, Ricardo Muñoz appeared at the gate.

"Gotta go," I told Brubeck.

"Bring home some shrimp from Ecuador," he replied.

"DID YOU SEE this?" Muñoz asked, lifting a copy of *The Washington Post*. He pointed to the headlines.

Deadly Protein in Tainted Shrimp Kills 3, Sickens 9 Others

"Yes," I replied with discomfort. While riding to the airport, I had read the article, and seeing mention of XK59 on a front-page story had made me feel like a villain of sorts even though my name as discoverer of the protein hadn't been cited.

I shifted attention away from myself to Muñoz, saying, "I saw your quote about the source of the shrimp still being under investigation."

He nodded. "I didn't want the shrimp farm in Ecuador to know they had been targeted."

"Who's handling the press while we're in Ecuador?"

"A colleague of mine from CDC named Crystal Petersen. Glenn Bird recruited her." His eyes brightened. "She'll replace me after we complete our work in Ecuador so I can see my fiancée in Peru."

"When's the big day?"

"Two weeks." From his wallet he pulled a photo of a woman with long black hair and engaging eyes. "Lolita," he said. "I want to begin my life with her."

WE ARRIVED IN Quito at dusk. Two men met us at baggage claim, one spindly and gaunt, the other portly and unkempt. The spindly one introduced himself as Alex Winrod of *Eagle Wings*.

On the flight, Muñoz had informed me that *Eagle Wings* was a CIA contractor that flew the jungles of Colombia to conduct surveillance on political insurgents. Winrod was a former U.S. Navy pilot with a long career of flying in hostile zones. He knew Muñoz and I were in Ecuador only for intelligence purposes.

Winrod eyed our bags. "Good, traveling light." And pointing now: "My colleague, Redondo."

Muñoz exchanged greetings in Spanish.

As we followed Winrod to the tarmac, Muñoz gleaned from Redondo that he hailed from a town called El Coco located near the shrimp farm and owned a fishing business. For years, the man had also worked as a CIA informant, passing on tips regarding the whereabouts of insurgents.

"Risky," I said. "Was he the one who arranged the visit to the shrimp farm?"

"No, I did that while you were in California. I used a Miami mobile number to make it appear I was calling from my business in Florida. I told the owner of the shrimp farm that I had opened a new seafood business in Miami and was swinging through South America to look for suppliers. I asked if I could drop by with a client." He gestured. "You're the client."

On the tarmac, we passed idle jets belonging to *Avianca*, *Lan Chile*, and *Varig* before reaching a section where cargo and military aircraft were stationed. Winrod pointed to an ancient airplane. "Recognize it?" he asked me.

"No."

"Best damn machine ever built."

It didn't look like it. It sat at a thirty-degree angle and had soot lines staining its dented fuselage behind twin propellers.

"DC-3," Winrod continued. "Few still remain, but for decades they served as workhorses for the aviation business."

"We're not flying one, are we?"

He grinned. "Nope, that Cessna over there is ours."

A far cry from the DC-3, it was sleek and new. Winrod opened a rear compartment. "Throw your gear in."

He assigned Muñoz and me to the rear, closed the doors, and revved the engines.

"No drinks, no lavatory," he called. "Puke into your shirt if you get sick." He donned a headset.

Before reaching the runway, we paused to let a Boeing 767 pass. It made me feel like a minnow beside a whale. Before long, we took off, and I gazed at the lights of Quito shining through a crystal clear sky.

We made a long, smooth arc to the southwest to cross the Andes. To the east, a snow-capped Mt. Cotopaxi came into view, its dome draped in moonlight. To my dismay, the stars soon disappeared and we bounced through clouds. Lightning cracked and thunder shook the plane. I clutched an armrest as the Cessna dove. Within seconds, Winrod steadied the plane in an eerie calm.

"That's nothing," he called. "Mild turbulence from cold Pacific air colliding with hot inland currents; happens all the time."

Outside, a range of low-lying hills came into view through thinning clouds while, beyond them, the Pacific appeared as a vast expanse of foreboding dark. As we descended, I cleared my ears with a gaping yawn, refusing to release the armrests.

"Keep your eyes peeled," Winrod advised. "We're going to buzz the shrimp farm."

He made a turn that brought us over the coastline, so low I saw brown pelicans flee their nests. The junction of water and land was blurred by mangroves that formed an endless patchwork of islands with interlacing inlets.

Redondo addressed Muñoz, who interpreted for me. "He says the entire coastline used to look like this before the shrimp farm dredged the mangroves and dug earthen holes for shrimp pools. It's an environmental nightmare because the mangroves serve as a sanctuary for marine life—especially juvenile fish—and when they're destroyed, the fish leave. Before the shrimp farm came, he used to catch all the fish he needed along the coast, but now he has to go far out to sea. Not only that, but the farm has soiled the sea with fertilizer, antibiotics, and chemicals."

Below, a series of rectangular pools appeared along the coast, each a bit larger than a basketball court. A silver sheen reflected from all but one, a solitary round pond apart from the others that emitted a bioluminescence. A warehouse and trailer shot by, and then the shrimp farm disappeared, replaced by a trash heap with a plume of smoke rising from its center. An instant later, we flew over a collection of shacks, a plaza, and a church whose steeple almost pierced us.

"El Coco," Winrod called.

A small bay came into view, its periphery rimmed with fishing boats, and then, inland, a villa on a hill. As I craned my neck to catch a glimpse of a swimming pool beside the villa, my stomach shot to my chest as the airplane swooned onto a knobby pasture.

"Gentlemen," Winrod said, "please remain in your seats until the seat belt sign has been turned off and the airplane has come to a complete halt at the terminal."

Some terminal, I thought: a hole-ridden hut with a windsock.

Winrod killed the engine on Redondo's side but left the opposite one running for a quick getaway. "Out you go," he ordered.

I hopped out into a blast of equatorial air.

"This way," Muñoz yelled, following Redondo's lead.

As we made our way to a flatbed truck, the Cessna purred into the night. I jumped into the middle seat of the cab, and after a short ride through a banana plantation, we arrived at the *Hotel Buenos Sueños*, which, despite its name, was anything but a dream hotel. It had a drab façade that faced the plaza and a dank lobby with mildew-covered walls. A mousetrap sat on an unattended counter beside an ash tray laden with butts.

Redondo spoke to Muñoz.

"He apologizes for the state of the hotel," Muñoz said. "It's a poor town with few visitors. About the only thing of value here is the shrimp farm."

Redondo gave each of us a set of keys and left.

I followed Muñoz up a rickety staircase to the second floor. He stopped beside his room and tapped his watch. "Seven a.m. sharp. Meet you in the lobby."

I bid him goodnight and stepped into my room. It was an austere space holding a bed, wooden chair, and sink with a crack in it large enough to vie with the drain. Along the wall, a beige gecko lizard scurried toward the ceiling in gravity-defying fashion.

I set my belongings down, undressed, and climbed into bed. It met me with a mattress unlike any before, one with contours of a wave pool. Lacking box springs, the mattress sagged to become a hammock. After an hour of fitful sleep, I awoke to rain pelting the window. In the humidity, I felt I was in a sauna rather than a hotel. I spent a few hours tossing about until settling on a diagonal stretch. Above me, in the flickering light from a street lamp, the gecko moved along the ceiling.

Day 4.

I MET MUÑOZ in the lobby at daybreak. He descended the steps gingerly, and when he reached the bottom, stretched his back one way, then the other.

"I need coffee bad," he moaned.

We walked across the street to the plaza where a vendor tended a cart. After buying coffee and rolls, we sat on a bench and dipped bread into our steaming brews as we listened to the rustle of El Coco's palms. It was a hot, tropical breeze that prevented one from moving faster than a crawl.

Muñoz peered across the plaza. "Time to go," he said, pointing to Rendondo's truck.

We joined our colleague and drove through town, a trip that afforded a closer view than that provided by the airplane. Here, the inescapable blemishes of poverty were ubiquitous: ramshackle stilted huts; canals run afoul with raw sewage; and mangy, bedraggled dogs lurking about. At one point, we drove past a group of barefoot boys playing soccer on a dirt street, and as we passed, I waved at one. At first, my target hesitated to return the gesture, as if a socio-cultural divide too wide to span separated us, but then, as we rounded a bend, I saw him break forth with a beaming smile. If visitors were common here, it wasn't apparent; the looks I received made me feel I came from a distant planet.

We left the shanties for sugar cane fields, eventually climbing a hill that looked over El Coco in the distance. With the exception of the church and plaza, it looked like a ragged heap, a dumpster overturned by the Pacific. Along the northern edge of town was the mountain of refuse I had seen the night before, its fire still smoldering, yet even in daylight, it was difficult to tell where the trash ended and the shanties began.

The road from the summit turned toward the coast, exposing a festoon of pools that comprised the shrimp farm. In short order, we came to a sign pointing toward the *Enterpresa de Mariscos*, or shrimp farm, but rather than follow the arrow, we turned onto a less-traveled route.

We passed more sugar cane along a road that narrowed to the point I had to pull my arm in to keep from getting cut by leaves. After a while, the stalks ended and we came to a field of shrubs sloping toward the sea.

We left the truck and followed a path to the coast where Redondo pulled on a rope secured to a pole. A small boat emerged from the mangroves. He held it steady as I clambered aboard. Muñoz followed suit, only he almost fell from the weight of the duffle bag he toted. Redondo, in contrast, hopped in with ease and, taking a seat at the rear, started the engine with a few pulls of the cord. Before long, we set out on a sinuous course through a canopy of red mangroves, taking care to dodge their bowed roots. The water, olive-brown, looked like a nutrient-rich soup simmering in an equatorial kettle. Here and there, bubbles burped to the surface as if some furtive fermentation were concocting a marine cocktail. Along each channel, networks of cinnamon-colored roots coalesced into trunks, which, in turn, splayed into lattices of branches with thick, oval leaves.

After rounding one of many bends, I was startled when a flamingo lifted from the water, its legs retracting like landing gear. I tried to follow its path but lost it beyond the tops of mangroves that had grown tall enough to obscure the coastal hills. At one point, when the water became shallow, Redondo cut the motor and tilted it forward. As we glided along, my ears tuned to a new chorus: buzzing insects, chirping birds, and mysterious splashes from unseen creatures.

"*Cangrejo*," Redondo said, pointing to a crab resting on a branch. Using a paddle, he steered us through the forest, the shade offering a cool respite from the sun.

Upon leaving the canopy, the boat jiggled. I looked back and saw Redondo donning a pair of booties. He eased into the water and came to the bow to pull us toward a muddy mound. Before we reached it, however, a thick sulfur smell filled the air, the sort I recalled from childhood whenever my mother prepared egg salad sandwiches for lunch. I buried my nose in my shirt and marveled at Redondo's imperviousness to the odor.

When we reached the mound, he pushed an arm into the mud.

Lifting it, he displayed an enormous clam, larger than any I'd ever seen. He brought it to the boat.

"A meal itself," I chuckled.

Redondo spoke solemnly.

"He says they're rarely that size anymore. The big ones are disappearing."

"*Chímicos*," Redondo retorted.

It made me think he understood more English than he let on. He launched an impassioned speech.

"Pollution from the farm," Muñoz reported. "Fertilizers, insecticides, oil and diesel, all washing into the sea … stunting shellfish … driving fish to deeper waters."

Redondo returned the clam to its home. With remarkable ease, he slipped back into the boat and restarted the motor, although this time, we headed toward open water. After skirting the shore for a distance, we came to the first of the farm's pools, its earthen levy reaching above a cement wall that abutted the sea. Rising along the cement was a stairway leading to the levy's rim. Redondo steered the boat to the steps and moored along a rail.

"We'll take a quick view of a pool before we continue to the office," Muñoz said.

I followed the duo up the steps. At the top, we came to a sign warning, *Propiedad privada*. Beyond it, myriad pools stretched along the coast with each connected to the next by walkways, pipes, and hoses. Here and there, plumbing leaks sent miniature fountains skyward as an incessant hum of aeration devices, pumps, and generators drowned the sound of lapping waves.

I knelt and surveyed a pool before us. It appeared to be shallow at one end—three feet or so—yet progressively deeper toward the other. The water teemed with shrimp, most six- to nine-inches long, their antennae dark brown and bodies grayish-white. Sprouting from their abdomens were busy legs and a dark tail fan rimmed in yellowish green—all in all, most attractive, I thought.

"Is that the glowing pond we saw last night?" I asked, pointing ahead.

It was a lone circular body set back from the other pools, and in the daylight, its bioluminescence was no longer apparent.

I removed a vial from the duffle bag along with a small net and a pair of shoulder-length rubber gloves.

"What are you doing?" Muñoz asked.

"Getting a sample from that pond," I replied.

"Later," he advised. "We haven't gotten permission yet to take samples."

"What if they prevent us from sampling that pond?"

He frowned. "Work fast!"

I scrambled to the pond where I donned both gloves. Kneeling, I dipped the vial into the water with one hand while I swept the net through the water with the other. It proved to be more challenging than I expected to ensnare shrimp, so I stretched onto my stomach to make wider swaths with the net. I seemed only to startle the critters which shot past the net with dexterous speed. At one point, when several shrimp bumped the net's rim, I recoiled and dropped the vial. Helplessly, I watched it sink to the bottom.

"Hurry!" Muñoz called.

I waved to him for help.

He appeared at my side. Seeing my predicament, he said: "Why'd you drop it?"

"I didn't mean to! Hold my legs while I stretch for it."

I submerged my arm toward the vial and braced for shrimp to bump me, but none did. After retrieving the vial, I handed it to Muñoz and adopted a new strategy, this time holding the net still as the passing current extended its tapered end. Before long, several shrimp swam into the net, and I transferred them to the vial.

"Let's go!" Muñoz implored.

I removed the gloves and scurried to the boat. As we headed off, I labeled the vial and packed it on ice. Before long, we reached a pier where a husky, fair-skinned man waved to us. He had sandy blonde hair that flitted over his eyes, leading him to flick his head to clear the view. A pair of binoculars hung from his neck.

"I'm Dudley Zot," he called, "owner of the shrimp farm. You're my visitors from the U.S., I assume?"

"Yes, I'm Milo Ramírez," Muñoz said, stepping off the boat. "And this is Oscar Fields."

We shook hands.

With a dismissive nod, Zot acknowledged Redondo who, in turn, quickly turned the boat to sea.

To us, Zot said: "I thought you'd be coming by land." His face turned stern.

"We toured the mangroves," Muñoz replied. "They speak to the health of the sea."

"And what did you find?"

"They're in good shape."

"You saw more than mangroves," Zot noted, tapping his binoculars.

"Indeed, we viewed the pools at the distant end."

"And took a sample."

"Which I told you by phone I intended to do for quality control purposes," Muñoz said.

Offset, it seemed, by the confrontational nature of our meeting, Zot broke into a smile. "Not a problem."

He led us to a cluttered modular unit ill-equipped to handle visitors. After clearing off a pair of seats, he said, "I lived here until my business produced sufficient revenues to build a home. Perhaps you saw it on the hill last night from the airplane."

"Yes," Muñoz replied. "Business appears to be good."

Zot leaned back. "Now, perhaps, but it wasn't always that way; the export market is a competitive place."

"Do you export all your shrimp?"

"Yes, to the U.S. currently, but I'm hoping to begin exporting to Japan shortly."

"Have you had any problems with white spot disease?" I asked. On the flight south, I had read about ailments that afflicted shrimp, white spot among them, a viral infection that led to progressive calcium deposition that caused shrimp to become emaciated before dying.

"Not an issue," Zot said, "because we raise our own larvae to keep the farm virus-free."

"No wild shrimp?"

"None."

"Yet, you pump seawater into the pools," I noted.

"True, but we treat it with ultraviolet light to kill any pathogens that might be present."

"Where's the hatchery for your larvae?" Muñoz asked.

"In the warehouse. I'll show you."

We followed Zot outside but stopped at the nearest pool. Like the ones we had seen earlier, it brimmed with shrimp.

"It may look crowded, but don't fret," Zot said. "We stock our pools at a lower density than industry standards to reduce stress on the shrimp." He pointed to the water. "Those are white shrimp, or *Litopenaeus vannamei*."

An employee approached the pool with a bag from which he tossed pellets into the water.

"We use the highest-quality feed," Zot boasted. "No rubbish or waste; only premium nutrients."

I glanced at the label on the bag and my heart leapt—*Manufactured by BioVironics Pharmaceuticals and Neutraceuticals, Germantown, Maryland*; it was the same firm that had produced the juice Danny Rogers consumed.

"Your feed," I stammered, "how long have you used that brand?"

"For several years. Its' an excellent product."

He led us toward a shed at the end of the pool, and as we walked, Muñoz and I exchanged glances. It was clear he was as shaken as I to have seen the name *BioVironics*.

Zot opened the door to the shed. It held a dizzying array of lights and instruments.

"With forty outdoor pools, each roughly the size of Olympic swimming pools, we deal with close to 70,000 cubic meters of water at any given moment," he proclaimed. "That's equal to 70 million liters."

"What's your water exchange rate?" Muñoz asked.

"Twenty-five percent volume per day, which equates to 12,000 liters per minute."

"And how much shrimp do you produce each year?"

"About 100 tons." He closed the door. "To the hatchery …"

"Your accent," I said as we walked. "I can't place it."

"I grew up in Poland but wanderlust took me around the globe. Every few months, I stopped to work to earn cash." He lit a cigarette. "I dug clams in France, canned salmon in Alaska, and worked on a shrimp boat off Texas. Then I got the urge to start my own business, so I bought this farm."

The warehouse we entered had a sliding door and vinyl siding. Inside, it reminded me of an aquarium—not the public viewing area, but behind-the-scenes where motors hummed, hoses hissed, and dials displayed secretive readings. There were open tanks, too, multiple ones, different sizes all, each purring with an aerating device. White-coated technicians buzzing about gave the place the feel of a laboratory.

We stopped before a waist-high tank.

"We grow selected males and females here before breeding them via artificial insemination," Zot explained. "It gives us control over the genetic outcome of the offspring."

"But I've read the yields are lower with artificial insemination than with natural mating," I observed, recalling another paper I perused on the airplane.

"True, but we trade lower yields for superior genes."

We approached another tank, this one lined with fine mesh. In the water were tiny creatures that looked more like aquatic spiders than shrimp.

"Those are 'nauplii,' " Zot explained, "freshly hatched from shrimp eggs. Being poor swimmers, they risk getting sucked by filters or injured by bubbles. The mesh protects them from that."

We moved to a series of tanks of progressively larger size, each housing shrimp in different life stages. At the final tank, Zot said: "These shrimp are called 'postlarvae.' They are the product of two more molts following the nauplii stage."

Unlike the more juvenile forms, to my eye, the postlarvae looked like adult shrimp, albeit smaller in size.

"At the proper time, we transfer postlarvae to an area called the nursery where they grow under carefully-controlled conditions. Following that, we move them to the larger pools outdoors for the so-called grow-out phase, a period that lasts four to five months before the shrimp are harvested."

He led us to another building, this one refrigerated throughout, where employees packed shrimp on ice. A man with a discernible limp approached us.

"Ah, allow me to make an introduction," Zot said. "This is Mr. Anton Manovic, a visiting scientist from the United States who is helping us deal with a venomous snake that has been making its way from the mangroves to our pools." Zot looked at me. "You and Mr. Manovic come from the same neck of the woods."

"Are you from Maryland?" Manovic asked. He spoke with an east European accent.

"Yes, from Frederick." I handed him a card.

As he read it, I noticed the skin about his eyes and nose was mottled and swollen, making me think he had recent sinus surgery. His hair was two-tone from bleaching, the older growth yellow and the newer black.

"Ah, we're neighbors," he exclaimed. "I live about twenty-five miles away from your office in Frederick." His green eyes, tinted by contacts, looked animated, as if they had found a long-lost friend.

"Where do you live?" I asked.

"Germantown."

My stomach twisted. The Washington, D.C. suburb with fewer than a hundred thousand residents had, in the past three days, raised its profile alarmingly—on a bottle of juice collected from Danny Rogers' home; on a business card deposited on my door mat; on a bag of shrimp feed I noticed moments earlier; and now in voice form from a visiting scientist in remote Ecuador. The encounters defied chance alone.

"How nice," I said. "I wish I got there more often, but my seafood business keeps me in Frederick."

"Gentlemen," Zot said, "I encourage you to continue your discussion, but I must attend to a delegation of Japanese visitors. I trust you'll join us later for lunch."

"An honor," Muñoz said. "In the meantime, we'll look about a bit more."

ALISTAIR BRUBECK HAD packed our duffel bag carefully. In addition to equipping it with vials to collect samples, he included swabs, tubes containing media to promote the growth of bacteria and viruses, and packing material. Muñoz and I spent the morning collecting samples from pools, fertilizers, chemicals, and other aides used to maintain the pools. We were left to our own with little interest from others.

Early that afternoon, Zot summoned us to lunch on a grassy knoll among mango trees. I set the duffle bag down and, wiping my brow, joined Muñoz in drinking a beer. Beside us, a chef grilled steaks, his corpulence suggesting he'd enjoyed the spoils of his trade for decades.

Zot approached us with a woman by his side. She was petite with long black hair highlighted red along its lower curls and wore matching red eyeliner. "My wife, Carmen," he said.

She smiled in a fashion that tried, I suspected, to conceal teeth that needed work. "I hope you'll enjoy the food," she said, her accent Latin.

"But first *drinks!*" Zot blurted. "You worked hard this morning." He left us to socialize with other guests.

I took up on his offer of a second drink, meeting a Japanese man at the cooler.

"From America?" he asked.

"Yes, and you?"

"Okinawa."

We shook hands. He motioned to his colleagues. "Friends … all from Japan. Come to see shrimp farm."

"What do you think of it?" I asked.

"State-of-art."

A silver tray with hors d'oeuvres appeared, held, no less, by the visiting scientist we spoke to earlier, Anton Manovic.

"You must try one of these shrimp," he said. "Fresh as can be."

I took one out of courtesy but vowed not to eat it in light of the evidence that shrimp from this very farm had caused the outbreak of XK59-associated bleeding in the United States.

"Very kind of you to help Mr. Zot with his guests," I said.

As I lifted the shrimp, my eyes darted to a generous portion of Manovic's chest laid bare by a largely unbuttoned guayabera shirt.

Manovic smiled. "Not a problem; the least I can do." He moved on, displaying a waddle to his gait, as if one leg was shorter than the other.

"Please, come!" Zot bellowed from the grill. "The meat is cooked."

I ate a steak with fried plantains and corn on the cob. Sitting in a chair with a cool breeze blowing from the sea, I savored the food, the view, and the hum of easy talk.

THE LUNCH PROVED to be a protracted affair with a band playing well into the afternoon. Muñoz and I excused ourselves quietly, however, to collect more samples. Upon completing the task, we went to Zot's office.

"May I count on your business?" he asked.

Muñoz tapped the duffle bag. "With favorable results, I should think so."

"And what about you, Mr. Fields?" Zot asked me.

"How could I say no after eating your shrimp?"

"I may have other clients who would like to purchase your product as well," Muñoz said.

"Oh?" Zot leaned forward. "Who are they?"

"I'd be happy to discuss them with you," Muñoz said, "but we needn't tie Mr. Fields up as we do so. He would like to return to El Coco to inspect Redondo's fishing business before the day ends."

Although I was uncomfortable with the idea of parting ways with Muñoz, he had convinced me earlier to leave the shrimp farm before he did to arrange a pickup time with Winrod.

"No problem," Zot replied. "We'll send Mr. Fields with our Japanese friends."

"How will Mr. Ramírez get back?" I asked, eyeing my colleague.

"We'll arrange a ride for him," Zot assured me.

I thanked Zot and carried the duffle bag to a bus where the Japanese had already taken their seats. It was a noisy ride to town with a group still abuzz from liquor that had flowed freely at lunch. I received a cheer of good will as I departed at Redondo's fish market. Redondo, cutting steaks behind a counter, came out to greet me.

"*¿Como estás, amigo?*"

I dug deep for remnants of high school Spanish. "*Bien, y usted?*"

"Where is señor Ramírez?" he asked, the first I'd heard of his English.

"At the farm. He should be back soon. In the meantime, he asked that we call Winrod to plan an evening departure."

"I do that." He escorted me into his shop where he called Winrod. After a brief discussion in Spanish, he said, "He arrive at midnight to collect you." He removed his apron. "*¿Quieres una cerveza?*"

"*Si, por favor.*"

We walked to the plaza and sat at an outdoor café under a *Cinzano* umbrella and ordered beers.

"We watch pretty *señoritas*," Redondo suggested.

There were plenty to be seen, for it appeared that the town had assembled at the plaza for sunset. Across the street, at the fountain, a bevy of girls giggled at a group of boys poised on the steps. Music from a loudspeaker blared nearby.

Night fell quickly and after downing the fourth beer of the day, I switched to mineral water as empty bottles collected on the table like bowling pins.

"I go now," Redondo said. "I meet you and Ramírez at your hotel later to take you to air field."

I thanked him and said goodbye, but rather than return to the forlorn hotel, I remained at the café to wait for Muñoz to arrive. Under a sputtering street lamp, I drew comfort from watching people pass. At the last light of day, a flashy jeep with a roll bar finally turned into the plaza. As it drove by, I saw Manovic in the driver's seat with Muñoz beside him. Neither noticed me at the café.

I paid the bill and started across the plaza. As I walked, I saw the jeep come to a stop before the hotel. Oddly, the driver's face was covered by a ski mask now and the headlights had extinguished. I called to Muñoz but he didn't hear me through the rustling palms, or if he did, he didn't reply because he was preoccupied with freeing his seatbelt. Suddenly, the driver bolted from the jeep and ran into the hotel, and as he disappeared, an explosion ruptured the night, shooting fiery streaks from the jeep.

"My God!" I shrieked.

I sprinted, shouting "Muñoz, Muñoz!," oblivious to his alias. Through smoke billowing from the jeep, I saw the vehicle had flipped onto its roll bar. Parts were strewn about the ground—a shattered headlight, a door, a seat. The heat from the chassis was so intense I couldn't approach it, yet from twenty yards, I saw Muñoz's lifeless form charred to the frame. A severed arm lay on the street only feet away.

I looked up and down the street for help. An amorphous crowd had formed at the end of the block, yet no one stepped forth. I turned my eyes to the hotel, thinking help would surely come from there, but again, none did. Instead, a light flicked on in a second-floor window from the very room I had slept in. A masked figure appeared at the window and opened it, revealing the barrel of a rifle. I turned to run, but before I could take a second step, a shot rang out. The duffle bag beside my body jerked. Then another shot, one striking the sidewalk.

I dove behind a palm tree. My throat burned for air. In the silence, I knew I had to flee, so I dashed to the next tree. Another shot dug into the soil beside me. I took another tree, this time peeking around the trunk to find the window barren.

I rushed across the street, duffle bag in tow, and raced along a dark, narrow lane away from the plaza. Here and there, I stopped to catch my breath, but as I did, I pressed my body into doorways. When I looked back I expected to see a pursuer, but none came, so I ran again, diving behind a dumpster at one point when a truck approached. To my relief, it turned onto another street, allowing me to continue. As I ran, I passed windows through which I saw people eating dinner or putting children to bed.

My legs ached by the time I reached the outskirts of town. As I continued, the dwellings were replaced by sugar cane fields, one of which I took refuge in as I groped for my cell phone. An eternity passed before the party answered.

"Krispix, is that you?" the voice asked.

"You almost got me killed!"

"Calm down!" Glenn Bird shot back. "Where are you?"

"In a godforsaken field out of town!"

"Is Muñoz with you?"

"He's dead!"

"*What?*"

"They blew up the jeep he was riding in and tried to shoot me, but I escaped."

"Listen!" he commanded. "Stay on the phone; I'm going to get someone else to join us."

Mosquitoes descended upon me, bringing thoughts of malaria, dengue, and yellow fever.

"Krispix," Bird finally said. "Alex Winrod has joined us. Are you there, Alex?"

"Yes," he replied.

"Tell Krispix what you want him to do."

"I'm coming," Winrod said, "but you're going to have to find your way to a different field from the one we landed on; they'll be looking for you there."

"Where do you want me to go?"

"What road did you take out of town?" he asked.

"The first one I could find!"

"Give me landmarks."

I peered out from the edge of the field into the moonlit night. "I'm near a hill with part of its side dug out."

"Ah, the quarry!" he said. "I know exactly where you are. You've got a hike ahead."

"With a duffle bag that weighs a ton!"

He continued: "You'll scale that hill you see, and when you reach the other side, there'll be a valley where I'll pick you up." He asked what the weather was like.

"Calm wind, clear sky."

"Good, I'll meet you in an hour and a half."

It took me almost that long to get to the valley. The weight of the duffle bag threw me off balance and I fell repeatedly from the treacherous footing. By the time I reached the destination, my trousers were torn and my arms bruised, but the sound of an airplane dropping from the sky was a balm as soothing as any. It was a rapid descent Winrod made, and one without lights. He taxied up to me and stopped abruptly. With both propellers still spinning, he left the pilot's seat to appear at the rear door.

"Get in!" he shouted. "I saw a pair of headlights coming around the hill."

In moments, we were airborne. I sat beside Winrod as he turned the airplane one way, then another to dodge thunderstorms.

"Back to Quito?" I asked.

"Nope, to Colombia." He was quiet for a moment. "Sorry about your partner."

An hour passed before we began our descent, and I watched the hands of the altimeter turn. After piercing a layer of clouds, we entered a pitch-black sky sequestered from the moon. Winrod banked us to one side and then leveled the airplane before the wheels touched ground. We stopped beside an immense aircraft.

"C-130 *Hercules*," Winrod said, preempting my question.

The tail at its rear had been lowered, revealing a helicopter inside. At the base of the ramp was a jeep with the insignia *United States Air Force*.

"One war zone to another," Winrod grumbled. "We'll get you out of here soon."

We crossed a tarmac surrounded by jungle to a one-floor building. An armed sentry waved us through to a room where a group of men played cards. An officer in a flight suit acknowledged me with a nod. "Hang tight," he said.

With no seats available, I stood in a corner and used the time to check on the contents of the duffle bag. The bullet that struck the bag earlier had pierced the thick rubber gloves Muñoz and I used to collect specimens but left the individual containers unharmed.

"Full house," a player said, slapping his cards on the table.

Cursing followed, and with it the game ended. The officer approached. "Pete Nelson," he said. "I'll be flying you to Andrews Air Force Base outside Washington." He glanced at the duffle bag. "That's it?"

I nodded.

"Onward."

He led me to the C-130 and we climbed its ramp. At the top, an enlisted loadmaster took the duffle bag and packed it securely. Inside, with the seating modules removed, the helicopter filled the cavernous space. Our feet gripped the non-skid surface as we made our way forward.

After scaling a ladder to the flight cabin, I was greeted with a nod from the co-pilot.

"Take that seat," Nelson said, pointing to the rear of the cockpit.

Outside, the turboprops fired up, and it wasn't long before we took off. After a steep ascent through a layer of clouds that bumped us about, we leveled off. The co-pilot summoned me to his side where he gave me a headset. "Incoming call," he explained.

It was from Glenn Bird. "I heard you're on your way."

"Yes."

"Muñoz blew your cover down there. That's why they killed him."

"What are you talking about?"

"He left a photo of himself and his fiancée at the shrimp farm. An employee found it in one of the pools. On the back was a note saying, *To Ricardo Muñoz, my husband to be, at CDC now, but forever in my heart.*"

"*Shit*," I whispered. I suspected it had fallen from his pocket when he leaned over to hold my legs at the round pond. "Who told you about the photo?"

"Winrod. He got a call from some guy named Redondo, who, in turn, learned of the photo from a friend who works at the farm."

"Which means they're hiding something," I said. "Otherwise, why would they have killed him?"

"They're saying it was an accident. A guy named Manovic told Redondo the jeep was fueled by natural gas and that a spark ignited a leak."

"Bullshit! Manovic ran from the jeep before it exploded and later fired at me from a hotel room."

"We're sending a forensics team to El Coco," Bird said.

I grimaced. "Who's going to call Muñoz's fiancée?"

A pause, then: "That would be you, buddy."

Day 5.

I AWOKE TO the thump of the C-130's wheels touching ground, a jarring that made me sit bolt upright. Through the cockpit windows, I saw dawn cracking the sky.

When we came to a stop, the loadmaster escorted me to the tarmac where he handed me the duffle bag. An official from the UNIT approached me instantly.

"Follow me, sir," he said. "You're to see Dr. Brubeck urgently."

With rush hour yet to begin, we made it to town readily. Upon reaching the UNIT, I went to the lab where I found Randy Flagstaff and Brubeck huddled in discussion.

"Jason," Flagstaff said. "Welcome back." He shook my hand and held it longer than I expected, peering into my eyes as if to express regret for the mission he'd sent me on.

I handed Brubeck the duffel bag. "All yours."

"Bullet?" Brubeck asked, pointing to a hole in it.

"Better there than in me," I replied.

His face tightened. "God awful about Muñoz."

I said nothing.

He continued: "I was just reviewing with Randy the results of XK59 testing for Danny Rogers and the juice he drank."

"The *Electric Jolt*?"

"Yes." He frowned. "The numbers are eerily similar to those for the Seattle victim and leftover shrimp."

"How similiar?"

Brubeck inched forward. "One part per billion XK59 in *Electric Jolt* yet one part per *million* in Danny's blood."

"What I call the 'inverted thousand,' " Flagstaff said. "One would expect the concentration of XK59 to be a thousand-fold higher in food or drink as opposed to blood."

Brubeck's frown deepened. "And the two bacteria, *Vibrio parahaemolyticus* and *Aeromonas hydrophila*, were present in both samples—blood and *Electric Jolt*."

"How can that be?" I asked. "There's no connection between the juice and the sea."

"Product tampering," Flagstaff concluded. "No other option."

"If that's the case," I said, "we need to test the isolates of *Vibrio parahaemolyticus* from the victims, shrimp, and *Electric Jolt* to see if they're genetically identical. If they are, they probably came from the same source."

"Why test only the *Vibrio* and not *Aeromonas*?" Flagstaff asked.

"A fair question," Brubeck agreed.

"Because *Vibrio* has the record of being a true pathogen, not *Aeromonas*."

Brubeck frowned. "Very well, we'll run whole genome sequencing." For Flagstaff's benefit, he explained: "WGS, or whole genome sequencing, determines the exact sequence of DNA building blocks—or nucleic acids—that comprise the bacteria's genes. It's the most accurate test that exists for characterizing DNA; a gold standard genetic fingerprinting system."

"As with all bacteria," I added, "we'd expect a variety of different strains of *Vibrio parahaemolyticus* to exist in nature, each strain possessing a unique sequence of nucleic acids. We can use those differences to distinguish among strains. If WGS shows the isolates from the victims, shrimp, and *Electric Jolt* to be identical, they most likely came from a common source."

I pointed to the duffel bag. "Let me know what you find in there."

BEFORE I LEFT the lab, Flagstaff said he wanted to meet with Glenn Bird and me in Bethesda after I had a chance to see Eve.

"Why not now?" I asked.

"Bethesda's better."

I hopped onto Metro to head home. As I rode the train, I scanned the newspaper and found an article with quotes from Crystal Petersen, the CDC physician Glenn Bird recruited to replace Muñoz. She implicated Ecuadorean shrimp as the cause of the poisonings and announced efforts to recall implicated lots from market shelves and freezers around the nation. To my dismay, she referred to a thirteenth victim, a man who fell ill on July

22nd after eating raw shrimp at a sushi bar in Omaha, Nebraska.

I removed a copy of the epidemic curve Muñoz gave me and penciled an additional bar.

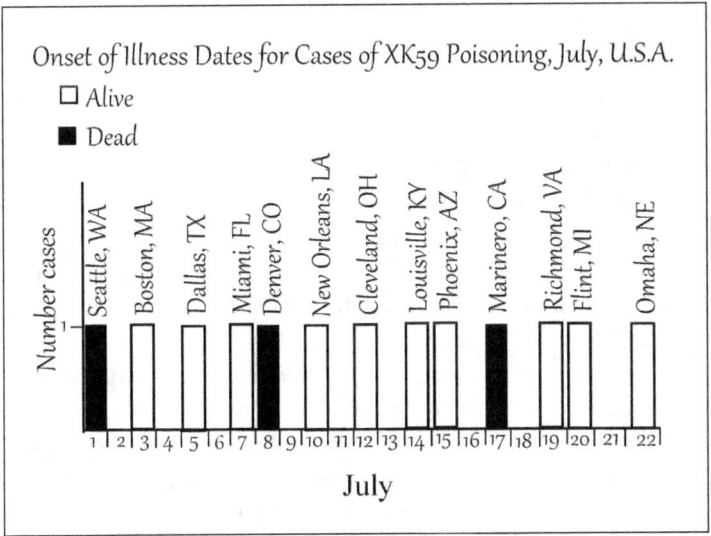

At home, I found Eve in the bedroom affixing a mobile over the crib. It held an array of colorful fish encircling a music box which played melodic lullabies. With her belly pressed against the crib, she had to stretch to maneuver the mobile into place. She left it askew while we hugged.

"I don't like what's going on," she said, holding me tightly. "First, Danny Rogers, and now, Dr. Muñoz. I fear for your life."

"I'm staying close to home," I replied.

She released me and pulled a business card from her pocket. "I found this on our doorstep last night."

"Another one?" I inspected it …

Giva Bhanjee, M.S.
BioVironics Pharmaceuticals and Neutraceuticals
Germantown, Maryland

"My God," I whispered.

"Jay ... son ..." Eve growled, dissecting my name the way she did when she was upset. "Who is that person?"

"I don't know, but the name of the company has popped up too often in the past few days." I recounted the episodes.

She sighed.

I squeezed her hand. "How are *you*?"

She looked away.

"Eve ..."

"Something changed: the skin over the breast mass."

I asked to take a look.

"Forever the doctor," she grumbled.

I didn't like what I saw. The skin had taken the appearance of an orange peel, slightly swollen and dimpled.

She looked at me inquisitively.

"Several things can do that, including simple inflammation." I feigned optimism, avoiding mention of more worrisome causes of a condition often referred to as *peau d'orange*, or "orange skin."

She looked past me, her eyes at peace. "All things in their time."

I wondered how she could say that. There was *no* time for cancer for a woman on the brink of motherhood. This was a time for discovery, for awe, for shepherding a baby into the world. For a moment, I felt like Job of Biblical lore but rejected the notion because it was Eve, not I, who faced the larger struggle.

AFTER A SHOWER and nap, I met Flagstaff and Bird at a coffee shop in Bethesda. I waved a newspaper at them as I sat.

"Why did Crystal Petersen exonerate domestic shrimp?" I asked.

"That was McCloskey's decision," Bird replied.

"Based on what?"

"Invoices from restaurants and stores where the victims purchased shrimp. They all pointed to shrimp shipped from the Ecuadorean farm."

I was livid. "What if the invoices are wrong? And besides, McCloskey has a potential conflict of interest: He represents the shrimp industry in Louisiana."

"Good God, Krispix!" Bird snapped. "He represents the *con-stituents* of Louisiana! You think his colleagues on the Task Force would allow him to jeopardize the American public to protect domestic shrimpers?" He glared at me. "Besides, why would they have killed Muñoz if the operation was clean in Ecuador?"

"Someone from the U.S. could have orchestrated the murder to make the Ecuadoreans look dirty."

"But the invoices—"

"—could have been doctored or someone could have slipped tainted U.S. shrimp into shipments of Ecuadorean shrimp. It's too early to conclude where the shrimp came from. McCloskey should've waited until we have results from the samples I collected in Ecuador."

"And leave the public hanging from a ledge when we *know* it was shrimp that caused the poisonings? We *had* to identify the most likely source and recall it from the market."

Flagstaff lifted a hand. "Water under the bridge, guys. We need to hit the road."

"Where to?" I asked.

"Germantown."

"*Why?*"

"To meet Charles E. Oxford, the CEO of *BioVironics Phar-maceuticals and Neutraceuticals*."

I extracted the card Eve had discovered on our doorstep. "Did the security detail see who left this one at our house?"

Bird, quiet initially as he examined the card, asked: "Who is this person, Giva Bhanjee?"

I shrugged.

Flagstaff led us from the coffee shop to a UNIT vehicle. We left Bethesda for Interstate-270 north, a corridor lined by pharmaceutical firms funded, in part, by the National Institutes of Health nearby. Even in an SUV, Flagstaff outsized the vehicle, his brawn and sinew filling the seat and then some. Had he chosen to, he could have driven with his head out the sunroof.

"I looked into *BioVironics*," he said presently. "Do you know what a 'neutraceutical' is?"

"No."

"The term derives from 'nutritional' and 'pharmaceutical' and refers to a variety of products that supposedly provide extra health benefits. Examples include dietary supplements, processed foods, individual nutrients, and herbal products."

Fifteen miles up the road, we left I-270 for Germantown, a glorified strip mall where we turned right at the second light. After climbing a hill, we dropped into a shallow valley housing a vast glass dome sprouting eight sinuous appendages. A glitzy sign in front announced, *BioVironics Pharmaceuticals and Neutraceuticals.*

We parked in the visitor's lot and entered the dome where a woman behind a counter greeted us.

"Here to see Dr. Oxford," Flagstaff told her.

We displayed our CDC badges.

"I'll let Dr. Oxford know you're here."

While we waited, I gazed at a massive aquarium that occupied the atrium, a glass roundabout two stories tall housing a variety of pelagic fish that swam about unhurriedly—sharks, bonito, yellow-fin tuna, and more. A sign informed viewers that it was one of the largest salt water aquariums in the country and was maintained by a team of research marine biologists who worked at the firm. Although no numbers were provided, reference was made to the high costs involved in keeping up the structure.

"Dr. Oxford will see you," a second voice called.

We followed an escort past the aquarium into one of the building's appendages. After a short elevator ride, we traversed a long winding corridor to a lobby where luxuriant potted plants stretched toward the ceiling. Water from a fountain trickled down a cascade.

A brunette at a reception desk said, "Messieurs Flagstaff, Bird, and Krispix. Dr. Oxford is waiting for you." She stood and curved her torso around a doorway. "Your visitors, sir."

A trim, athletic man with impeccable hair appeared. He wore a cream-colored suit and matching Gucci shoes of the sort a model might don at a hillside Riviera villa. Rings adorned his fingers, enough to make his hands look knobby.

"Ah, the investigative contingent," he said warmly. "I'm Charles Oxford."

After introductions, we followed him to a sitting area that

resembled the cozy nook of a television news show. I looked about for a meteorologist to break-in with the weather.

We sank into comfortable chairs. With his legs crossed, Oxford's socks showed the letters *CEO* embroidered across them. I wondered whether they were a play on his initials and his position at the firm.

"Gentlemen, I must admit, I'm puzzled why three members from the Centers for Disease Control and Prevention are here to see me," he said.

"Puzzled?" Bird repeated. "My colleague, Dr. Jason Krispix, was the recipient of two business cards from your firm. Both had been left on the doormat of his home in recent days."

"Business cards?" Oxford asked.

"Yes, one of yours and another from an employee named Giva Bhanjee. Do you know the name?"

"Of course, but I have no idea why the cards were left at Dr. Krispix's house."

"You didn't leave your card there?"

"By no means."

Flagstaff leaned forward in his chair. "So, let's change topics —to the accounts of illnesses linked to tainted shrimp. Have you seen the stories in the newspaper?"

"Of course; front page material!" he replied.

"That's why we're here. *BioVironics* produces shrimp food, doesn't it?"

"Certainly, but so do many other firms."

"You supply feed to a shrimp farm in Ecuador from which the tainted shrimp may have come."

"We're a leading manufacturer in the shrimp feed market," he said. "We have customers around the globe."

"What's in the feed?"

"Proteins, fatty acids, carbohydrates, and trace elements."

"Do you produce the feed here?"

"Yes, in wing D. You're not suggesting our feed was the source of the poisonings, are you?"

"We're just collecting facts. Does your company deal with XK59 in any way?"

He drew back. "The protein that caused the bleeding? Of course not!"

"That's interesting because we found XK59 in a bottle of one of your drinks."

He clasped his hands. "Which one?"

From his jacket, Flagstaff removed the now-empty bottle I retrieved from California.

"My God, *Electric Jolt*? Where did you get that?"

"From a victim's house. XK59 was present in the remnants."

"But I saw no mention of that in the papers!"

"We withheld the news," Flagstaff said. He relayed the details of Danny Rogers' death.

"Sir," Oxford said, boring his eyes into Flagstaff's, "I cannot help you because I know nothing about XK59. My goal is to run a world class company and XK59 has no part in that. Clearly, someone tampered with one of our products."

"Is there a reason for someone to have done so?" Flagstaff asked.

"I can only speculate. Our competitors may be threatened by our ability to develop innovative products from the sea. We've created a number of drugs from marine resources, and our achievements don't cease there. We've made mind-blowing discoveries. Did you know certain sponges grow glass fibers that can transmit light more efficiently than the fiber-optic cables used today?" He splayed his arms. "You saw the design of our plant. What did it remind you of?"

"An octopus," Bird said. "Eight arms branching from the dome."

"Yes, a design I chose because, while doing my post-doc in molecular biology, I discovered a novel substance secreted by octopi that kills a wide range of viruses. I turned the agent into our first commercial product."

"How do neutraceuticals fit into the picture?" I asked.

"Three-fourths of Americans resort to alternative remedies to treat their ailments, leading us to believe that neutraceuticals in the form of dietary supplements and medically-designed foods can provide immense benefits."

"*Electric Jolt* being an example?"

"Yes, it's an immune-booster for athletes." He glanced at his watch and stood. "But enough talk. Let me *show* you the exceptional standards we employ here. Perhaps that will reassure you we have nothing to do with XK59."

Flagstaff nodded. "Very well, a short tour, perhaps."

"Follow me," the CEO said.

We returned to the dome and entered a different arm of the facility, a vast, open space that contained steel and vinyl tanks connected by a tangle of pipes. Amidst hissing steam and purring motors, we heard water gurgle, splash, and lap.

"Our aquariums hold collections as extensive as any," Oxford said. He led us to a tank the size of a basketball court. "Take a peek."

I scaled a ladder and peered over the ledge. Below, turquoise water brimmed with coral and tropical fish.

"See the anemones?" Oxford asked.

Nodding, I watched their tentacles wave in the current along a craggy perimeter.

"They hold great promise for wound healing. A compound within them dissolves scabs, which, as you know, impede healing by serving as depots for dirt and bacteria. We've developed an ointment containing a substance from anemones that speeds wound healing."

I exchanged places with Bird, and after each of us had a chance to view the tank, we moved to another that held seahorses meandering through marine grass.

"Curious creatures," Oxford said from an observation deck. "They have prehensile tails which they use to grasp things and snouts that suck food, but what I find most amazing is their loyalty. After the female bears her eggs in the male's pouch, the monogamous male carries the eggs until they hatch and then assumes the brunt of childrearing." He paused. "A model for us all."

"What are you doing with the seahorses?" Flagstaff asked.

"They have a unique substance in their lateral lines that could be an antidote to vertigo." He turned. "Come, there's more."

We double-backed to the dome to enter yet another arm, but before doing so, stepped first into a chamber that reminded me of the entryway to tennis bubbles used during winters. The chamber had two doorways, one connected to the outside world and another leading deeper into the wing. Along the inner doorway was a sign that read, *Pressurized—Ensure only one door opened at a time!*

"We keep our drug manufacturing arms under continuous positive pressure to prevent contaminants from entering," Oxford explained. He went to a sticky mat and placed both feet on it. Lifting one foot, he donned a shoe cover before repeating the process with the second shoe. He then put on a hair net, gown, mask, and gloves.

Following his lead, we did the same. A rush of air blew at us when we opened the second door. The area we entered was vast and contained stainless steel compartments the size of small houses that were connected by conveyer belts enclosed in glass sleeves. Replacing the tranquil notes of lapping waves were clanks, whirrs, and beeps.

We passed a belt carrying a stream of capsules.

"*NoVir*," Oxford proclaimed, "a novel drug to treat dengue fever." Yet another belt displayed jiggling blue tablets. "An anti-influenza drug called *EradaVir*."

We moved to a station where plastic bottles were filled, labeled, and boxed. Forklifts darted about like flitting insects.

"We ship to about half the nations on the globe and plan to add the rest before long."

We made a loop to the exit chamber where we disrobed. A brief sojourn through the dome brought us to the noisiest arm yet, a place with rattling cans, clanking bottles, and snapping lids.

"Our neutraceutical division," Oxford announced. He guided us to a machine from which a creamy beige fluid flowed into plastic single-service containers. "That's a pudding with calcium from oyster shells and chitin, a thickening agent from lobsters."

A short stroll brought us to another product labeled *AllUNeed*.

"A medical food that contains shark liver oil for omega-3-fatty acids and squid ink for color and flavor. Very popular at nursing homes."

We looped back to the dome where we caught an elevator to yet another arm housing the firm's laboratories.

"We're big on research," Oxford noted, "which explains why we have a wing dedicated to labs."

We came to a section where a man with a goatee and intense dark eyes rose from a stool to meet us.

"Dr. Gerald Mannino," Oxford said, "director of virology."

As I shook hands with the man, I noticed a woman behind him glare at me from a microscope the instant Oxford mentioned my name. She had long black hair and a pierced nose holding a silver bead. A sari flowed from beneath her lab coat.

"Dr. Mannino, I trust you will confirm that we have nothing to do with the protein XK59 here," Oxford said.

The man's eyebrows rose. "The protein in the newspaper?"

"Right."

"Of course not! We focus on viruses here."

"Which ones?" I asked.

"Marine viruses, chiefly. For example, we're developing an antimalarial drug using a virus we found in ocean sediments."

"Tell them about your anglerfish," Oxford said.

Mannino beamed. "Ah, yes! We discovered a virus in anglerfish that kills *Salmonella*, a common foodborne bacterium." He pointed to a photograph of the fish on the wall. "The virus came from that beast—the 'black devil' or, if you prefer its scientific name, *Melanocetus*."

It was a ghoulish creature with a stubby body and a large head angled backwards. It seemed nature hadn't intended the fish to close its mouth for its razor-sharp teeth were too long for it to do so. A pair of small pectoral fins jutted from its sides while a single dorsal fin, replete with spear-like projections, lined its back.

"We discovered the virus by chance," Mannino continued. "A technician cleaned an anglerfish and inadvertently dripped intestinal contents onto an agar plate growing *Salmonella*. Within an hour, the *Salmonella* began dying."

"How did you know it was a virus that killed the bacteria?" I asked.

"We blended the intestines from the fish and then divided the slurry into two portions, irradiating one to sterilize it. We then added aliquots from each portion to agar plates growing *Salmonella*.

We discovered that only the non-irradiated portion was lethal, which led us to conclude a microbe was responsible for killing the *Salmonella*. That led us to the virus."

"But, that wasn't the novel finding," Oxford interjected. "Microbiologists have known for years about 'bacteriophages,' viruses that infect bacteria. The novelty was the way we genetically engineered the virus to enhance its killing of not only *Salmonella*, but several other diarrhea-causing bacteria, and we did it in a way that prevented the virus from harming the helpful bacteria that reside in our guts. We hope to market this virus as a new form of antibiotic."

"Did you genetically engineer the virus here?" I asked.

"Yes," Mannino replied. "We have several geneticists here." He looked me over. "What sort of physician are you?"

"A hematologist."

He mulled the response. "Are you looking for a job? We're hoping to expand into the hematologic realm, and with one of our scientists abroad currently, we could use the help."

"Not the right time," I replied.

"Dr. Mannino, if you'll escort these gentlemen out, I have a meeting to attend," Oxford said. To Flagstaff: "I hope you're convinced we have nothing to do with XK59 here."

Flagstaff nodded. "It appears that way, but before you go, let me ask you this: You have a consortium of boating interests called *Starboard* that funds you, in part, don't you?"

Oxford nodded. "You've seen our Web site."

"What is it, exactly, they're funding?"

"Development of a product to kill an aggressive seaweed plugging parts of the Intracoastal Waterway. As you know, that's a navigable inland waterway that extends 3,000 miles along the Atlantic and Gulf of Mexico coasts. With global warming, the seaweed has become a major issue."

"But why's *Starboard* paying for the project when the federal government maintains the waterway?" Bird asked.

"The feds *used* to maintain the waterway," Oxford replied, suddenly animated. "The government's destitute now. You can see that from our decaying infrastructure—bridges, dams, roads, and the like. The American Society of Civil Engineers recently assigned a grade of D- to America's navigable waterways. Seaweed plugging the Intracoastal Waterway isn't a priority even though it's ruining beaches, stifling fishing, and causing havoc with boats." He sighed. "Now Dr. Mannino, if you'll see our guests to the lobby."

Oxford shook our hands and left.

"Gentlemen, give me a moment to collect something before we depart," Mannino said. He disappeared into an adjacent office.

While Bird and Flagstaff attended their phones, I reviewed a poster on a wall that summarized a project Mannino's staff had presented at a conference. As I read it, I sensed someone approach me. It was the Indian woman I saw earlier at the microscope. She stopped at a sink beside me, but rather than wash a beaker she held, she looked at me with urgency.

"When can I see you?" she whispered, her accent British.

"Have we met?"

"I'm Giva Bhanjee. I left the business cards at your house." She glanced over her shoulder.

"Cards?" I asked.

"Yes, one for Dr. Oxford and one for me." She turned on the water. "We need to talk!"

"About what?"

"I'll explain tonight. Meet me at the *Still Waters Inn* at midnight. Come alone."

"Where?"

"The restaurant on MacArthur Boulevard near the Potomac River."

"But—"

"Be there!"

She returned to the microscope.

"Gentlemen," Mannino called. "Shall we go?"

As we left, I glanced over my shoulder and saw the young woman's eyes locked on mine. Fear was written across her face.

WHILE WALKING TO our car, I mulled whether to tell Bird and Flagstaff about the encounter with Giva Bhanjee. I opted against it because I suspected they would advise me not to meet her alone, a precondition she insisted on.

"Damn, it's hot," Flagstaff grumbled.

"You're from Arizona," I reminded him.

"No humidity there."

It seemed the sun hadn't budged since we arrived. It hovered over the smog, heating it to a cocktail that burned the eyes. I dabbed my brow. "Why did you bring up *Starboard* in there?"

"Because they're headquartered in Currituck, North Carolina."

"So?"

We reached the car. "Get in," Flagstaff said. With Bird at the wheel, he rummaged through his briefcase and handed me a sheet of paper. "Take a look …"

July 10 – Charleston, SC
July 12 – Georgetown, SC
July 15 – Carolina Beach, NC
July 18– Wrightsville Beach, NC
July 20 – Morehead City, NC
July 22 – Currituck, NC
July 24 – Norfolk, VA

"What's this?" I asked.

"Postmarks on missives received by the XK59 victims; Currituck was one of them."

" 'Postmarks' as in locations where stamps were canceled by the U.S. Postal Service on outgoing mail?"

"Correct."

I reviewed the list carefully. "The last missive was sent just over a week ago," I observed.

"Right, and all came from points along the Intracoastal Waterway in a south-north progression."

"Are you suggesting *Starboard* played a role in the poisonings?"

"*Starboard* paid *BioVironics* ten million dollars to fix a seaweed problem in the waterway. If *BioVironics* hasn't shown sufficient results, perhaps a disgruntled party affiliated with *Starboard* tampered with a *BioVironics* product in retribution. To that end, we need to identify where *Starboard* raised its money."

"How?"

"You'll see shortly."

Bird drove quickly, weaving through cars to bring us to the Hyatt Hotel in Bethesda. In the lobby, a wiry middle-aged man with a luxurious rim around an otherwise bald head approached us with a bounce to his gait.

"Marcus Calendar, please meet Dr. Jason Krispix," Flagstaff said.

Calendar's handshake was protracted and firm.

"*Distamus ab aliis*" he said as we shook hands.

"*Proprius orbis*," I replied.

We sat at a bar in the lobby away from other patrons.

"Calendar works for the Federal Reserve Bank," Flagstaff explained. "At our request, he's identifying *Starboard* donors."

"Heard of the Automated Clearing House, or ACH?" Calendar asked me.

"No."

"Then imagine a sprawling, windowless room with rows of humming mainframe computers. That's the ACH. In the old days, when checks served as the backbone of commerce, it took a massive effort to process them. Enter the ACH, a payment system designed to eliminate checks with electronic funds transfers—clean, efficient, and rapid. It became the largest payments system in the country, processing billions of items each year valued in trillions."

He sipped a gin and tonic.

"The ACH is Grand Central for America's financial exchanges, a site where a record exists for every transaction that takes place between depository institutions—banks, credit unions, and the like." He pulled a notebook from his briefcase and opened it to a drawing.

Bird and Flagstaff slid their stools closer.

"We begin here," Calendar said, fingering a box labeled *BioVironics*. An arrow pointed to it from another designated *Starboard*. "*BioVironics* received ten million from *Starboard* eight months ago.

Starboard is a consortium of lobbyists, interest groups, and organizations dedicated to expanding the Intracoastal Waterway to spur economic growth."

"Don't we have enough development on our coasts already?" I objected.

"*Starboard* would say, no."

Calendar pointed to a series of boxes with names like *Blue Wake*, *Paradise Canal*, *Water Meister*, and *Heaven's Gate*, each designated by location with an arrow pointing to *Starboard*. "All of these groups contribute financially to *Starboard*, but we have a problem here."

"What is it?" Bird asked.

"The ten million *Starboard* sent to *BioVironics* was an uncharacteristically large sum." He paused as if to reflect the quandary. "*Starboard*'s a small entity despite the fact that it receives funds from a number of groups. I checked their finances over the past few years using data from the ACH and discovered they made no payments over fifty thousand dollars before that ten million zinger went to *BioVironics*." He fingered the boxes on the page. "So now I'm tracing with utmost care every payment that went to *Starboard* to track where the ten million came from."

I eyed the locations of the consortium members that comprised *Starboard*, reading some aloud: "Charleston, Georgetown, Wrightsville Beach ..."

"Curious, isn't it," Flagstaff interjected, "that they should be towns along the Intracoastal Waterway where missives were postmarked?"

IT WAS A short stroll from the Hyatt to my home, and when I reached it, I found Eve's father sitting on a rocking chair on the porch. He had arrived from Australia that afternoon to help us transition to parenthood. Having raised four daughters, he knew the routine.

"How are you Spud?" I asked, calling him by a moniker derived from his name, Steven P. Udley.

He enveloped me with arms hardened from years of raising horses. "How's my favorite American son-in-law?"

"Fine," I replied, the stray Yankee to marry into his family.

"Eve's grown large."

"Yes ... any day now."

We went inside and had dinner. While doing the dishes, I told Eve about my encounter with Giva Bhanjee at *BioVironics* and her request to meet at midnight.

"You're going with the security team," she cautioned.

"I can't."

Exasperated, she asked: "Why not?"

"Bhanjee insisted I come alone. I'd scare her off if the security detail joined me."

She shook her head. "After what happened to Danny and to Muñoz, you're willing to take that risk?"

"I feel I *have* to."

"What does she want?"

"I don't know, but she looked desperate."

She turned away. "I'm not happy about this."

Several hours later, before leaving the house, I kissed Eve's forehead as she slept. From the living room window, I saw a black SUV parked along the street several doors down. I tiptoed to the dining room and opened a window overlooking an alley that ran along the rear of our home. Jumping out, I crept through the darkness toward an old pickup we parked several blocks away. It was a decrepit vehicle I had owned for years for sentimental reasons as both my brother and I learned to drive in it.

At the end of the alley, I peeked both ways to look for a second contingent to the security detail. Seeing none, I made my way to the pickup and began driving through tree-lined streets to a deserted MacArthur Boulevard that headed out of town. At one point, I had to wait for an approaching car to clear a one-lane bridge, but from then on, the road belonged to me. For companionship, I listened to music as an oppressive breeze blew through the window.

The houses grew further apart as I drove. Here and there, the boughs of unrestrained maples blocked the light from lonely street lamps. Then, at an abrupt clearing, a firehouse appeared holding two shiny engines with their front doors open. A short distance later, I passed the Naval Surface Warfare Center with its long, tunnel-like structure running parallel to the road. My GPS indicated the *Still Waters Inn* was approaching quickly.

After rounding a bend, I saw the cozy restaurant nestled amongst trees—sylvan, quiet, subdued. The rush of dinner had long passed, leaving only a handful of patrons seated at tables on an outdoor patio. Behind them, a doorway led to the inn itself, an appealing manor tucked under stately trees, its windows casting soft light upon the ground outside.

I parked the pickup below the inn and remained seated, scanning the tables along the patio. My watch read 11:58. Leaving the vehicle, I began walking toward the tables, gravel shifting under my feet, when I heard a voice from a nearby car call, "Dr. Krispix."

I turned to find a slender woman with skin only a shade lighter than the night. She stood beside a lime green Volkswagon Beetle. She was dressed in a dark blouse and pants that blended with the forest behind her. Moonlight formed a corona on her black hair.

She approached me. "Are you alone?"

"Yes," I replied, noting the American accent she spoke with now, a change from the British pronunciation she spoke with at *BioVironics*. Gone, too, were the sari and nose bead, replaced by denim and boots.

Giva Bhanjee relaxed her shoulders and embraced me, a greeting I found to be uncomfortably cordial. As she dropped her arms to my side, I heard her bangles jingle. She wore a garish gold necklace and a set of headphones pushed back from her ears.

"Where would you like to talk?" I asked.

"Not here," she replied. "The place will close soon." She pointed across the street. "There, along the towpath, we'll be alone."

We crossed the street and traversed a bridge over the Chesapeake and Ohio Canal which ran some 184 miles from Washington, D.C.'s Georgetown district to Cumberland, Maryland. The gravel path we set foot on stretched along the canal in both directions. A month earlier, Eve and I had trekked the portion in Georgetown, a section with locks, stone walls, and signs with historical snippets. In days past, horse-drawn barges ferried goods along the canal to avoid the perilous Potomac River nearby, but those days were gone, leaving the trail and canal for pedestrians, bicyclists, and kayakers.

We walked away from the inn, moonlight guiding our way. Giva flicked a cautious look behind her. "Good, it's quiet."

"Dead," I observed.

"Please, not that word!" she cried. "My fiancé is dying!"

"Dying from what?"

"XK59 poisoning!" she exclaimed. "Someone injected it into him!"

"*Injected* it? XK59?" I grasped her arm. "Who injected him?"

"Please," she cried. "You're hurting me!"

I released her. "Tell me who injected him with XK59!"

"I don't know," she stammered. "He wouldn't tell me because he said if I knew, they'd kill me, too. He insisted you speak to him before he dies. His name is Minal Chandrapur, and he left his job at *BioVironics* to die at home."

"Where does he live?"

"India."

"*India*?" I shouted. "Are you saying he left the United States to go to India to die?"

"Yes."

"But he'd be in no shape to travel! And, besides, even if he did travel, he'd die well before he reached India! Did he call 9-1-1?"

She looked about anxiously. "No, he didn't, and please don't shout. I don't want anyone to hear us."

"Fine," I growled in a lower voice, "all I'm saying is that XK59 would kill him in as little as an hour."

"You're the expert. All I know is Minal worked with XK59 at *BioVironics* before they injected him with it."

"Impossible! Drs. Mannino and Oxford told us no one at *BioVironics* handled the protein!"

"They don't know about Minal's project."

"What was he doing with XK59?"

"I'm not sure, but he told me he acquired the protein a year ago. He's a geneticist."

"A year ago? Not a chance! I just published my paper six months ago and I didn't divulge the sequence of amino acids that constitute the protein."

"He knew about XK59 before your paper came out, and even before you gave a talk about the protein at a conference in Singapore. But his supervisor sent him to Singapore nonetheless to hear the presentation."

"Are you referring to Dr. Mannino, the chief of virology?" I asked.

"No, another man who reports to Mannino."

"What's his name?"

She said nothing, pulling an envelope from her purse. "Here, take this. It explains how you can get in touch with Minal."

I ripped the envelope open and lifted my cell phone to illuminate the contents but felt Bhanjee grasp my arm.

"Not now! We need to go before anyone sees us here!"

Day 6.

AT 5 A.M., the phone in my pajama pocket buzzed like an angry bug trying to escape. Before going to bed, I'd set it to vibrate mode for incoming calls but, mercifully, none arrived until now, leaving me with three hours of sleep after returning from the *Still Waters Inn*.

I stumbled to the bathroom. "What is it?" I asked the caller.

"Can you get here fast?" Alistair Brubeck asked. "I've got something to show you."

"Do you normally keep these hours?"

"The day's well under way," he chirped.

I showered and began to dress, noticing then I hadn't placed my wallet in its usual spot on the dresser. Retrieving the khakis I wore the previous night to meet Bhanjee, I found the wallet in a front pocket, an unaccustomed site. For a moment, I frowned, wondering why I had diverted from a lifelong routine. Stress, I concluded.

I finished dressing and grabbed a bite to eat before taking Metro downtown. I found Brubeck leaning over a counter in the lab, his eyes riveted to a photo. Beside him, Randy Flagstaff stood with a cup of steaming coffee.

"I'll take mine with cream," I told him.

Flagstaff pointed to a pot. "Get it yourself."

"No, look at this first," Brubeck insisted. He beckoned me to his side. "You're a lab guy. What do you make of it?"

I glanced at the photo ...

Pulsed-field gel electrophoresis (PFGE), *Vibrio parahaemolyticus*, Outbreak vs. Non-outbreak Strains

	1	2	3	4
Weight scale	Leftover shrimp	*Electric Jolt*	Victim's blood	Non-outbreak isolate

"It's a gel electrophoresis," I said sleepily.

"Yes, but what does it show?"

I rubbed my eyes and examined it more closely. Through the blur of fatigue, the findings emerged. "It appears that a genetically identical strain of *Vibrio parahaemolyticus* was present in the leftover shrimp, *Electric Jolt*, and a victim's blood."

"Whoa!" Flagstaff protested. "Speak English."

Brubeck seized the moment: "We're looking at a laboratory tool called a 'pulsed-field gel electrophoresis,' or 'PFGE.' Think of it as a fingerprinting system for bacterial DNA; it's not as good as the gold standard, whole genome sequencing, or WGS, as a system for fingerprinting, but it's helpful to undertake while we wait for WGS results."

He paused to look at Flagstaff who, in turn, nodded slowly as if digesting every word Brubeck had spoken.

"Okay," Brubeck continued, "so in this case, we have a PFGE fingerprint of DNA from *Vibrio parahaemolyticus* recovered from leftover shrimp, *Electric Jolt*, and the blood of a victim. To create it, we first broke apart *Vibrio parahaemolyticus* cells from each source to isolate the DNA. We then added an enzyme called a 'restriction endonuclease' that works like a pair of scissors to snip DNA into fragments of varying sizes. Next, we applied a pulsating electric charge to the DNA fragments in a gel setting that made the fragments migrate different distances according to their size, with the smallest fragments moving the farthest down the gel. After turning off the electricity, we took a picture of where the fragments ended in the gel. Each band you see represents a fragment of DNA. What's key here is that we're seeing identical DNA band patterns for *Vibrio parahaemolyticus* recovered from the leftover shrimp, in Lane 1; from the *Electric Jolt*, in lane 2; and from the blood of a victim who ate undercooked shrimp, in lane 3. What this suggests is the same strain of *Vibrio parahaemolyticus* was present in the shrimp, drink, and blood, meaning the bacterium most likely came from the same place. For the sake of comparison, I ran a lane comprised of a strain of *Vibrio parahaemolyticus* not linked to the outbreak; as you can see, its fingerprint is totally different from the outbreak strain." He pointed to a column along the far left. "These are simply molecular weight markers." He stood back from the counter.

"Let me get this straight," Flagstaff said. "What you're saying is that, in nature, a number of different strains of *Vibrio parahae-molyticus* exist, each with its own DNA fingerprint, yet what we're seeing here in lanes 1 through 3 are identical fingerprints, suggesting the same strain of bacterium was in the shrimp, juice, and victim."

"Precisely, and we've run gels on *Vibrio parahaemolyticus* recovered from blood specimens from all of the other victims, and they're identical to what we're seeing here."

Flagstaff pondered the notion. "You're suggesting someone planted the bacteria in the shrimp and *Electric Jolt*?"

"Yes."

Flagstaff shook his head. "But, why would they have added *Vibrio parahaemolyticus* to the shrimp and juice if they had already been spiked with XK59?"

Neither Brubeck nor I had an answer.

"Our next step," Brubeck said, "will be to check databases of PFGEs to see if the strain of *Vibrio parahaemolyticus* we're seeing in the shrimp, juice, and victims has been seen before and, if so, where."

"Which databases?" Flagstaff asked.

"One at CDC and another at a large research hospital in Bangladesh where they diagnose *Vibrio parahaemolyticus* infection routinely."

"In the meantime," I said, "we wait for whole genome sequencing results on *Vibrio parahaemolyticus*."

I started for the coffee pot, noticing the duffle bag I'd toted from Ecuador. "Do you have any results for the specimens I brought back?"

"Not yet," Brubeck replied, "but I'll call you as soon as I get them."

FROM THE LAB, I went to the Amygdala with Flagstaff where Glenn Bird joined us in Flagstaff's office. He wore bags under his eyes and slumped his shoulders.

"I just got news," he said. "Dudley Zot, the owner of the shrimp farm in Ecuador, was found dead last night."

"*What?*" I gasped.

"His wife found him in bed with weird marks over his body."

"What sort of marks?"

"Bites of some type."

"From an animal?"

"I've told you what I know. The forensics team we sent to Ecuador will do an autopsy."

With that, Bird plodded off.

"Forgive him," Flagstaff said. "He's dealing with a problem within the Task Force."

"What sort?"

"Do you recall Congressman Nick Kosta?"

I thought for a moment. "The gray-haired man with the quivering moustache?"

"Yes," he replied, leading me into his office. He closed the door. "Marcus Calendar called last night to inform us that *BioVironics* wired a million dollars to an account Kosta opened in the Caribbean nation of Antigua and Barbuda. The transfer took place two days ago."

"That's a bit untimely, isn't it, given the spotlight on the firm?"

"To say the least, but McCloskey has instructed us not to confront Kosta on the issue until the WAFTA vote has taken place. He and Kosta are on opposite sides of the bill and he doesn't want to inflame matters before the vote."

"What's McCloskey's stance on WAFTA?"

"He's against it. He thinks tariffs play a vital role in protecting domestic industries."

"Like his Louisiana shrimpers?" I suggested.

Flagstaff nodded. "Among others."

"And Kosta's for it?"

"Very much so. He views WAFTA as the equivalent of a foot on the economic accelerator."

"And the other Task Force members?"

"Evenly split, but not along party lines; that's what's different about WAFTA: it has driven a wedge within each party."

He opened a drawer and pulled out a slip of paper with an address on it, sliding it across the desk. "Your agenda for today: plug this into GPS and go find it."

I glanced at the address. "Annapolis?"

"Congressman Kosta's summer home on the water." He drummed his fingers on the desk. "Although we have to wait for the WAFTA vote before we approach Kosta about the transfer of funds, nothing says we can't drop by his summer home to see what's there."

"Why me?"

"Because the rest of us are tied up."

"What could possibly be there?"

"For starters, a cabin cruiser; Kosta moors it there in summer. Go check it out."

"I'm not a detective."

"Become one."

I started for the door. "By the way, there's something I need to tell you." I described the encounter with Giva Bhanjee at the *Still Waters Inn*.

"Good God, you went there *alone*?"

I nodded.

He shook his head. "What did she say?"

"Her boyfriend, a guy named Minal Chandrapur, worked with XK59 at *BioVironics* before someone injected him with the protein. She said he went home to India to die."

Flagstaff turned crimson. "*Injected* him? Charles Oxford told us no one at *BioVironics* worked with XK59!"

"Chandrapur worked with it secretly."

"*Who* injected him?"

"Bhanjee didn't know."

"Then call this Chandrapur man now before he dies!" He pushed the phone across his desk.

"I don't have his number, only directions to his home in a town called Vellore in south India."

"Bhanjee met you for a midnight stroll to give you directions to his house without providing a phone number?" He trembled with anger. "We're bringing her in!"

"Not yet!" I pleaded. "She risked her life to see me. Let me address her one more time."

He frowned. "Did you see the screen out there this morning? Two new poisonings!"

"And Bhanjee may have information that can help us figure out who's behind them."

"*One* more chance with her, then she comes in."

AS I MADE my way to the UNIT garage to collect a car, my phone rang.

"Hello," a melodious voice said, pronouncing it as "Yellow." I recognized the voice instantly.

"Dr. Squills, what's up?"

"I found what you're looking for," the English professor said.

"The source of the missives?" My pulse hummed in my ears.

"I believe so." A paper crumpled. "What do you think about the choice of words?"

I opened my satchel and retrieved the missives. "Unsettling," I replied.

"Give me an example."

"… *your father's cruelty*,"

"Yes, there's a theme throughout the missives of dominance, as in *power* and *strength* and *surrendering*."

"So, where does this take us?"

"To writings from an earlier era," he replied. "Any Greek poets come to mind?"

"Homer …"

"Another one—one who went to lengths to express himself with abstractions in personified terms. The missives bear his signature."

"Greek poets aren't my forte."

"Do you know the name 'Hesiod'?"

"No."

"Then we failed to educate you properly. He was a Greek poet who wrote a piece called *Theogony*, and every missive but one came from this work."

"*Theogony?*"

"Yes, a detailed genealogy of the Greek gods written sometime around the eighth century B.C. Violent and gory, but a masterpiece."

"Which missive was the exception?"

"… *not that rich chimaera*. Those were William Faulkner's words. The only reason I recognized them was because I did my dissertation on Faulkner. I know his works well."

"Where do those words appear?"

"In *The Sound and the Fury*. Have you read it?"

"No."

"Some consider the novel disjointed, but I rather like it. It describes life in the south in the early 1900s: lazy days, shady lawns, white houses, buzzing bees, and sun-sprayed trees leaning over walls." He chuckled. "Faulkner spoke of the novel as his 'most splendid failure.' "

"Where is the clause in the book?"

"In my version, on page 132 in a scene where the character, Quentin Compson, is walking through the countryside. Faulkner writes: *Like it were put to makeshift for enough green to go around among the trees and even the blue of distance not that rich chimaera.*"

He paused. "It's intriguing that Hesiod should speak of a chimera as well in *Theogony*. Let me read it to you: *But she bore Chimaera, who breathed invincible fire, a terrible great-creature, swift-footed and strong. She had three heads: one of a fierce lion, one of a she-goat, and one of a powerful serpent.*" Another pause. "Listen, gotta run; another call coming in. We need to talk later about the missives in more detail."

"Call me when you can."

I hung up and scribbled *Theogony* on the sheet of missives, making a mental note to purchase the book later that day. I then called Flagstaff and left a voice mail informing him about what Squills had told me.

IN THE UNIT garage, I found my assigned vehicle and drove it onto the streets of Washington. With GPS guiding me out of the city, I stopped in the parking lot of a fast-food outlet before I reached the freeway to double-check the card Giva Bhanjee had given me the previous night.

Reaching into my satchel, I lifted the envelope made from rice paper upon which she had penned my name. The paper was grainy and pleasing to the touch. Here and there, the trail of ink took jagged turns over clumps of pulp, like the one underlying my middle initial, *E*. As it had done the previous night, the sight of the initial unnerved me because I hadn't used the initial since childhood. I shunned it because it stood for *Eggbert*, a name I found ungracious even though it traced deep into my lineage. It disturbed me that Giva Bhanjee had come upon it somehow.

I removed the card from the envelope. A drawing of a sari-clad woman feeding a peacock adorned the front, while on the back were directions to Chandrapur's home in India …

> *By air, arrive Chennai*
> *Taxi to central rail station*
> *Train to Katpadi Junction (closest stop to Vellore)*
> *In Vellore, check into Hotel Ranga*

From hotel, walk:
→ *north one block (past post office)*
→ *east two blocks (to temple)*
→ *left onto narrow street*
→ *5 doors down to brick building with red gate*
Ask for Chandrapur apartment
Minal's parents: Prathiba and Govind Chandrapur

I turned the card over hoping that I had missed a telephone number for Minal Chandrapur on its back, but none was there. Puzzled still by its absence, I dialed the number Bhanjee had penned on the business card she left on the doormat of my house. When a receptionist at *BioVironics* answered, I asked to speak to Bhanjee.

The call transferred, and a woman's voice came on the line.

"Is Giva there?" I asked.

"No."

"When will she be back?"

"I don't know."

"Who am I speaking with?"

"A colleague of Giva's."

"Did I see you yesterday at your lab?"

A muffled sound came forth, as if the receiver had been cupped. "Were you with the group from the CDC?" she whispered.

"Yes, it was a routine visit, no more. Please tell Giva I'll call later."

"Wait!" the voice pleaded. "I'm worried about her!"

"Why?"

"Because, she *never* misses work without telling me, and I haven't heard from her today."

"Did you call her?"

"Yes, but she didn't answer."

"Does she live alone?"

"Yes."

"Where?"

"Not far … in Germantown."

"What's her address?"

"I … don't …"

"I need to speak to her!"

Silence before an address came forth.

"Thank you," I said. "Last question: Do you know Minal Chandrapur?"

"Of course, he works here."

"Who's his supervisor?"

"A man named Grainger."

My pulse quickened. "His first name?"

"Frank."

"*No!*"

"It is."

I sat bolt-upright. "May I speak to him?"

"He's out of town."

"When will he return?"

"I'm not sure."

"Can I leave him a message? It's urgent."

"Yes, of course."

I trembled as I spoke. "Tell him to call Jason Krispix at his earliest convenience." I gave her my number.

"I'll make sure he gets the message," she replied.

PARKED STILL IN the lot of a fast-food outlet close to the freeway, I felt pins and needles pierce my hands as I dialed the University Medical Center in Las Vegas, a number I knew by heart. When the operator answered, I said, "Who's on-call for hematology-oncology?"

A pause, then: "Dr. Saxby."

"Ah, Jeff Saxby," I said. He had entered the hematology-oncology fellowship at the beginning of my final year of training there, and we worked together often. I informed the operator of our relationship and asked her to page him.

"One moment," she said.

Seconds passed like hours. Then: "Saxby."

"Jeff! Jason Krispix calling."

"I *thought* the operator said it was you, but she said it so quickly I wasn't sure." He chuckled, an effusive, belly-deep gurgle that had always impressed me for its sincerity. "How are you doing, buddy?"

"I'm working hard on a manuscript."

"Krispix, you don't *need* publications anymore; you left academia."

"I know but I want to finish this final paper, and you can help me get it done."

"How?"

"I need a lab value for a patient I evaluated several years ago. I'd like you to check his record."

"What's the patient's name?" he asked.

"Grainger." I spelled it.

"First name?"

"Frank."

"Birth date?"

"Give me a break! Just look up *Frank Grainger*. There can't be too many of them."

"Hang on."

Taps on the keyboard before: "Found it. What value do you need?"

"First, verify he was admitted to the hospital about two and a half years ago."

"That's right … to the surgical service for a swollen thigh."

"That's him! Give me his blood sodium from the emergency department." A red herring to convince him I was writing the paper.

More key-punching.

"Hey," Saxby exclaimed. "This is the guy who launched your XK59 career! Says right here: *Patient brought piece of bark that he claims caused bleeding death of a colleague in Madagascar.* I remember the work you did with the bark!"

"Right, got the sodium value?"

"I'm getting there … ah, here it is—136 milligrams per deciliter."

"Now go to the admission history and physical. I need a couple things there."

"Hey, this was supposed to be simple!"

"It will be."

"Fine," he groused. "Okay, got it …"

"Which leg did he injure—left or right?" I asked.

"Right."

"Now, read the part of the physical examination about his skin. Does it mention any tattoos?"

"Let's see."

My jaw tightened.

"Yeah," he said finally. "There *is* mention of a tattoo! Damn, you've got a good memory!"

"Does it describe the tattoo?"

"Yes, I'll read it verbatim: *Tattoo of pistol in sternal notch.*"

"*Shit!*"

"What is it?" Saxby asked.

My heart pounded at the base of my skull.

"Krispix, are you still there?"

"Yeah, hang on," I begged.

"I've hung on long enough!"

"Okay, we're done," I relented. "I owe you a dinner the next time we meet."

"A *nice* dinner!"

AFTER HANGING UP with Saxby, I called Flagstaff at the UNIT.

"I know who killed Muñoz!" I exclaimed. Even with the engine idling and windows raised, my shout was loud enough to draw the attention of a passerby heading toward the fast-food outlet nearby.

"Easy, Krispix!" Flagstaff replied.

"*Easy*? The guy could be in town coming after me right now!"

"Who are you referring to?"

"A man named Frank Grainger who was the patient I met in Las Vegas two and half years ago that loaned me the bark from which I discovered XK59. He was at the shrimp farm but went by the name 'Anton Manovic.' He now works at *BioVironics* in Germantown!"

"You're saying a former patient of yours killed Muñoz?"

"I'm positive of it."

"Why would he have done that?"

"I don't know, but I intend to find out."

"And you didn't recognize him as your former patient when you were in Ecuador?"

"No, because he had undergone dramatic changes from when I first met him." I listed the changes: "The Frank Grainger I met in Las Vegas had normal ears, yet those of the scientist in Ecuador were shriveled and wrinkled. In Nevada, the nose was straight as opposed to crooked, and while Grainger's lips were full and red in Las Vegas, they were thin and bluish in Ecuador. Even his chin had changed from a protruding one to cleft. And his jaw, square initially, became rounded."

"What about his eyes?"

"They were odd—raccoon-like, as if he'd had recent sinus surgery."

"And the eye color?"

"I don't recall what they were in Nevada, but they were green in Ecuador. Keep in mind, though, that contacts can change eye color."

"And his voice?" Flagstaff asked.

"The pitch had changed: kind of whiny in Nevada but deep and matter-of-fact in Ecuador. But pitches can be feigned."

"So why are you convinced Manovic and Grainger are one?"

"Because both had the same distinct tattoo."

"A *tattoo*? That's your proof?"

"Yes, an elaborate one of a pistol located in the sternal notch just below the neck; it has multiple colors and intricate details."

"You remember a tattoo from a patient you evaluated two and a half years ago?"

"Yes!" I replied. "This was no ordinary patient; he loaned me the bark that launched my career."

"But it doesn't make sense!" Flagstaff objected. "If Grainger went through all those anatomical changes to assume a different appearance, why would he have left the tattoo intact?"

I had no answer.

"Besides," Flagstaff added, "what if there's an artist out there who's done thousands of those tattoos?"

"It's not just the tattoo that convinces me Manovic and Grainger are the same person," I insisted. "I talked to a lab technician at *BioVironics* today after I tried to reach Giva Bhanjee. When I asked the technician who Minal Chandrapur's boss was, she told me it was a man named Frank Grainger. Curiously, she also said Grainger happened to be out of town when I called. That's when I called the hospital where I trained in Las Vegas. A former colleague of mine there pulled Grainger's medical record and verified that Grainger had a tattoo of a pistol in his sternal notch, one identical to the one I saw on Manovic in Ecuador."

"Yes, but—"

"Hold on, there's more!" I said, cutting Flagstaff off. "In Ecuador, Manovic limped from what appeared to be an injury to his right leg, and a review of the medical records by my colleague indicated that Grainger had been admitted to the hospital for a swollen right thigh."

I paused to allow Flagstaff to object, but hearing only silence, I continued. "Add to this the assertion by Zot that Manovic had gone to the shrimp farm to deal with a venomous snake that was making its way into the shrimp pools from the mangroves. Frank Grainger's PhD research was on snake venom. That's the reason he went to Madagascar in the first place: to collect snake venom!"

A pause left both of us speechless until Flagstaff asked: "But why would he have tried to hide his identity in Ecuador?"

"To cover his role in the XK59 poisonings, I'm guessing."

"Alright, let me do this," Flagstaff said. "I'll call Charles E. Oxford at *BioVironics* to inquire about this. In the meantime, we just heard from our folks in Ecuador that Zot died from massive muscle breakdown resulting from spider bites."

"*Spider bites?*"

"Yes. Our pathologist wasn't sure what type of spider it was, but he's convinced spiders killed Zot. That part of Ecuador is known to harbor a poisonous species in the cane fields, and I understand there was a field behind Zot's house."

"Are they testing Zot's tissues for venom?"

"Yes."

"Was he allergic to spiders?"

"Don't know. The pathologist is going to interview Zot's wife today. Gotta run. Call me from Annapolis."

I MADE MY way to Route 50 outside Washington where I joined a throng of cars destined for resorts along the coast. It was a hot summer Saturday, and many cars toted beach chairs, bicycles and vacation goods. I took my place among them, the odd man out.

At the outskirts of Annapolis, I received a call from Alistair Brubeck. I pulled off the road to take the call.

"I've been talking to you more than to my wife," I lamented.

"Lots to discuss."

"What now?"

"I have results on the samples you brought from Ecuador. The shrimp are hot."

"With XK59?"

"Yes, but only shrimp from the source you labeled, *Round, glowing pond*. Why would that be?"

"I *knew* something was odd about that pond!" I described its bioluminescence.

"Could be innocent," Brubeck replied. "A number of marine organisms emit bioluminescence—worms, squid, and bacteria, all of which have a chemical system similar to fireflies. In fact, people have been startled to find fish filets glowing in the dark on kitchen counters after they let the fish sit out at room temperature. Bioluminescent bacteria multiply to create the glow."

"How much XK59 was in the shrimp?" I asked.

"The same level we detected in the Seattle victim's leftover shrimp—one part per billion."

"Did the shrimp glow?"

"Hang on, let me check." He came back shortly. "Yes, they glow, but, again, only the ones from the round pond."

"Was *Vibrio parahaemolyticus* present in the shrimp you tested?"

"Yes, along with *Aeromonas hydrophila*, but again, only in shrimp from the round pond."

"I'm becoming convinced the *Vibrio* played a role somehow in producing the levels of XK59 we're seeing in the victims."

"How?"

"I'm not sure; it's just a gut feeling. Which reminds me: Did you check the *Vibrio* databases to determine whether the strain we're dealing with has been seen elsewhere in the world?"

"Not yet."

"Let me know when you find out."

I set off again, soon reaching the Annapolis waterfront with its sleek yachts and parking lots filled with Mercedes, Jaguars, and BMWs. Before long, I turned onto a lane with staid, ivy-lined homes and coiffed lawns. From each side, boughs from ancient oaks reached over the road to form a canopy that extended several blocks to a marsh thick with cat tails. I lowered my window and gazed beyond the marsh to a tributary of the Chesapeake Bay, inhaling the salty air.

More eloquent homes with screened porches and gazebos set along the waterfront sailed by as I drove, but I stopped when I came to a mailbox hosting the letters *N.K.* It stood at the entry to a driveway lined by rhododendrons taller than the SUV, but before turning onto the property, I rehearsed a response in case someone asked why I was there. Satisfied, I followed the driveway into a vast tract where a stately manor overlooking the water came into view. The drawn blinds and empty parking spaces suggested I was alone, but I left the car warily to approach the front door where I rang the bell.

With no response ensuing, I walked around the house to find locked windows and doors about. A path in back stretched toward a thicket of woods, and when I followed it, I came to a secluded inlet that opened to the Chesapeake Bay. A blue heron perched in shallow water nearby eyed me cautiously before resuming its hunt for fish.

My eyes turned to a sleek cabin cruiser moored nearby, its name *Down Under*. She had a long main cabin and a snappy fly-bridge for the helm station, and her windows were tinted, making it impossible to see inside. Confident I was alone, I ventured up a set of steps onto the rear deck and called, "Anyone here?"

In the silence, I opened the glass door to the salon and entered a natty room with teak trim and cream-colored chairs. Beyond the salon, one step down, a galley boasted an electric stove with glass-top hot plates, a microwave and conventional oven, and a full-sized refrigerator with freezer. Keeping the cream-colored theme, a padded vinyl bench surrounded a generous marble table in a dining area adjacent to the galley.

I explored a pair of staterooms, one with bunk beds and the other with berths fore and aft. The master suite was located beyond them at the bow, equipped with king bed, private head, and a host of shelves which, like those in the staterooms and salon, were stacked end-to-end with the works of Greek authors. I felt as if I were in a library, for the books spanned multiple genres: poetry, medicine, history, comedy, tragedy, philosophy, and more. While many names I recognized—Aristotle, Plato, Homer, Sophocles—some I did not—Callimachus, Apollonius of Rhodes, Aeschylus. As for titles, a number were new to me: *On the Heavens, Lysistrata, The Birds, The Clouds*, and many more. I was astonished not only by the volume of books, but by the impeccable care taken to preserve them, each housed in a clear plastic box to shield against the elements.

A bedside photo in the master suite caught my eye, one in which three dark-haired men stood beside a boy with the Parthenon of Athens behind them. I examined the boy's face more carefully. He was an adolescent, but his features were familiar: dignified nose, full lips, and a widow's peak that reminded me of a freighter's bow plowing the sea.

I turned the frame ...

To Nicholas Kostanopoulos,
beloved nephew:
Never forget your heritage
nor your birthplace.
—Your Uncles:
Cristoforo, Damian, and Sebastian Kostanopoulos

I set the photo down, admiring Kosta for scaling the immigration ladder to reach the lofty heights of Congress.

Returning to the deck, I climbed to the flybridge, a partially-covered platform above the main cabin that held a wheel and navigational equipment. Surrounding the helm was a semi-circular cushioned bench under which cabinets held life jackets and tools. In one, I noticed a stack of maps and, beside them, a marine battery with a cable running to a solar panel.

I pushed my head further into the storage space. Behind the battery, I saw a laptop and a printer. I lifted the computer and turned it on, surprised to see the icons appear without need for a password.

I opened the word processor, but it contained no files. The same was true for the spreadsheet and graphics programs, leading me to believe the laptop had been abandoned. Curious to see if the system worked, I typed a few words and printed the results.

Growing uneasy, I started for the ladder to return to the main deck but stopped short when I eyed a briefcase behind a cooler next to the helm. It was an odd placement, I thought, for it was exposed to the elements. I set it atop the bench and opened it. It contained a logbook entitled *Down Under*.

I leafed through its hand-written notes, ones describing excursions dating back to a maiden voyage from Australia to Annapolis five years earlier. Each entry provided a date, summary of marine conditions, distance traveled, key sightings, and a closing signature, *N. Kosta*. I was impressed by the Congressman's extensive travels along the Atlantic coast and to destinations beyond in the Windward and Leeward Islands, Dutch Antilles, Belize, and Yucatán. Also noted were regular excursions to Galveston where he owned a beach house from which he courted constituents on fishing trips.

As I examined the pages, I noticed the lettering turned increasingly scraggy as the script strayed from the lines. It was as if the more recent entries had been made in the dark, on shaky surfaces, or under the influence of alcohol (a bar in the salon was generously stocked). And then, for some reason, the latest data came in the form of computer-printed entries stapled into the book. The nature of the excursions changed over time as well, being confined largely to the Chesapeake Bay—all, that is, but a final, multi-stop jaunt that ended the previous week. For this excursion, there were no daily narratives, only a list of ports of call ...

July 7—10 Annapolis to Charleston, SC
July 12—Georgetown, SC
July 15—Carolina Beach, NC
July 18—Wrightsville Beach, NC
July 20—Morehead City, NC
July 22—Currituck, NC
July 24—Norfolk, VA

The list hit me like a body blow because I recognized each town as a missive postmark site. From my pocket, I extracted a sealable plastic bag of the sort used to pack sandwiches in which I kept notes from the investigation. Reviewing the missive postmarks, I saw that, without exception, the dates and locations matched the days the *Down Under* had moored in each town. Breathless, I snapped a photo of the names and dates.

Because figures helped me visualize details, I drew a new epidemic curve to which I added the missive postmarks. For simplicity, I included only the original twelve cases for which I had complete information. Once again, I noticed that only seven victims had received a missive ...

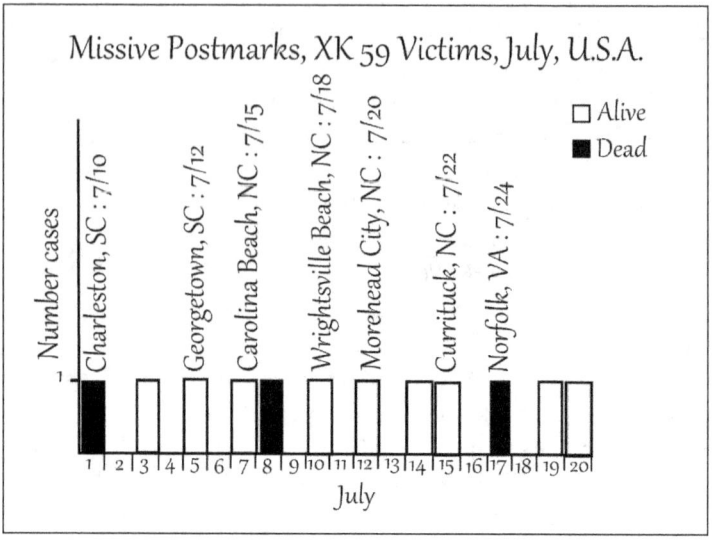

Missive Postmarks, XK 59 Victims, July, U.S.A.

Studying the curve, I saw a pattern wherein victims with later illness onsets received missives postmarked at successively northern locations. Of particular concern were the short periods between illness onset dates and missive postmarks. For example, the first victim fell ill on July 1st yet his missive was postmarked in Charleston, SC only nine days later, on July 10th. Similar short intervals occurred with other victims, suggesting someone with intimate knowledge of the outbreak investigation—an "insider"—had sent the missives. Congressman Nick Kosta came to mind immediately.

"*Impossible!*" I whispered.

How was it that a *Congressman*—a member of a super-secret federal Task Force, no less—mailed the missives? What motive could he possibly have had for doing so? Surely he knew the tracks of a Congressman were indelible, all the more so given his position on an elite anti-terrorism unit. Moreover, Congressmen didn't commit acts like this. They partook in lewd and lascivious behavior and peddled influence, but they didn't poison the public and then issue bizarre missives.

I pondered whether Kosta was a new breed of Congressmen, one turned against his fellow citizens. Or could it be that, in exchange for a million dollars deposited in his Antigua bank account, he was protecting an employee at *BioVironics* who orchestrated the poisonings?

The question dangled as I replaced the logbook. Returning to the main deck, I began perusing the shelved books, and because they were arranged in genres in alphabetical order by author, I kept an eye out for a poetry section that might hold Hesiod's *Theogony*.

I started in the salon and, seeing the genres *Astronomy* and *History*, moved to the guest cabins where I found *Tragedy* and *Comedy*. I fretted that if the master suite left me empty-handed, I would be forced to restart the search and comb through books individually in the event *Theogony* had been misplaced. I entered the final cabin and raked my eyes across its voluminous titles, ones housed in sections labeled *Philosophy*, *Medicine*, and, to my relief, *Poetry*. In the final section, I discovered two works by Hesiod, *Shield of Heracles* and *Works and Days*, but my heart sank when I noticed a gap between them, one I suspected belonged to *Theogony*.

I headed for the galley because, strangely, while traversing it earlier, I noticed what appeared to be a book propped along the counter. It appeared in the form of a reflection in a mirror beside the toaster. I rushed to the spot now and, sliding the toaster aside, discovered a paperback with a weathered cover and pages littered with sticky notes. Its title: *Theogony*.

I opened it to the first sticky on the copyright page. In typed letters, it read ...

Dr. Krispix,
Distamus ab aliis.
Follow the mirrors.

I grimaced at the sight of my name alongside a Latin code designed to guard my secrecy. The juxtaposition reinforced my conviction that someone on the Congressional Task Force, or perhaps in the UNIT itself, had played a role in sending the missives. But it flummoxed me that someone knew *I* would be the one to discover the book in its elusive position behind the toaster. Was Flagstaff to be trusted, I wondered. After all, it was he who had sent me here.

I took a photo of the sticky to preserve the evidence.

My attention turned to the third line. What "mirrors" was I to follow other than this one? I picked up the small rectangular glass and peered at its chipped edges, flipping it over to see if it held another message. It didn't.

I returned my attention to the book. It was 50 pages long and little larger than my palm. I leafed through the *Table of Contents*, *Introduction*, and a brief *Note on the Translation*. The text of *Theogony* followed, its length 33 pages. I read the first line of text, *From the Muses of Helicon let us begin our singing,* but my eyes drifted to handwritten notes in the margin. I was startled to see they displayed the same penmanship from Kosta's logbook prior to the deterioration of the writing. Like *CliffsNotes*, they explained the text and added perspective and definitions. Regarding *Hera of Argos*, for example, a note stated, *goddess of marriage as well as a wife and older sister of Zeus*; for *Phoebus Apollo*: *god of the sun*; and for *Poseidon*: *ruler of the sea.*

I flipped to the next sticky ...

Byron Rudolf
8672 Mason Avenue, Seattle, WA 98106
Start VP35—3,129

The name rang a bell. Extracting a list of victims' names, I saw it belonged to the first person poisoned, a 36-year-old software engineer in Seattle. I presumed the address was one to which the missive had been sent, but the third line, a cryptic code of some sort, left me baffled.

I turned to the text immediately beside the sticky where three words were underlined: *your father's cruelty.* I recognized them as the first missive. Mentally, I applauded Squills for identifying *Theogony* as the missives' source.

I lifted my eyes to a header on the page which read *Lines 163–191.* Similar headers appeared on other pages, and when I turned to the final page, I saw 1,026 lines comprised the text of *Theogony.* The words, *your father's cruelty.*, fell on line 169.

I examined the remaining sticky notes dispersed through the text and a final one occupying the inside of the back cover. Each sticky within the text listed a victim's name, address, and cryptic code, and each was attached to the page where the words forming the missive had been underlined. One sticky, in particular, gave me great distress; it had the name *Danny Rogers* typed across it along with his address in Marinero, CA and a cryptic code, *Start VP30—8,509*. The page to which it was attached contained the words, … *who lives under the earth,*. The final sticky on the inside of the back cover listed a victim's name, address, and a missive, … *not that rich chimaera.*, but no cryptic code. I recalled Squills identifying its source as *The Sound and the Fury* by William Faulkner.

To visualize in one place the missives, line numbers, and cryptic codes, I copied them on a sheet of paper …

… *your father's cruelty. Line 169. Start VP35—3,129*
… *of the lovely cheeks, Line 242. Start VP40—4,479*
But she, surrendering to … Line 326. Start GP—6,039
But she, surrendering to … Line 326. Start GP—6,039
… *Power and Strength, Line 385. Stop GP—7,133*
… *who lives under the earth, Line 460. Start VP30—8,509*
… *not that rich chimaera.*

The cryptic codes intrigued me because the presence of the initials, *VP*, in three of them fortified my belief that *Vibrio parahaemolyticus* played some role in the poisonings. Less clear were the numbers attached to the initials, as in *VP35*, *VP40*, and *VP30*, or for that matter, the subsequent larger numbers in the cryptic codes—*3,129*, *4,479*, *6,039*, *7,133*, and *8,509*. I entertained the notion that *Vibrio parahaemolyticus* had been genetically engineered to produce XK59 in the victims, and if that were true, then perhaps the large numbers in the cryptic codes referred to specific regions of the bacterium's DNA that had been altered.

A clicking sound from outside startled me. Tucking my notes away, I returned *Theogony* to its place behind the toaster and reset the mirror to its original position. To hide from the doorway, I ducked behind a chair and waited for the intruder to enter. In the sweltering heat, sweat beads formed along my brows before dropping to the floor. Hearing only silence, I peered around the chair through the salon doorway to see dark clouds gathering in an angry sky, and it was then I realized the clicking came from a wooden chime blowing in the gusts. Beyond the stern, the once docile inlet churned now in frothy whitecaps.

I left the boat and rushed into a forest of howling trees. When I reached the garden behind the house, a lightning bolt made me dive to the ground. As I lay there, cheek-to-soil, I listened to the rumble of thunder as the scent of wetted earth wafted up. I remained still until the thunder ceased only to see a tall blonde woman enter the house and close the door behind her.

I kept my position until I was confident she had moved into the interior of the house. Upon standing, I stepped over a stream that had formed in the garden and raced to my car without looking back. When I got in, I turned the key and sped away, sending a shower of gravel toward a red Ferrari parked behind me.

I FLED KOSTA'S house with one eye on the road and the other on the rear view mirror, expecting a red Ferrari to pull up at any moment. Only when I reached a bustling thoroughfare did I feel sufficiently anonymous to pull aside to place a call. It took me several attempts with trembling fingers to hit the numerical sequence.

"Krispix, what's happening?" Randy Flagstaff said.

"You guys are rotten to the core!" I shouted.

"What bent you out of shape?"

I told him about the copy of *Theogony* on Kosta's boat and the first sticky note that read …

Dr. Krispix,
Distamus ab aliis.
Follow the mirrors.

"Kosta poisoned the victims!" I exclaimed.

"Too early to conclude that; no proof Kosta wrote that sticky."

"If it wasn't Kosta, it was someone on the Task Force or in

the UNIT."

"It's troubling," he acknowledged, "and we'll get to the bottom of this, but I want you to keep your eye on XK59. We'll deal with Kosta."

"Tell me this, then: Does Kosta own a red Ferrari?"

"Yup, that's his baby."

ALTHOUGH I NEVER became a merchant marine, my fondness for the sea remained strong, and the visit to Kosta's boat rekindled the bond. Even though the vessel was moored when I boarded it, it made me reminisce an experience I had years earlier while ferrying across Lake Michigan during middle school. Each deck on the ferry imbued a different outlook on life: On lower levels, with the water almost in reach, I appreciated the need—metaphorically speaking—to roll with the waves whereas on higher decks with horizon vistas, I saw the value of long-term living.

Tense as the visit to Kosta's boat had been, the breeze from the bay had a relaxing effect, enough so to make me long for the sea. Bypassing an onramp for Washington, D.C., I steered the SUV onto another that led me out of Annapolis toward the eastern shore of Maryland. With beach-going throngs diminished, I crossed the Chesapeake Bay Bridge with ease before stopping at a mall-side ATM to withdraw two thousand dollars. The wad of cash pressed against my thigh as I drove on.

At the seaside town of Lewes, Delaware, I joined a queue waiting for a car ferry to cross the Delaware Bay to Cape May, New Jersey. With vessels departing every ninety minutes, it wasn't long before I drove onto a sleek ship with a tinted-window observation salon poised three decks above the sea. The mood aboard was festive, similar to that on ocean liners before they set off to sea. I abandoned the SUV to take a place beside a rail on the main deck where I called Eve as the last of the passengers boarded.

"Everything fine?" I asked her.

"The contractions are getting more organized," she replied.

"Should I come home?" I held my breath.

"Not yet, but stay close."

Below me, the hatch to the stern closed.

"Will do. Love you."

"Love you, too," she replied.

A breeze whipped up as we left port. Sweetness tinged the air, as if the wind had picked up strands of cotton candy from beachside vendors and carried them to sea. I remained outside until we approached Cape May, only then leaving the rail for the SUV. After mooring, I drove north, relieved to have the sea as a partner in travel. Here and there, I passed carefree towns that beckoned me to visit their sand and waves.

A call interrupted my soirée with serenity.

"How come you didn't answer an hour ago?" Alistair Brubeck asked.

"Busy," I replied. The call registered as the ferry left port but I ignored it to savor my freedom.

"News," he said.

"What sort?"

"I heard from CDC and Bangladesh. Our strain of *Vibrio parahaemolyticus* has never been seen in the U.S. but it was recovered in Bangladesh a few years ago."

"The *same* strain?"

"Yes, isolated from a patient who developed diarrhea while visiting India."

"What part of India?"

"Southern—a town called Vellore."

"*No!*"

"Heard of it?" he asked.

I told him about Minal Chandrapur, who hailed from Vellore.

"Do you think he supplied the strain that tainted the shrimp?" Brubeck asked.

"Possibly."

Switching topics, I told Brubeck about the copy of *Theogony* with its cryptic codes.

"Got them handy?" he asked.

I retrieved my list and read aloud the codes containing the initials *VP*: "*VP35–3,129*; *VP40–4,479*; and *VP30–8,509*. What else could *VP* stand for other than *Vibrio parahaemolyticus*?" I asked.

He said nothing.

"On the other hand, there were some codes with *GP*, rather than *VP*, before them, namely, 6,039, which appeared twice, and 7,133."

"Weird," Brubeck mumbled. "Let me mull this over."

WHEN GAMBLING, I seek action, not décor; a casino's digs mean nothing. It's the cards that matter, the dice, and spinning wheels. For me, the line between winning and losing is an exhilarating tightrope walk, a life-infusing jaunt.

I lit a cigar and sipped a Martini at a blackjack table in Atlantic City. Neither smoke nor drink brought me luck, however. Within an hour, I burned through my pot of two thousand. All was not lost, though, for I drew comfort from gambling with kindred souls. It was a family reunion of sorts, only without names—a gathering of like-minded.

Broke but content, I left the casino and returned to my car where I checked my phone to find a message waiting from Eve.

"Why aren't you picking up?" she asked. "I need to reach you."

I called her to apologize. "My phone slipped from my pocket in the vehicle while I was working in Annapolis."

"That can't happen," she said. "Not now." Her tone was edgy.

"I'm sorry."

"Something else: Did you withdraw two thousand dollars today? I was balancing our account and just noticed it."

My knuckles formed a white arc along the steering wheel.

"Jay ... son," she said. "Our agreement ..."

Eve was aware of my gambling history, the debts I had accrued before we met, and how I had paid them off with the sale of XK59 to *Natow Pharmaceuticals*. She insisted I seek help, which I did, but rehabilitation came fitfully. With time, I accepted that I couldn't gamble without jeopardizing our relationship, but the past few days had pushed me over the edge.

"I bought some things for the baby," I said, ashamed of myself for lying.

"With cash?"

"Yes."

"Like what?"

"A stroller, crib, and mobile."

"A *mobile*? We have one! You saw me hanging it the other day."

"I know, but that was a used one. I thought we should have a new one."

"We *did* our buying! Besides, it's unlike you to shop."

"These were things I couldn't pass up."

"Where did you find them?"

"Here in Annapolis."

"*Two thousand* dollars?"

"You'll love the stuff."

She clucked her tongue. "I don't like this, Jason …"

"I understand. Gotta run; another call coming. See you tonight."

She sighed. "Drive safely."

It was Bird and Flagstaff who called on a speakerphone.

"Where are you?" Bird asked. "Expected you back by now."

"Got delayed by a storm. A violent cell passed through Annapolis."

"Heard about it. Funnel cloud reported."

Flagstaff: "We've got more results from Dudley Zot's autopsy in Ecuador."

"Oh?"

"They found venom in the guy."

"Snake venom?"

"No, XK59."

"I'm sorry, I didn't hear you right," I said.

"XK59," he repeated. "At high levels under the bite marks."

"XK59's not a venom! Someone must've injected the protein as they did with Chandrapur."

"We have two experts who identified the marks on Zot's body as spider bites, and XK59 was beneath them."

"But Zot didn't bleed! He had muscle breakdown. And what about *Vibrio parahaemolyticus* and *Aeromonas hydrophila*? Were they present?"

"No, just XK59."

"There's more," Bird said. "They found some small bones and a rodent's pelt in Zot's bed."

"Bizarre," I muttered. "What sort of rodent?"

"Something akin to a mouse or vole."

"*Totally* bizarre!"

IT WAS EARLY evening when I reached the UNIT laboratory. I found Alistair Brubeck in his white coat, crisp as ever.

"You heard the news about Zot?" he asked.

"I don't buy it."

"What part?"

"Spider bites and XK59."

"Why not?"

"Because XK59 comes from the bark of a tree, not from a spider. Are they sure it was XK59?"

He displayed a print of results from an instrument called a mass spectrometer that identified specific molecules, and it showed the indisputable signature pattern of XK59. "Fresh from Ecuador. Convinced?"

Reluctantly, I nodded. "But, why didn't Zot bleed?"

"You got me. Perhaps XK59 is a strange case of Dr. Jekyll and Mr. Hyde—behaving one way in venom and another in the company of *Vibrio parahaemolyticus*."

"We need to run some tests," I said.

"What sort?"

"Feeding studies in guinea pigs. I learned recently the animals serve as an excellent model in which to study the disease-causing mechanisms of *Vibrio parahaemolyticus*." I took a pen and outlined a plan ...

Group 1: controls (chow without XK59)
Group 2: chow + XK59 (1 part per billion)
Group 3: chow + XK59 (1 part per billion) + Vibrio parahaemolyticus

"What do you think?" I asked Brubeck.

"I see what you're getting at. It'll show how the animals fare after eating XK59 at the concentration found in shrimp, and what effect, if any, *Vibrio parahaemolyticus* has in making them sick."

"Can you get guinea pigs?"

"Not a problem."

DARKNESS HAD FALLEN by the time I left the UNIT, and as I walked toward Metro, I joined a steady stream of anti-WAFTA protestors returning home from a massive demonstration that had taken place on the mall earlier in the day. I squeezed into a crowded train and rode to Bethesda with a heavy heart, convinced the time for lies had long passed and that I needed to tell Eve the truth. At home, I found her lying on the sofa with her feet propped on a pillow. I kissed her forehead.

"Do you have a fever?" I asked her.

She nodded. "A hundred point five."

My mind raced into doctor-mode. A fever late in the third trimester raised the possibility of an infection of the membranes that enclosed the amniotic fluid, a condition that could complicate delivery. But other causes were possible, too. "Sore throat?" I asked her.

"No," she replied.

"Urinary symptoms?"

She shook her head.

"Bleeding or discharge?"

She raised a hand. "Jason, I'd tell you if I had those things."

"Let me listen to your lungs and belly."

She rolled her eyes.

I fetched a stethoscope, meeting her father in the hallway.

"Ah, good," he whispered, seeing the device. "I told her to call you earlier about the fever, but you know Eve—stoic as ever."

"Has she had a cough?"

"Not that I've heard."

"Stiff neck or headache?"

"Don't think so."

I returned to the living room. Eve's heart and lungs were clear, and the baby's heart rate was normal. "I'd like to check a couple of other things," I said, nodding toward the bedroom.

"Doctors … prod and poke …"

In the bedroom, I felt her breast mass for signs of change but found none. "Did you call the obstetrician about your temperature?"

"I'll do it in the morning if it remains." She set her head on the pillow. "There's lasagna in the refrigerator. Daddy and I ate earlier."

I kissed her again. "Sorry I was late."

She nodded forgivingly, but her expression soon changed. I braced myself for the question about the baby items.

"There's a message out there from Giva Bhanjee," she said. "You need to call her."

"Did she say where she was?"

"Yes, in London."

"What's she doing there?"

"I didn't ask. She asked you to call her as soon as possible."

I started for the door.

"Jason."

I turned. "Yes?"

"Would you close the door? I'm going to sleep now."

IN THE DINING room, I viewed the message on the table from Bhanjee as a tiny window with drapes pulled shut. If I wanted to see beyond the drapes, I had to call the number yet I hesitated to do so for fear of seeing what lay beyond the curtains.

I placed the call. Bhanjee answered after the first ring. "What took you?" she asked.

"I only received the message now."

"I don't have long. My flight to India leaves shortly."

"Why didn't you tell me you were leaving?"

"Because I left as fast as I could. It was horrible!"

"What was?"

"What they left in my home!"

"What was it?"

"Oh, God, it's too awful to talk about!"

"Giva—"

"Listen! Chandrapur is on a respirator. His doctors don't know how long he has to live. Why didn't you go see him?"

"You think I can drop what I'm doing to go to India?"

"I did!"

"Then call me when you get there."

"But you need to know what the codes mean now, and Minal can tell you."

"Wait! What codes are you referring to?"

"The ones you found on the Congressman's boat."

"How do *you* know about that?"

"Chandrapur told me."

"How does *he* know?"

"He knows everything! That's why you need to see him!"

"Give me his telephone number! I'll call him!"

"No, he insists you see him! That's how secret the codes are!" An announcement in the background competed with her words. "I need to go. My flight's boarding."

"Hold on! Let me ask you something: Frank Grainger is your boss at *BioVironics*, isn't he?"

"How did you find out?"

"Doesn't matter! What I want to know is whether Frank Grainger has a tattoo of a pistol in his sternal notch, at the top of his chest. Does he?"

"I wouldn't know; he always wears a tie."

"But it was Grainger who told you what my middle initial is, right? You used it on the envelope with directions to Chandrapur's home in India."

"I need to go!" she wailed. "I'll call you from India."

IN THE SILENCE, my stomach rumbled in protest of missing lunch and dinner. Heeding the call, I went to the kitchen and served myself a heaping plate of lasagna, but I consumed it in perfunctory fashion for my thoughts dwelled on how to break into Bhanjee's home.

From my satchel, I retrieved the address Bhanjee's lab partner had given me. Tucking it into my pocket, I peeked into the bedroom and saw that Eve had fallen asleep, the sheet over her belly rising and falling with each breath. Down the hall, her father had retired also, allowing me to leave unnoticed.

Fearing the security detail now had an eye on both of our vehicles, I slipped out the dining room window into the alley and snuck into Bethesda's commercial center. A car rental agency maintained a small fleet there that I reached just as its staff prepared to shutter for the night.

After renting a car, I made my way through Bethesda to I-270 north. I followed the freeway out of town, passing the exit Flagstaff, Bird, and I had taken the day before to meet with Charles E. Oxford at *BioVironics*. Beyond the exit, the freeway climbed a hill atop which a moonlit Sugarloaf Mountain came into view in the distance. After making a long, steady descent, I left the freeway for a quiet road that cut between housing developments so new bulldozers and backhoes still lingered in the shadows.

Three traffic lights later, I turned into an area I recognized from an outing Eve and I had taken two weeks earlier when we spent a Saturday morning picking blueberries at a farm. The region was a curious blend of rural and urban, its pastures surrounded by expanding suburbs. I passed a park rimmed by cornfields before coming to my destination, *Wayland Drive*, a freshly paved road that led to a condominium complex.

I stopped the car in a space reserved for visitors and inspected the buildings before me. They formed a "U" about the parking lot, each four floors and rimmed with spacious balconies. A single entrance served as a portal for each complex, and I entered the one where Bhanjee lived. Inside, I came to a lobby with rows of mailboxes, one of which, to my relief, had a card reading *G. Bhanjee* over the number *325*.

I climbed the stairs to the third floor and stopped before door *325*. Glancing at my watch, I saw it was 11:25 p.m. I tapped the door softly and stepped back. No one answered. Placing my ear to the door, I listened for sounds inside; none ensued. Knocking harder, I waited again. A neighbor's door opened.

"Bit late, isn't it?" a woman's voice said. I approached her door but could see only part of her face through the crack. A security chain obscured her nose altogether.

"I'm looking for Giva Bhanjee," I said.

"At this hour?"

"It's critical." Even though I knew Bhanjee wouldn't be there, I felt compelled to find out what it was that had been left in her home that was so "horrible" she fled the country.

"Who are you?" she asked.

"An acquaintance; I met her last night."

She eyed me warily, narrowing the gap when I inched closer.

"Please, I need your help," I insisted.

"With *what*?"

"I need to find Giva. I was told she didn't show up for work today."

"Who told you that?"

"A colleague of hers at work."

The gap widened, allowing me to view a lock of brown hair and a set of hazel eyes.

"I *knew* I should have checked on her this morning," the woman said.

"Why do you say that?"

"Because, we almost always leave for work at the same time, yet I didn't see her today."

"Do you know her well?"

"We've walked together almost every weekend for the past two years."

"Did you call her after not seeing her this morning?"

"Yes, but she didn't answer."

"Have you noticed anything unusual around here the past few days—visitors, deliveries, suspicious cars?"

She ran her eyes over me.

"Other than me. I promise, I'm trying to help her."

The door closed. A moment later, I heard the sound of a clinking chain reverse. The door opened. A middle-aged woman in a nightgown appeared, one hand on the door as if ready to shut it at any time.

"It's odd," she said, "but I heard sounds coming from under Giva's door around 11 p.m. last night after I returned from walking the dog. It's not like Giva to be up at that hour. She goes to bed early."

"She asked to see me last night at midnight," I replied. "That was probably her leaving for our meeting."

"You keep late hours, don't you?"

"This was at her request."

She seemed disarmed now, stepping into the hallway, a petite woman.

"Can you do me a favor?" I asked.

"What?"

"Let me into Giva's condo. Do you have a key?"

Another once-over, more intense than before. "It wouldn't be right," she said.

"Please, trust me, it's crucial. Giva told me her boyfriend's ill, and I want to help him."

"Minal Chandrapur?" she gasped.

"You know him?"

"Of course! What's wrong with him?"

"He may be dying."

"God, no!" she cried, loud enough to look both ways for neighbors.

"Please, open her door for me."

She peered at me before stepping into her home without closing the door. After disappearing for a moment, she returned. "*You* open it," she said, handing me a key.

I took it and unlocked the door. "Giva?" I called from the entryway.

Hearing nothing, I stepped into a studio apartment—kitchen right, bathroom left, living room-bedroom ahead.

"She and Chandrapur were planning to get a bigger place after marrying."

I turned abruptly, unaware the petite woman had accompanied me. "I didn't think you were coming," I said.

"I changed my mind."

I switched on a light. "How do things look to you?" I asked.
She shook her head. "Something's wrong."

"What?"

Cowering, she went to the kitchen and pointed to the dish rack. "No cereal bowl, which means she skipped breakfast this morning. She dries her bowl there every day." She looked across the room and then pointed. "And what's that?"

I followed her around a small table with two chairs that constituted the dining room. An un-smoked cigarette lay on the floor beside the table.

"Giva doesn't smoke!" She grasped my arm.

"Then, whose—"

"I don't know!" she cried, her eyes zeroing in on the bed. "And *that's* strange! The way the bed's made; Giva doesn't do it that way."

"Stay put," I told her.

I went to the bed and examined it. The bedspread had been pulled neatly over the pillows although there appeared to be a small object pushing the bedspread up over one of the pillows.

"Giva folds the bedspread back," my shadow said, peering over my shoulder.

Beside the bed, leaning against the wall, was a decorative cane that I used to lift the bedspread. Peeling it back, I saw a small mirror fall and slip along the pillow onto the mattress.

"What the hell?" I asked. I shuddered as I recalled the words of the sticky in Kosta's copy of *Theogony*: *Follow the mirrors.*

I saw a reflection in the mirror of something move under the bedspread. Lifting it further, several handsome, bluish-green spiders came into view. They had large bodies, over an inch wide, although my view of them was fleeting given their rapid retreat.

"Did you see that?" I asked with disbelief.

"See what?" my partner replied.

"Those spiders!"

"Oh, God, I'm outta here!" She ran out the door.

I dropped the cane and stepped back, aghast by the discovery of the spiders and mirror.

Trembling, I went to the kitchen, emptied a large glass jar holding rice in it, and returned to the bed where I flicked on a bedside lamp for better viewing. Using the cane again, I lifted the bedspread and pulled it back until the first spider emerged. I lowered the jar over it and pressed the rim to the bed to snare the creature without harming it. Slipping a sheet of paper under the rim, I quickly turned the jar upright and screwed on the lid. With the spider captive, I held the jar up and peered at its contents. Save for tarantulas, it was the largest spider I'd seen, larger than the wolf spiders we had in Wisconsin. Two features struck me: the crab-like motion—as I held the jar up, the spider scurried sideways and then backwards, much as crabs do on sand when confronted—and the blend of blue-green hues.

I lowered the jar to get another view, recalling the anatomy of invertebrates. I recognized the spider's two sections—cephalothorax and abdomen, the two connected by a thin waist, or pedicel. Given its size, even the smallest parts were discernible, including the finger-like spinnerets that secreted silk. But it was the mouthparts that drew my attention, for the jaws and fangs were enormous, sword-like extensions.

Lifting the jar to see the spider's underside, a bright flicker along the bedside table diverted my eyes. Angling the jar back and forth, I soon realized the flicker came from lamplight reflecting off a series of plates along the underside of the spider's thorax.

Just then, Bhanjee's neighbor reappeared, her eyes wild.

"I called the police!" she announced.

"*Why?*"

"Because this is a crime scene—spiders in Giva's bed!"

I bolted for the door.

"No!" she cried. "You need to stay!"

"Can't!"

"Tell me your name!" she called.

From the stairwell, I shouted, "Oscar Fields!"

I raced down the stairs and sped away in my car, driving the first half mile without lights to preserve my anonymity. When I reached the thoroughfare leading to the freeway, I saw the flashing lights of a wailing police car rushing the opposite way.

"*Damn!*" I whispered, fearing Bhanjee's neighbor had recorded my license plate.

Day 7

IT WAS CLOSE to 2 a.m. by the time I returned the rental car and made my way home after visiting Bhanjee's condo, and I tiptoed through the house to confirm that both Eve and her father were asleep. Relieved to have time to myself, I stored the jar with the spider in a secure spot and poured myself some rum.

The alcohol numbed my nerves as my thoughts returned to the Frank Grainger—Anton Manovic nexus. I poured more rum and, navigating the haze of drink, recollected my initial encounter with Grainger ...

Before entering his room at the hospital in Las Vegas two and a half years earlier, I had reviewed his chart and learned he was in his thirties and was pursuing a PhD in biochemistry at the University of Nevada in Reno.

"You must be the hematologist," he said as I approached his bed. "The surgeons said you'd be coming."

I eyed his swollen thigh that lay above the sheets.

"Yes, I wanted to hear about the bleeding that killed your colleague in Madagascar."

"Nothing *you* can do about it," he said.

"Nonetheless, I'd like to hear why you think a substance in the bark may have caused the bleeding."

"Not *may have* ... definitely did."

"How can you be sure?"

"Why else would a perfectly healthy man in his twenties bleed to death within an hour after being lacerated—bleeding not just from his wound, but from every orifice in his body?"

"Did he have a history of easy bleeding?"

"No."

"Was he taking any medications that might induce bleeding?"

"None."

"What about alcohol? Was he a drinker?"

"Not a chance; he was a devout Mormon."

"Strange," I said, shaking my head.

"No, it's simple: a toxin in the bark caused the bleeding."

"What toxin would that be?"

"I don't know, but I intend to find out. That's why I brought some bark back with me." He reached for a container that held the bark packed inside two plastic bags. It was a foot long and had sharp ridges, miniature blades almost. "You can see how this would cut someone." He fingered a ridge gingerly.

"Could I show that to my colleagues?" I asked.

He coveted the bark as a mother would a newborn. "I don't know; I don't want to lose it."

"I'll return it, I promise."

"You gotta understand, I went through hell to bring this back—limping through forests, hiding it in luggage, smuggling it through customs."

"I appreciate that, but we might be able to provide you with some ideas of toxins to look for."

"*I've* got ideas!" he shot back. "I work with poisons from venomous creatures for my doctorate."

"That's not a creature; it's bark."

He grimaced, exposing his teeth like a growling dog. "You're an arrogant son of a bitch, just like all doctors."

"I'm sorry, I didn't mean to question your abilities. I'm sure you're more than capable of analyzing the bark."

"Damn right I am."

I pointed to his thigh. "That's a nasty wound there, one the surgeons think may have turned into 'compartment syndrome', a condition—"

"I know what compartment syndrome is!" he lashed out. "It results from trauma and entails a buildup of pressure within a wound to the point that blood flow stops. Tissues begin to die from lack of oxygen. If the swelling advances, it can compromise blood flow to the rest of the limb." He snarled. "Why do you think I came to the hospital?"

"You're well-versed, I see."

"No, it's just that you doctors think you're the only ones who know these things, so you talk *down* to people. You're cut-throat sons of bitches molded to act that way. I learned that in college when I was a pre-med."

"You were thinking of becoming a physician?"

"They chose not to take me."

"So you pursued a PhD."

He nodded.

"I used to dissect snakes I found as road kill," I said.

"Like I said, you doctors know *everything*."

"Not I."

He searched me as if to see whether I was being sincere. "Well, Madagascar is a haven for snakes."

"I'm sure."

I glanced at my watch.

"Am I boring you?" he asked.

"Not at all, but I have other patients to see." I pointed to the bark. "Are you sure you wouldn't allow me to show that to my colleagues?"

He wrinkled his brow. "I have your word you'll return it?"

"You do."

"For what that's worth," he replied.

He set the bark in the container, sealed it, and handed it to me. "You'll find yourself in big trouble if I don't get that back."

WITH NERVES PICKLED by rum, I slipped into the bedroom, donned pajamas, and snuggled up to Eve whose heavy breathing told me she was fast asleep. I kissed her forehead and turned to my side, but something was awry: a foreign presence pervaded the room, one conveyed through gyrating air currents, radiating body heat, and a sense that spaces normally free were filled. I shut my eyes and listened intently, hearing the sound of a door open.

Bolting upright, I turned on the lamp to find the dark hole of a silencer pointed at me from across the room. The masked man who held the weapon straddled the doorway of our walk-in closet, waving the gun for me to stand. As I did, he issued another command, this one to extinguish the lamp. I reached for the switch, but before turning it, stole a glance at Eve who remained asleep.

I stepped around the bed and felt a cold cylinder press against my neck. It shifted when we reached the hallway, jabbing me in the back as I marched toward the living room. When my left side suddenly felt the barrel, I knew to turn right, stopping only when I reached a window in the dining room.

"Open it!" a voice whispered.

I scolded myself for leaving the window unlocked after meeting Bhanjee the night before.

"Jump and wait for me. I'll kill you if you try anything stupid."

I maneuvered my way out with my captor close behind.

We walked the alley in tandem to the street where we stopped. Circling me with the gun, he looked about before waving me on. After traversing a block, I felt a tap on my back. Turning, I found a man of medium build dressed in leather trousers, coat, and boots. With his mask off, he revealed himself to be the visiting scientist I met in Ecuador.

"How should I address you?" I asked. "As Frank Grainger or Anton Manovic?"

"Good, you made the connection." He spoke without an accent, a sea change from the Slavic pronunciation he voiced in Ecuador.

"Your tattoo betrayed you," I said.

"Get in," he ordered, pointing to a white van.

I sat across from him with the gun pointed at me.

"Are you a voyeur or a burglar, hiding in the closet as you did?"

He waved the gun at me. "You haven't changed, I see—just as arrogant as in Las Vegas."

"Did you break into Giva Bhanjee's condo, too?"

"Who are you, Sherlock Holmes?"

"Answer this, then: Who altered your appearance?"

He glanced into the mirror. "Ah, the miracles of plastic surgery; I even had my vocal chords adjusted."

"A violation of the body."

He pulled the trigger, shattering the window beside me.

"What are you *doing*?" I cried.

"The next one won't miss."

He shifted the gun to his left hand and held up his right. "What hand is this?"

"Right," I replied, my heart heaving.

Turning the mirror toward me, he held the hand up again, asking, "Which hand does it appear to be in the mirror?"

"Left," I replied.

"Yes, mirror images." He started the van. "Remember that."

As he prepared to drive, I glanced at his leg. Between hem and boot, I saw a titanium rod.

"A prosthesis," I observed.

"Yes, because of a below-the-knee amputation due to compartment syndrome."

"You may not have needed that if you'd stayed at my hospital; instead, you left against medical advice."

"Because of the demeaning way you doctors treated me there."

"Where did you go?"

"Elsewhere where they were more polite."

We drove through desolate streets.

"Where are we going?" I asked.

"You'll see."

"Why did you poison the shrimp?"

He pointed to the mirror which was still directed toward me. "Can you see yourself?"

I squinted. "Yes."

"Mirrors have much to teach you."

"You're obsessed with them. You planted one in Kosta's boat and in Bhanjee's bed. Are there others I missed?"

He said nothing.

We entered Washington, D.C. which, at that hour, had traffic lights flashing yellow.

"Who gave you permission to work with XK59 at *BioVironics*?" I asked.

"No one."

"Where did you get the protein?"

He sneered.

"We found XK59 in Zot but he didn't bleed," I informed him.

"Because spider venom doesn't work that way."

"Forget spiders!"

"You know *nothing*!" he shouted.

After driving in silence, we approached an intersection that required him to place both hands on the wheel. As we rounded a corner, I released my belt and lunged for the weapon.

He hit the brakes which sent me flying forward.

"You want to die?" he shouted as I collected myself from the floor.

"Isn't that what you have in store for me?" I replied. "After all, you killed my partner in Ecuador and my best friend, Danny Rogers!"

He accelerated and once again slammed the brakes before I could refasten my belt, sending me lashing against the dash. As I slumped to the floor, I felt something strike the side of my head.

Darkness befell me.

THE CEMENT FLOOR on which I lay was inhospitable to a throbbing head and sore neck. In my stupor, I found myself under a portico, its immaculate plaster ceiling holding a dazzling chandelier. The morning's first rays shone between columns of the porch, while above me, a brass knob gleamed from a tall oak door.

When I sat up, I winced from a pain in my upper arm just below the shoulder. Raising my pajama sleeve, I noticed a red dot that resembled an injection mark. I shuddered at the prospect that a needle had pierced my skin. Chandrapur's decent toward death came to mind and I wondered whether I might die, too, at the hands of the protein I had discovered.

Looking about, I saw a stairway descend from the porch to a cobblestone street where a red sports car was parked. I cleared my eyes for a second look, confirming it to be the same flaming F430 Spider Ferrari I saw the day before at Kosta's home in Annapolis. Beyond the car, a pair of trolley tracks lay in disrepair. A passing car swayed from side to side as its tires slipped from tracks to stones and back again. At the end of the block, a bus traversed a busy intersection. The entire area had a familiar look to it, and when I peered at the street signs, I saw ones indicating 35th and P Streets, N.W. in Washington, D.C.'s Georgetown district.

With the sun on the rise, I heard the front door open. A tall, sleek woman with icy blue eyes and fair skin stood in the entry. "Dr. Krispix!" she exclaimed.

I nodded.

Sigrid Bjornstad narrowed her eyes. "Why are you in your— " She pulled her bathrobe tighter.

"Where am I?" I asked.

"At Congressman Nick Kosta's home."

"Why are *you* here?" I asked, coming to my senses.

"I'm his guest."

As if on cue, the Congressman appeared, gaunt and weak. He grasped the door for support. "By God," he said, "you're the doctor Glenn Bird brought to Capitol Hill."

"Yes, Jason Krispix," Bjornstad noted.

Kosta held his gaze on me. With sunlight streaming through the doorway, he shielded his eyes, yet in the shadow under his brows, he exhibited a subtle yet undeniable side-to-side oscillation of the eyeballs.

"You've bled from your head!" Kosta said with concern. "Should I call an ambulance?"

I ran my fingers over my temple where Grainger had struck me. I felt clots but there appeared to be no active bleeding. After considering the pros and cons of going to an emergency room, I said, "Let me be for a bit."

"At least come in for some coffee," Kosta insisted. He beckoned me feebly.

I entered the house.

"I don't mean to be rude, but do you generally go about in your pajamas?" Kosta asked.

I told him about what had happened. "Do you know the name, 'Frank Grainger'?" I asked. "He dumped me here."

Kosta shook his head.

"What about you?" I asked Bjornstad.

She pointed to a library off the foyer. "Let's get your coffee." She led the way.

"Yes, please serve Dr. Krispix a fresh cup while I finish dressing," Kosta said. He departed at a tepid pace, lifting his arms for balance. At the stairway, he gripped the banister, ascended a step, and then rested before taking the next.

In the library, Bjornstad offered me a seat at a table that held two sets of breakfast dishes. "I'll brew a fresh pot."

She left a wave of perfume as she departed. In her absence, I glanced at the shelves replete with books, nary a space empty. Again, the theme was Greek, only there were no genre markers. I searched for the title, *Theogony*, but Bjornstad cut me short.

"I'm very concerned about what happened to you last night," she said. "Just yesterday I learned about this man, Frank Grainger. Chairman McCloskey informed me that Grainger was in Ecuador under an alias. Investigators sent by the UNIT to Ecuador discovered Grainger's driver's license at the shrimp farm. A background check verified he holds a PhD in biochemistry from the University of Nevada where he did research on snake venom."

"Are you aware that he works at *BioVironics* in Germantown?"

"I am, indeed. I encouraged Chairman McCloskey to apprehend Grainger so that he may be questioned in detail. In the meantime, I'd like you to know I identified the source of the missives the victims received. They came from a Greek work by Hesiod called *Theogony*."

"You must have learned that from Randy Flagstaff because I told him that." I informed her of the conversations I'd had with my English professor from college, Lawrence P. Squills.

She bristled. "Actually, I discovered it on my own."

"Really?" I tested her: "Did *all* the missives come from *Theogony*?" It was a detail I hadn't shared with Flagstaff.

"No, one came from a separate source."

"Which missive was it?"

"… *not that rich chimaera*."

"And where did it come from?"

"William Faulkner's *The Sound and the Fury*." She recited the passage …

Like it were put to makeshift for enough green to go around among the trees and even the blue of distance not that rich chimaera.

Impressed, I asked her: "Why do you think Grainger left me here?"

"I don't know; that's one of the questions we need to ask him." Looking over her shoulder, she leaned closer and whispered: "And we need to keep an eye on Congressman Kosta, too. He may be working with Grainger."

Just then, the Congressman appeared. Clean-shaven and wearing a suit, he looked invigorated, as if a shower had revived him. "I'd love to join you, but I cannot because of WAFTA. The vote is approaching quickly."

"What side are you on?" I asked him.

He cleared his throat in a series of grunts. "I've always been pro-WAFTA. Tariffs impede trade, and I want to clean the slate of them." He reached into his pocket and handed me forty dollars. "Call a taxi."

WITHOUT EXCEPTION, EVE meditated each morning in our den, a room set apart where she sat for variable periods before emerging with tranquility to meet the new day. Ours was a contrast in greeting the sun—she a philosopher, peace-seeker, minister; I a pragmatist, warrior, strategist.

"Jason!" she called from the den as I entered the house. "Where *were* you?"

A newspaper crinkled from the living room as her father's head appeared. "You went out in your *pajamas*?" he asked.

I went to Eve and hugged her, telling her what had happened. I used the opportunity to inform Spud about my work as well since he couldn't be left in the dark any longer.

Eve cupped my face in her hands. "You think Grainger *injected* you with something?"

I removed my pajama top and ran a finger over the site. "I'm thinking it was a tranquilizer, nothing more."

"How are you feeling?"

"Sore and tired, but otherwise alright."

If Grainger had injected me, roughly five hours had passed from the time of the injection. An interlude of that length without the appearance of more serious signs and symptoms gave me hope that it wasn't XK59 he injected.

"I'm taking you to the emergency ward!" Eve declared.

"Not needed," I replied. "Let me take a hot shower and see how I feel."

Eve frowned. "We can't take any chances, Jason!"

"Believe me, I'll go to the ER if I deteriorate."

Her frown deepened. "I found that scary spider you brought back last night in a jar sitting on our kitchen counter," she said. "Why did you bring it here?"

"Because I found it in Bhanjee's bed. What did you do with it?"

"I called Randy Flagstaff. He sent someone here to collect it."

She went to our bedroom and returned with a manila envelope. "Did you leave this in our closet?"

"No," I replied. "I don't recognize it."

I opened the envelope and found a series of photographs. The first was a close-up of the type of spider I found in Bhanjee's bed. A ruler along the bottom measured the spider's body, excluding legs, to be four inches in length. A small frame outlining part of the front section, or cephalothorax, was magnified in the next photo. It showed a pair of jaws with protruding fangs that resembled tapered hoses capable of delivering torrents of venom. Continuing the pattern of greater magnification, the photos zeroed in on the poison gland, a venom-producing sac composed of several pouches. Three layers comprised the venom sac: an outermost muscle layer; a middle component labeled "basal lamina"; and an innermost single row of cells labeled, "epithelium—produces venom." The remaining photos brought the epithelium to life in increasing detail, the last one taken by electron microscopy. It depicted a series of dots budding from the end of the epithelial cells into the venom sac.

A final sheet was not a photo but, rather, a penned message stating, *More details to follow.*

"Grainger," I murmured. "He must've left these when he broke into our house last night. I need to tell Flagstaff about this."

"Good, because he called this morning. I saw his name flash on your phone."

I went to the medicine cabinet and gulped down two tablets of acetaminophen. In the mirror, I saw bags under my eyes and wrinkles that looked as if they'd leapt there from a crumpled paper.

Eve offered me my phone.

I took her entire hand. "You're warm," I said.

"I still have a temperature: hundred point five."

I swallowed hard. "Better call the obstetrician."

"I will this morning."

I sighed.

"Do you know what day this is?" Eve asked.

In mill-like fashion, my mind ground slowly. "Your due date."

"Yes." She kissed me. "Call Flagstaff."

Wearily, I placed the call.

After answering, Flagstaff put me on speaker with Bird.

"We heard about what happened last night!" Flagstaff said. "How are you?"

"I've felt better. Where was your security team?"

"Outside your home!"

"What about in *back*? That's how Grainger got in."

"We'll check on it," Bird said.

"Why was Bjornstad at Kosta's house?" I asked.

"Because Kosta offered to put her up while she's in town."

"Bit awkward, isn't it, given that Kosta may have sent the missives?"

"We can't draw that conclusion yet," Bird cautioned.

"Back to last night," Flagstaff said. "In your words, tell us what happened."

I recounted the events, confirming the Grainger-Manovic connection. "Since you found his driver's license at the shrimp farm, why didn't you apprehend him at the border when he returned to the U.S.?"

"We were too late; he'd already entered the country."

"But we're looking for him now," Bird added. "McCloskey is adamant we apprehend him."

I described Grainger's van, including the shattered passenger-side window.

"That's helpful," Flagstaff said, "In the meantime, McCloskey joined us on a phone call to Charles E. Oxford at *BioVironics*."

"Did Oxford know Grainger was in Ecuador?"

"Of course, the company sent him there to deal with a venomous snake that's infiltrated the shrimp pools from the mangroves."

"Did you tell Oxford that an employee of his named Minal Chandrapur worked with XK59?"

"That's hearsay at this point," Bird said. "We need to confirm that."

"Sounds like you learned little from Oxford," I said.

"Not entirely. We confirmed the company knew about Grainger's arrest record before they hired him."

"What was he arrested for?"

"Breaking and entering."

"Where?"

"In Nevada while he was a grad student there. He told the police he was trying to reclaim a laptop another student stole from him."

I thought for a moment. "Sounds like a pattern."

"What do you mean?"

I told them about how the diaries in which I kept detailed notes had been stolen from my townhouse shortly after moving to Bethesda. A window beside my computer had been broken. At the time, I thought it was odd that only my diaries should disappear when we had art work and cash at home, too.

"That's how he learned about Danny Rogers," I surmised.

"Why would he harm Rogers?" Bird asked.

I shook my head. "Don't know. What about Kosta? Anything new since we last spoke?"

"Yes," Flagstaff replied. "We learned he earmarked a bill to fund *Starboard*'s campaign to clear the Intracoastal Waterway of seaweed."

"Congress funded *Starboard*, not individual donors?"

"Correct. Kosta inserted a clause requiring *Starboard* to hire *BioVironics* to undertake the job."

"Some Congressional pork!" I said. "Kosta earmarked a bill and then embezzled a million from its funds while he motored up the Inland Waterway mailing missives."

A SHOWER AND a fresh set of clothes made me feel somewhat better. It relieved me tremendously to conclude that the injection I'd received—assuming it *was* an injection, which I was convinced it had been—consisted of something other than XK59.

After downing a stack of French toast for breakfast, I placed a call. Normally, Congress would have been recessed in August but with WAFTA due for a vote, I suspected Paul DeTrigger would be at his desk, even on a Sunday. He answered the phone promptly.

"Got a minute?" I asked.

"Make it fast; WAFTA's about to explode. Barely got to the office through the protestors out there."

"On the flight to Ecuador, Muñoz told me you had called him on Kosta's behalf for updates on victims' names and addresses. Why did you do that?"

"Because Kosta's a Task Force member."

"So are others, but they didn't request that information."

"They didn't have a constituent who was poisoned; Kosta did."

"Muñoz said Kosta was traveling a lot at the time he requested the updates."

"We multi-task here."

"Where did he travel to?" I asked.

"I don't keep his calendar."

"Is he a boat enthusiast?"

"Of course, for good reason: Before coming to Congress, he was a Coast Guard officer assigned to the Intracoastal Waterway."

OUTSIDE, IT WAS a "code orange" day, a meteorological euphemism for hot, putrid air. Even the short walk from our house to the car left Eve and me in sweat.

We drove to the emergency department of the hospital where the obstetrician on-call for the weekend from the practice taking care of Eve had instructed us to meet him. I stopped at the front entrance to leave Eve off and told her I would join her after parking.

"No," she insisted, kissing me goodbye.

"I'm staying!" I repeated. "I want to be with you!"

"I'll be fine," she said. "He just wants to check me for a low-grade fever."

Along the way, we had argued about whether I should remain. The doctor, husband, and father-to-be in me insisted I stay.

"I'd rather you get your work done so you won't be absent later," she said. "I'll get daddy to pick me up."

"Then, call me," I said, reluctant to depart.

We hugged cheek-to-cheek, her skin warm.

I drove back home, parked the car, and walked to Metro, my shirt becoming a towel along the way. In the cool of the train, the fabric dried only to moisten anew as I trod the familiar route to the UNIT. Inside, I made my way to the lab where I found Brubeck wearing a pair of goggles. He looked up at the last moment, setting down a pipette.

"Jason, just the man I want to see!" He nodded over his shoulder. "I've got preliminary results on the guinea pigs."

He led me to another section of the laboratory where, after donning gowns and gloves, we entered a windowless room with metal shelves stacked to the ceiling. At intervals, step-ladders stretched to the highest levels. The sound of pit-patting feet carried through the musty air. We stopped before three cages set apart from the others.

"As you recall," Brubeck said, "we agreed to test three groups. In each group, we have six guinea pigs." He pointed to a cage labeled, *Group 1: controls (chow without XK59)*. "How do the animals look to you?"

I watched them move about briskly. "Healthy."

He nodded, pointing to the next cage labeled, *Group 2: chow + XK59 (1 part per billion)*. "As you recall, this was the concentration of XK59 in the shrimp."

"How long have they been eating the chow?"

"Eight hours."

The animals appeared to be as healthy as those in the first cage, which didn't surprise me because in my mouse studies I had to spike the chow with 10 parts per million XK59 to produce fatal bleeding. That represented a concentration of XK59 10,000-fold greater than the level the guinea pigs had eaten.

"So what we're seeing here," I said, "is that chow laced with 1 part per billion XK59 is insufficient to cause bleeding. Taking it a step further, if we assume guinea pigs are a reasonable proxy for humans, 1 part per billion XK59 in shrimp would be insufficient to cause bleeding in humans. Something else boosted the level of XK59 in the victims a thousand-fold higher to 1 part per million."

"What do you think did it?" Brubeck asked.

"I'm still betting on *Vibrio parahaemolyticus*." I held my breath for the third cage.

Brubeck pointed to it, and my hopes were dashed. Behind a card reading, *Group 3: chow + XK59 (1 part per billion) + Vibrio parahaemolyticus,* six guinea pigs moved about energetically.

"*Damn*, they're healthy," I lamented. "That shoots my theory about *Vibrio parahaemolyticus* causing elevated levels of XK59 in the victims."

"Perhaps it's too early to see anything," Brubeck replied.

"To the contrary, every one of the humans fell ill within eight hours of eating shrimp, so we should be seeing similar results here."

"Let's ride it out a few more hours before we draw conclusions."

I saw no other choice.

AS I ENTERED the Amygdala, Eve called.

"I'm at the obstetrician's still," she said. "They examined me, drew blood, and took a urine sample. They want to do an ultrasound now of my chest to make sure there's nothing in the lungs or nearby that explains the fever and breast mass."

Unwelcome diagnoses entered my mind, including lymphoma, a cancer of the lymph system, and sarcoidosis, an autoimmune disorder that could affect the chest cavity. Both could explain the duo of fever and breast mass.

"Did they mention any specific possibilities?" I asked.

"No, only that they wanted to view the lungs and the compartment between them, the media … mediast …"

"Mediastinum."

"That's it. I'm going down the hall to get the ultrasound now."

"I should have stayed with you!"

"No, I called daddy. He's coming to join me."

"Call me when you're done, promise?"

She gave me her word and hung up, leaving me staring at the wall.

I WENT TO Flagstaff's office along the perimeter of the Amygdala. He had his legs propped on the desk, trousers riding to the top of cowboy boots that looked larger than life.

"What can I do for you?" he asked.

I closed the door. "I'm quitting."

He pointed to a chair.

"I'm having nightmares about Muñoz—jeep blowing up … body parts … blood-stains. Add to that my wife's pregnancy and breast mass."

He eyed me silently.

"What would *you* do in my situation?" I asked.

He seemed to look within before replying. "Ride it out."

"*You* weren't in Ecuador, and this isn't *your* wife."

"I was referring to horses," he explained. "In the past, I rode horses to get through tough times, and I was suggesting you resort to whatever method you have that might resolve your problems."

The first time I had ridden horses was with Eve in Australia. We went riding again during a visit to Zion National Park, but that was the only other time I'd been on a horse. On our farm in Wisconsin, we had a few cows and pigs, but no horses.

"I think it's best I quit," I repeated.

He lowered his feet and sat up. "Then go home. Be with your wife. Take the time you need."

"That easy, huh? Pick up and leave?"

"*I* did."

I scrunched my face. "I don't understand."

"I left the Marine Corps." He diverted his eyes, holding them in a steady stare on the wall. In the silence, I saw a look of solemn pain. When he turned back to me, his eyes had sunken.

"I was twenty-five at the time," he explained, "and had just completed a tour of duty. They offered me a bonus to re-enlist, but I refused because I'd lost my best friend in the Horn of Africa, another Marine we called 'Cherokee.' He and I were the sole Native Americans on our team, a group of equestrians. We spent months riding the gorges and canyons of Somalia rooting out extremist training camps. By day, the temperatures soared above 100 only to drop below freezing at night. One day, while crossing a river bed, we took fire. We galloped to a nearby slope, but when they shot our horses, we fled on foot. The only way to escape was to scale a series of terraces leading to a summit. The taller of us were able to climb faster than others. One by one, we succumbed to steady fire. Below me, several terraces down, Cherokee took a bullet to the back. To help him would have meant certain death. I pushed on. When I reached the summit, I looked back and saw a sickening sight: bullets riddling Cherokee's body to the point it looked like corn popping in a kettle. Only a handful of us made it out. When we returned with reinforcements, I found Cherokee impaled on a post like a scarecrow. It was then I decided to leave the Corps after my tour of duty. I returned to Arizona and took up my old job of breaking-in wild horses. After work, I rode in the desert for hours on end, wrestling with demons in my mind. I still fight them today."

He returned his eyes to the wall, a refuge, it seemed. When he spoke again, it was in a whisper: "There comes a time to walk, Jason—or, in my case, to ride—and this may be yours."

I said nothing; to do so would violate a sacred silence. I watched him grasp his forehead. He squeezed the skin until it turned white.

"Go," he said, pointing to the door.

I shook my head. "No."

He scowled. The demons, it seemed, were alive.

"Who'll take my place if I ditch?" I asked.

"What does it matter?"

"I want to know who it'll be."

"Crystal Petersen from CDC."

"What will you have her do?"

"A number of things, but first she'll follow-up on that spider you collected from Bhanjee's condo. We gave it to an expert at the Smithsonian. He's going to identify it."

"Who is the expert?"

He handed me a card. "Feel free to see him on your way home. But if you're not coming back, we need your ID and a signed pledge of silence about your detail."

I slipped the card into my pocket and left.

I WENT TO my office and retrieved a bag of cashews I had stored there earlier. Tossing a few into my mouth, I inspected the card Flagstaff had given me …

Gart Spilbat, Ph.D.
Arachnologist
Smithsonian Institution

I dialed the number on the card.

A whispery voice answered, "Spilbat."

I introduced myself. "You have my spider."

"I'm sorry, but have we met?"

"*Distamus ab aliis,*" I said.

He paused. "*Proprius orbis.* Yes, Flagstaff told me you collected the spider."

"What sort is it?"

"Dunno; still checking."

"Is it venomous?"

He laughed nervously. "Damn right it is! I pity its prey."

"Can I see it with you?"

"Of course."

"I'm on my way."

I crossed Pennsylvania Avenue and walked to the mall. When I reached the Natural History Museum, I climbed the steps with a throng of summertime visitors. Inside the foyer, I noticed a tall, lanky man standing beside a wooly mammoth. Wearing suspenders over a long-sleeve denim shirt, he was tall and gaunt and had a pointed beard that dropped a third of the way down his chest.

I approached him. "Dr. Spilbat?"

He leaned to my level. "*Distamus ab aliis.*"

"*Proprius orbis*," I replied, finding it awkward still to utter the words.

"Protocol," he apologized. "Come to my office."

Walking beside him, I saw little in the way of skin. In addition to the thick beard, he had an unruly crop of grey hair that extended well below the nape of his neck. Neither combing nor shaving seemed to be in his repertoire.

We passed through an entry marked *Private—Employees Only*. Drawing a pipe from his pocket, he slipped it between his lips. "Yes, I'm aware of the non-smoking policy, so I won't light it." He relaxed his shoulders and grinned, revealing a set of yellow incisors.

"How long have you worked here?" I asked.

"Thirty years."

"And when were you recruited to the UNIT?"

"Early this morning; they summoned me to collect the spider."

He seemed put off by small-talk for he picked up his pace, leaving me a step behind as we entered a dark, narrow passage that led to an expansive warehouse-like area that made me feel uncomfortable. We traversed it to an alcove at the distant end, an architectural after-thought that Spilbat claimed for an office. It had a lone window overlooking the mall, but the view was blocked by a tower of books. A cluttered desk filled much of the alcove, the remainder occupied by microscopes and cabinets with catalogued specimens.

He offered me a stool before pointing to four broad-based jars, each of which held an enormous spider with blue-green hues that moved about in crab-like fashion.

"Hey, how did you get so many of them? I collected only *one*!"

"*That* one," he agreed, pointing to a Petri dish. "I sacrificed it to study its anatomy. I collected the others from the Indian woman's house. Glenn Bird sent me there with someone from the UNIT. I'd just returned when you called."

"Were they under the bedspread?"

"Yes, a number of them." He frowned. "I feel for them—they didn't belong there."

I glanced at the Petri dish. "That one lost its color."

"Because of changes in oxygenation of its hemolymph," he explained. He tilted his head as if to test my knowledge.

" 'Hemolymph,' " I repeated. "The fluid that circulates through a spider's body?"

"Yes, analogous to blood in vertebrates. Instead of having hemoglobin, as in vertebrate blood, hemolymph holds a copper-based protein called hemocyanin that's blue when oxygenated—accounting for the color of live spiders—but grey when un-oxygenated." He looked at the jars. "Those critters have a boatload of hemocyanin."

He directed me to the table with the Petri dish. Pointing a lamp at the spider, he said, "I think you'll find this to be a most unusual creature." He circled a pair of tweezers over the body. "But first, basic anatomy—two major sections: cephalothorax and abdomen."

He handed me a magnifying glass which I held over the dish.

"*Incredible!*" I whispered, marveling at the complexity and beauty.

He lifted the Petri dish to expose the spider's underside.

"Got a penlight?" I asked.

"Why do you ask?"

"I'll show you."

He left the table and returned shortly with what I had requested.

I lifted the dish again and directed the penlight at the series of plates along the underside of the thorax that produced the flicker I had noticed at Bhanjee's condo. Light reflected from the plates to form tiny bars on the table. "See those?" I asked.

"Oh, yes, we'll discuss the reflective plates shortly, but let me turn your attention to several other features first." He set the dish down and placed the tip of the tweezers above a cluster of tiny spheres. "Fourteen in all, a very rare finding given that most spiders have eight or fewer eyes. This beast has excellent eyesight which, with its powerful legs, makes it a daunting hunter."

A telephone rang, but Spilbat ignored it, peering instead at the spider through his magnifying glass. A bead of sweat rolled off his brow and plopped onto the table beside the dish. Nothing, it seemed, could distract him.

"One mean arachnid," he observed.

He slid the dish under a microscope with two pairs of eyepieces. "Let's take a closer look."

I positioned myself to find the spider's head under the low-power objective.

"Venom's not the only factor to consider when assessing a spider's danger," Spilbat said. "How it *delivers* the venom is equally important." He flipped the spider over. Pointing to a pair of jutting appendages beneath the eyes, he said, "Those are the jaws, or 'chelicerae,' and they're exceedingly powerful in this case. If you've seen tongs used to pick up blocks of ice, you'll recall they start wide and come in from the sides to snare the ice. That's how this spider's jaws work, which allows it to attack large prey before injecting its venom."

"How large of prey?"

"Small rodents, I suspect." He lifted his head to engage me. "That's not unprecedented: tarantulas kill mice." His eyes widened as if to express a morbid delight. "I'm betting it was this spider that left those marks on Zot in Ecuador."

I shook my head. "I don't think so."

"Why not?"

"Because, if it was a spider that attacked Zot, why was XK59 present at the bite-sites?"

"Yes, Glenn Bird told me about your protein."

"I recovered it from *bark*, not from a spider." I pointed to the creature. "I assume you're examining the venom."

"As we speak." He peered into the microscope. "I should tell you that I measured the distance of its fully extended jaws and they match the bite marks on Zot. There's no other spider I know of with a bite so wide."

"Tarantulas?"

He waved me off. "Their jaws don't close from the sides as these do. They work like jackhammers, striking their prey from above."

He moved to a higher objective. "Look at the fangs at the end of the jaws. They're like hoses, capable of delivering a torrent of venom."

"You're impressed."

"*Awed*; never seen anything like this."

He brought a section of dissected abdomen into view. "As you can see, prominent silk glands and spinnerets located at the rear. I suspect its webs are vast."

He shifted to the reflective plates, the largest in the center with smaller ones about it.

"Yes, those," I said, my interest piquing.

Between the rectangles were patches of reddish brown hair that reminded me of lanugo, the soft, fine hair found on babies at birth.

"That's gotta be copper of some sort imbuing that color," he observed.

He went to the window, pulled the curtain, and turned off the lights, felling the alcove in darkness. Sitting again, he pushed the microscope aside and directed the penlight at the rectangles just as I had done earlier. With perfect clarity, the light reflected from the rectangles to create streaks across the ceiling.

"Mirrors," he said.

I shuddered.

He continued: "Each plate is made of specialized chitin endowed with exquisite reflective capacity."

I felt a pang of nausea from the repeated encounters with mirrors—one in the galley of Kosta's boat; another in Bhanjee's bed; the instructions to *Follow the mirrors* on a sticky in *Theogony*; and now the spider's.

"I suspect those reflective plates ward off predators," Spilbat suggested. "Just imagine the spider sitting on its web with sunlight striking the plates; no bird or mammal in its right sense would attack a creature reflecting such a bright light."

He opened the curtains. "Let's check the results on the venom."

He led me out of his office and up a flight of stairs to a laboratory hosting a vast array of instruments. Stopping before one, he produced a graph from a mass spectrometer. "That's it, the venom," he said.

"No *way!*" I gasped, studying the results. "That's almost pure XK59! How can that *be?*"

Spilbat shook his head. "Dunno, but I'm certain spiders killed Zot in Ecuador with their XK59 venom."

IT WAS EARLY afternoon when I left the Smithsonian to return to the UNIT. Without a breeze, the air was boggy and stained with exhaust. Honking cars and heat waves rising from the sidewalks made it difficult to concentrate, yet two questions bedeviled me: Was a spider the true source of XK59 rather than bark, and were the mirrors I encountered a cruel play on the chitin plates on the spider's cephalothorax?

At the base of the steps to the UNIT, I called Eve, concerned that she hadn't reached me while I was at the Smithsonian. As I waited for her to answer, I bit into a sandwich she had prepared for me before I left the house.

"Where are you?" I asked her. "I expected to hear from you."

"I'm sorry, I meant to call earlier. Daddy and I are home now."

"How did the ultrasound go?" I asked.

"Unrevealing except for some swollen lymph nodes in my chest."

"And the breast mass?"

"Unchanged."

"Lymph nodes ..." I mumbled.

"The doctor said it was a non-specific finding that could have resulted from a number of things."

Like the spread of cancer, I fretted. I clenched my teeth. "The plan?"

"Wait for the results of urine and blood cultures and take acetaminophen if the fever persists. Since the baby's fine, the doctor was comfortable sending me home although he wants to see me in the morning again. If I haven't gone into labor by then, he plans to hospitalize me to induce it."

"Alright, I'll come home when I can."

"Jason?"

"Yes?"

"Have you been gambling?"

My heart leapt. "Why do you ask?"

"Because I just received an email from a bank in Bethesda acknowledging the opening of a new joint account that received a hundred thousand dollar deposit."

I HURRIED TO my office in the UNIT to see if I had received a similar email but Eve called me before I could do so.

"Oh my God, Jason! A man just called our land line! It was horrible!

"Who was it?"

"The man who broke into our home last night."

"Frank Grainger?"

"Yes, he told me to relay a message to you."

"What was it?"

"I'll read it ... *You have until midnight to make amends. If you haven't done so by then, there'll be mass poisonings from XK59. You know what you need to do.*"

"That's it?" I asked.

"Yes, although he left a number for you to call."

"Give it to me."

She did, and then began to cry. "Why does he hate you so much?"

"He's deranged. We must be strong, Eve. We'll get through this. Remember, we've got a security detail watching us. I'm going to see Randy Flagstaff right now to tell him what happened. We'll track the guy down."

I hurried to Flagstaff's office where I found him talking with Glenn Bird.

"Grainger's out of control," I said. "He threatened to cause mass casualties with XK59." I told them about the call Eve relayed.

"What does he mean by, 'You know what you need to do?'"

I shook my head. "The guy's a lunatic. He poisoned people, some fatally. What more proof do we need?"

"We don't know *he* poisoned the shrimp," Bird said. "Did he admit to it last night?"

"No, but—"

"He may be a fall guy. Having an arrest record doesn't mean he poisoned the shrimp."

"All the more reason for you to stay with us," Flagstaff added. "We need your help."

I reached into my pocket for Spilbat's business card and set it on Flagstaff's desk.

"You're with us?" he asked.

I nodded. "I can't leave with the weight of XK59 on me."

I'D TAKEN NO more than a step from Flagstaff's office when Alistair Brubeck rushed me.

"You gotta see this! Come to the lab!"

Once there, we entered a temperature-controlled room with shelves holding agar plates growing various bacteria. Brubeck shut the door and turned off the light, engulfing us in darkness.

"Look around," he said. "See anything interesting?"

I scanned the area before noticing four bioluminescent circles. "Glowing," I said.

"Bingo! What do you think it is?"

"Something from the shrimp pond?"

"In part, yes, but what exactly?"

"*Vibrio parahaemolyticus*?"

"No, *Aeromonas hydrophila*! Four plates growing the bacteria—one each from a victim, leftover shrimp, *Electric Jolt*, and shrimp from the round pond."

Brubeck turned on the light.

"We discovered the glow by chance. One of my staff opened a refrigerator to find the light burned out yet noticed a glow in the remnants of *Electric Jolt* stored in a flask. That led her to check the agar plates in this room where she noticed the glowing *Aeromonas*."

"Bioluminescence isn't rare among marine organisms," I reminded him.

"So, you're unimpressed; then let me show you something else."

We went to his office where he displayed a pulsed-field gel electrophoresis ...

"What you're looking at is a photo of a gel plate with two strains of *Aeromonas hydrophila*. The one on the right was recovered from the victims—the 'outbreak strain'—while the one to its left, beside the weight scale, is the most common strain seen here in the U.S. While a PFGE is not the tool to tell us the quantity of DNA present in bacteria, it's interesting to see that the outbreak strain has far more DNA bands than the strain commonly seen. For that reason, we quantified the DNA from each strain and found the outbreak strain had far more DNA than its counterpart." He looked at me inquisitively. "What do you think that extra DNA is doing?"

"Coding for bioluminescence?"

"Very possibly, and what would be the purpose of that additional DNA?"

"Ask nature."

"Nature might know, but then again, a human might know, too."

"Are you suggesting someone spliced genes for bioluminescence into the outbreak strain of *Aeromonas*?"

"I'm not ruling it out."

"Why would they do that?"

"For two reasons. First, as you know, one or more genes for bioluminescence could have been inserted to serve as a marker to indicate another gene had successfully been introduced into the DNA of the outbreak strain."

"That's true, and the other?"

He frowned. "Someone may have *wanted* us to notice this strain, so they made it glow."

"To set it apart from *Vibrio parahaemolyticus*?"

"Exactly."

I pondered the notion. "That may be reading too much into the situation."

"Oh? Follow me," Brubeck said.

We wound our way to the animal section of the laboratory where we slipped on gowns and gloves. After entering the guinea pig room, we passed cages that we had examined earlier, the animals within healthy as could be. Beyond them, however, in a cage set apart, six guinea pigs lay in pools of blood. The stench of death was unmistakable.

"What *happened*?" I gasped.

"We added an extra group to the feeding study—one comprised of animals that ate chow containing 1 part per billion XK59 along with the outbreak strain of *Aeromonas hydrophila*."

"And they *died*?"

"Yes, from bleeding."

"What prompted you to focus on *Aeromonas*?"

"Lingering doubts about *Vibrio parahaemolyticus* … and the glowing."

"How long did it take them to die?"

"About six hours."

"Did you test them for XK59?"

"Yes, it was present at a concentration of 1 part per million, or a thousand-fold higher than that present in the chow."

"Just as in humans," I whispered.

We moved along the aisle, stopping before more guinea pigs in pools of blood.

"But this is what *really* troubles me," Brubeck said. "These animals ate chow containing the outbreak strain of *Aeromonas* alone."

"No XK59 in their chow?"

"*None.*"

I tilted my head as if to question what he'd said.

"You heard me right: *Aeromonas* alone and no XK59."

"And *that* happened?" I pointed to the bloody bog.

He nodded. "We found XK59 in blood and tissues at a concentration of 1 part per million."

"*Aeromonas* killed them by producing XK59 in their bodies," I said. I thought about the additional DNA Brubeck found in the outbreak strain. "Someone must have inserted the XK59 gene into *Aeromonas.*"

"Yup, along with a gene for bioluminescence. They doctored it up pretty good."

"But, if *Aeromonas* was engineered to produce XK59, why didn't it generate XK59 levels in the shrimp and juice equivalent to those found in the victims and guinea pigs?"

"Because shrimp and the juice lack the co-factors required for XK59 production."

In the silence, I retrieved the list I assembled on Kosta's boat of missives, cryptic codes, and line numbers from *Theogony*. Pointing to the carcasses, I said, "None of this explains the cryptic codes or line numbers." I snapped the paper in frustration.

Brubeck moved to my side to examine the sheet. His eyes widened as he studied it. "Why didn't you show me this earlier?"

"I told you about the codes when we talked by phone."

"But you didn't put it all together as it is here. May I make a copy of this?"

I held it up as he took a photo of the list.

Hurrying off, he said, "I'll be in touch!"

IN MY OFFICE in the Amygdala, I dialed the number Frank Grainger had left with Eve.

"Yes?" came the response.

"Where are you?" I asked.

"In your head."

"I'm not going to play your games, Grainger!"

"They're not games," he replied.

"Why do you hate people?"

"I hate *you*."

"Why?"

"You stole my bark and then claimed you discovered XK59. You didn't discover the protein! I did."

"You *found* the bark."

"I identified the protein before you did."

"I'm sorry, but I missed that publication."

"Arrogant bastard!"

"You left the hospital in Las Vegas against medical advice before I could return the bark."

"You knew how to reach me! I left my address with the nurse who took care of me. She told me she gave it to you. Not only that, but my address and telephone number were in the medical records."

My knuckles prickled. "I was busy."

"Too busy to answer the voice mails I left you?"

I said nothing.

"The only thing you were busy doing was stealing my dissertation."

"You helped advance science," I said. "For that, I commend you; thousands may benefit from your discovery one day."

He sneered. "You don't know the first thing about this protein."

"I described it in the *Journal of Pharmaceutical Metabolism*."

"The article's pathetic."

"In what way?"

"It's riddled with holes."

"Name one."

"There was no mention of spiders."

"I didn't know about them at the time."

"That's my point! You don't have the full picture. I do!"

"Then tell me why Zot didn't bleed. The venom from the spiders is essentially pure XK59."

"You've made progress, I see."

"Answer me! Why did the venom destroy Zot's muscles rather than cause him to bleed?"

"That's for *you* to sort out, Krispix, and you've got until midnight to do so. If you're as smart as you think, you'll answer that question, but if you fail to do so, thousands may die from this protein you claim to be yours."

"What do you mean by 'thousands may die'? Are you threatening to poison more food?"

Silence.

"What do you *want* from me?"

"Amends."

"For what?"

"For stealing my dissertation."

"The past is over; you have an incredible publication awaiting you that describes the spider."

"That's coming, but I still want contrition from you—a written statement in which you declare, first, that you stole my bark, and second, that it was I who discovered the protein. You'll submit that statement to the *Journal of Pharmaceutical Metabolism* so they may publish it."

"You can't be serious!"

"How many people have died from the shrimp so far?"

"Three," I replied.

"That's nothing compared to how many will die if you don't comply."

"I have no proof you discovered XK59!"

"I'll show you my lab records from grad school. They provide the dates for when I returned to Madagascar to get more bark and when I discovered XK59. I identified the protein before you did."

"But you never published your work!"

"Because you scooped me!"

"Life happens."

"And you're a thief!"

"If I send that statement to the journal as you request but they choose not to publish it, what'll keep you from saying I never sent it?"

"You'll send me a copy at the same time."

"And then we're done? No more threats?"

"No, you'll still need to provide correct answers to two questions before midnight to prevent thousands from dying. First, which of the two bacteria, *Vibrio parahaemolyticus* or *Aeromonas hydrophila*, played a more important role in causing the illnesses, and second, why did XK59 produce muscle breakdown in Zot rather than bleeding?"

A pause.

"The clock's running," he noted.

"I can answer the first question now," I said.

"Be careful; I'll take only one answer to each question, and both must be correct; no second chances."

I held my response.

"Midnight's your deadline," he reiterated.

"What happens if I miss it?"

Silence.

"I need more time for the second question!"

"No, you don't. I've given you the answer. It's in the mirrors. I brought you to the nation's capital to find them."

"What do you mean by you brought me to the nation's capital? I came on my own."

"No, I steered you here. I've controlled you like a puppet since you stole my bark."

"This is madness!"

"Not at all. Let's begin with *Natow Pharmaceuticals*. I led you there."

"No way! The CEO approached me in Singapore after I presented my paper there."

"He was just a pawn, nothing more, poor bastard."

"A pawn you killed!" I declared.

"*I* didn't kill him!"

"Then who did? He landed in a dumpster with a bullet in his head."

Grainger sighed. "That's a discussion for another day. For now, the point is I led you to *Natow* because I needed more XK59 after I lost my supply in the lab at grad school. They shut down my lab after I got arrested for a breaking into someone's apartment. But you were good enough to supply me through *Natow* until I could make more."

"Which you used to taint shrimp and Danny Rogers' bottle of *Electric Jolt.*"

"Yes, and which I've now mass-produced should you err in answering my questions correctly."

"And the Pan American Health Organization?" I asked. "Are you saying you led me there as well?"

"I did, by working with contacts in Washington, D.C. to ensure you received an offer too good to refuse. I knew you'd want to continue working with XK59."

"Was Nick Kosta one of your contacts?"

"Again, a discussion for another day. What's important is that I led you to Washington."

"Why?"

"To find the mirrors."

"To hell with your mirrors!"

"Enough tantrums!" he warned. "Jot this email address down." He read it. "Copy me on your statement to the journal and then answer my questions before midnight."

The phone went dead.

3:06 P.M.

An anvil hung from my neck, or so it felt. I viewed eight hours, fifty-four minutes as far too little time in which to meet Grainger's demands.

I rushed to Flagstaff's office and filled him in.

"You *stole* his bark?" he asked.

"I advanced science."

"Whatever. The point is, he's punishing society because you failed to return his bark."

"It appears."

"Then do as he said: Write that statement and answer his questions!"

"You're abetting Grainger!"

"I'm trying to protect the public!" He glanced at his watch.

"What other choice do we have in the eight hours and forty-nine minutes that remain before he unleashes God-knows-what?"

"Apprehend him!"

"We're trying!" He rubbed his forehead. "In the meantime, send that statement to the journal."

3:11 P.M.

I hurried to the lab.

"I was about to call you," Brubeck announced as I entered.

I joined him at a counter where he pointed to a distilled list of data ...

Line 169. Start VP35—3,129
Line 242. Start VP40—4,479
Line 326. Start GP—6,039
Line 326. Start GP—6,039
Line 385. Stop GP—7,133
Line 460. Start VP30—8,509

"You removed the missives, I see," I observed.

"Didn't need them; the action's in the numbers."

"What do you mean?"

He peered at me. "I think we're dealing with something far more ominous than *Vibrio parahaemolyticus* or *Aeromonas hydrophila.*"

"Like what?"

"I find it so alarming I'd rather not speculate until you go back to Kosta's boat to see if you can find more codes in *Theogony.*"

"I recorded them all."

"Are you sure?"

"Yes!"

"Did you go through each page individually?"

"No, I flipped through the text to the stickies."

"Go back and look at each page."

"*Back* to Annapolis? That'll take too much time." I told him about the deadline Grainger had imposed.

"It's critical that you go to Annapolis," he insisted.

"*How* critical?"

He looked away. "Let's put it this way: If those cryptic codes refer to what I think they do, we're doomed."

3:30 P.M.

With the passing of a day—from Saturday to Sunday—the traffic pattern on Route 50 had changed. More cars returned from the beach than went there now that a week of work loomed for most. I slipped into the flow of traffic easily, this time needing no directions to Annapolis. When I reached the city, I pulled to the side of the road to visit the website for the *Journal of Pharmaceutical Metabolism*. Six months had elapsed since my paper on XK59 had published, yet when I came to the journal's website, it seemed like yesterday that I submitted the work.

My fingers protested the email I composed …

Dear Editor:

With contrition, I write to acknowledge an event that transpired prior to publication of my article on XK59. The bark from which I recovered XK59 belonged to a graduate student hospitalized at the University Medical Center in Las Vegas. He never gave me permission to analyze the bark because he intended to do it himself as part of his doctoral dissertation. Despite repeated requests of me to return the bark, I kept it to advance my own research, ultimately submitting the manuscript you published. In doing so, I committed thievery and violated the Hippocratic Oath by inflicting anguish on a patient.

I put my fate in your hands. Should you insist I acknowledge this occurrence to your readers, I will do so in a venue of your choosing. I await your response.

I copied Grainger and sent the email, feeling my integrity vanish with it. Among those who would learn what I had done were colleagues in the lab in Las Vegas who assumed I had obtained permission to analyze the bark. Anger welled within me.

I resumed my way through Annapolis but parked a block from Kosta's house in case the Congressman was home. As I crept along the bushes lining the driveway, I saw a figure inside the house sweep past a window toward the front door. I crouched in fear but the only sound I heard was the occasional knock of a car engine cooling nearby. Through the leaves, I saw a red F430 Spider Ferrari.

With the house quiet, I bolted across the garden into the woods and slinked through the trees to the dock. I examined the boat for signs of activity and, seeing none, snuck aboard. An aroma of perfume greeted me in the salon, the same aroma I detected in Kosta's house when Bjornstad left the library to brew a fresh pot of coffee. I froze and listened for a footstep, a door to open or close, or a voice—anything to suggest I had company. Hearing none, I went to the galley to retrieve the copy of *Theogony* only to find it was no longer there. The small mirror had vanished as well.

Anguished, I searched the cabins but the book was nowhere to be found. With the mission of my trip to Annapolis scuttled, I fled the boat and retraced my steps to the car, but when I reached the bushes along the driveway, I heard the front door open. I dove for cover and watched as a man departed the house. He moved tentatively, taking one halting step after another in a feeble descent toward the Ferrari. When he reached the driveway, he paused for a moment as if to celebrate the achievement. He then opened the passenger-side door and, with great effort, deposited a small suitcase into the car before reaching into his pocket for a paperback book that he left as well.

I held my position as he painstakingly climbed the steps and disappeared into the house. After the door closed, I rose and sprinted to the Ferrari, noticing then the license plate: *TexRep*. With one eye on the house, I opened the passenger door to find the same copy of *Theogony* on the seat that I had perused before. As I grasped it, I heard a woman's voice through an open window of the house: "Nicolas, we must go."

I bolted to the bushes again and made a hasty retreat to my car. Eager to keep an eye on Kosta's driveway, I moved to a woodsy pullover nearby that afforded a surreptitious view. Through low-hanging bows, I kept a watchful eye but allowed myself brief respites to leaf through the book from start to finish in a search for additional cryptic codes. I found none.

Before long, I heard the humming of a boat engine. Peering through the boughs to the Chesapeake Bay at the end of the street, I saw a vessel cutting through the water, its long, sleek hull and flybridge immediately familiar. I reached for a pair of binoculars in the glove compartment and peered through the lenses to make out the name *Down Under* along the bow. On the flybridge, Nick Kosta tended the helm while Sigrid Bjornstad stood beside him.

I started the car to pursue them but stopped short when my mobile showed an incoming call from Giva Bhanjee.

"Jason, I'm in India at Minal's bedside," she cried. "He's bleeding from every orifice."

I envisioned the scene readily from my mice studies and those Brubeck had conducted on the guinea pigs.

"Can Minal talk?" I asked.

"No, he's on a ventilator."

"Is he responsive?"

"Barely," she sobbed, "but at least he recognizes me."

"Can he write?"

"No way! He's too weak."

"Can he lift a finger?"

A muffled voice, then: "He can, but with difficulty."

"Good. I want you to ask him some questions that he can answer by lifting one or two fingers: one for 'yes' and two for 'no.' "

"Okay."

"Ask him, 'Did you know that XK59 comes from a spider?' "

A pause, then: "One finger."

"Good! Next: 'Do you know how XK59 got into the bark?' "

"One finger," she replied.

"Did it leach there from the spider's venom?"

"One finger."

I now had an explanation for why I hadn't been able to find the DNA for XK59 in the bark: because it resided in the spider's venom gland.

Still, the series of 'yes' responses made me wonder whether Chandrapur was lucid or dutifully raising a finger upon command.

"Ask him if he's at home now," I said.

"Don't be foolish! He's in the hospital!"

"I need to make sure he's responding appropriately. Ask him!"

A murmur, followed by: "Two fingers. I told you so!"

"Now this: Did either *Vibrio parahaemolyticus* or *Aeromonas hydrophila* added to the shrimp and *Electric Jolt* serve to increase the amount of XK59 in the victims?"

A pause that seemed to last an eternity. "Yes."

To be sure, I asked: "One finger?"

"Yes!"

Had I been with Chandrapur, I would have shaken the answers from him. As it was, I felt I was chinking at a treasure chest with a toothpick.

"He's getting tired," Bhanjee warned. "We need to let him rest."

"Not yet! Ask him whether *both* bacteria increased the amount of XK59 in the victims."

After a moment: "No."

"Only one bacterium?"

"Yes."

"Was it *Aeromonas hydrophila*?"

No response.

"Giva?" I called out.

"I'm here!"

"Did he answer the question?"

She delayed before saying, "He raised two fingers."

"That *can't* be! Ask him again!"

A moment later, "Two fingers!"

"Is he saying *Vibrio parahaemolyticus* caused the elevated levels of XK59 in the victims?"

A deafening silence, then, "Yes."

"Oh, my *God*!" I fretted. "Can Brubeck be wrong?"

"Who's Brubeck?"

"Never mind! Does he know *how* the *Vibrio* contributed to the elevated levels of XK59 in the victims?"

"No."

"Come *on*! How could he *not* know? Ask him whether he obtained the *Vibrio* used to poison the shrimp and *Electric Jolt*."

"He did."

"Did he get it in India?"

"Yes."

"And he gave it to Grainger?"

"Yes."

"And did Grainger plant it in the shrimp and *Electric Jolt*?"

"Yes."

"Can he tell me what the terms *VP35*, *VP40*, and *VP30* mean?"

"Oh, God, he's having a seizure!" Bhanjee shrieked. "Look what you've done to him!"

"Don't hang up!"

I heard a click, and the line went dead.

"*No!*" I shouted. How could it be that the guinea pig studies implicated *Aeromonas hydrophila* as the cause of elevated XK59 levels in the victims whereas Chandrapur fingered the *Vibrio*?

As for the second question regarding why Zot had died from muscle breakdown after being bitten by spiders, I hadn't a clue about the answer.

I looked out the window and noticed the sun arching over the tree tops.

4:43 P.M.

With Kosta's boat long gone, I called Brubeck.

"I'm confused!" I told him when he answered.

"About what?"

"Whether *Vibrio parahaemolyticus* is truly innocent."

"You saw the guinea pigs! They bled to death after eating chow laced with *Aeromonas* but not with *Vibrio*."

I told him about what I had learned from Chandrapur. "He insisted *Vibrio parahaemolyticus* was responsible for elevating XK59 levels in the victims."

"How could that be?"

"I couldn't get details because he was on his deathbed."

"Perhaps he wasn't thinking straight; what he said makes no sense." Brubeck paused, then: "Are you in Annapolis?"

"Yes, outside Kosta's."

"Did you find his copy of *Theogony*?"

"Yes."

"Were there any more codes you hadn't seen earlier?"

"No."

"Then, we work with what we have, but it'll be in a very different direction from the route we've taken thus far. Do you recall the missive, … *not that rich chimaera*.?"

"From Faulkner's *The Sound and the Fury*."

"Yes, the operative word being *chimaera*. I suspect we're dealing with a combined bacterium-virus here."

"The bacterium being—"

"*Aeromonas hydrophila*."

"And the virus?"

"One of the deadliest in the world."

A lump formed in my throat.

"Marburg or Ebola," he continued. "I'm not sure which."

"Impossible! On Capitol Hill, Muñoz said all tests were negative for viruses that cause bleeding."

"I'm not saying the victims were infected with *actual* Ebola or Marburg virus but, rather, they were infected with a bacterium engineered to contain genetic *elements* from one of the two viruses."

"Wouldn't your tests for hemorrhagic viruses have ruled that possibility out?"

"Not necessarily. We tested the victims for six of the seven genes that comprise Ebola and Marburg viruses."

"What about the seventh?"

"That's where things get tricky. As you know, for the past six months, we've had raging epidemics of viral hemorrhagic fever in Africa due to different viruses—Ebola, Lassa fever, and Crimean-Congo fever. That's unprecedented, and it's put a crimp on diagnostic supplies, including tests for one of the genes common to Ebola and Marburg."

"Which gene?"

"One called *GP*. Got a pen? I want you to sketch the genes so we can discuss them."

"Go ahead ..."

"Start by labeling the schematic *Filovirus genome*. Ebola and Marburg are members of the same family called *Filoviridae*. Then sketch a bar and divide it into seven segments, the number of genes in Ebola and Marburg. The genes share names but differ in genetic sequences, of course."

"Go on ..."

"Now the gene names; begin at the left and move right."

As he read the names, I completed the diagram ...

Filovirus Genome

NP	VP35	VP40	GP	VP30	VP24	L

"As you can see, three of the names—*VP35, VP40, and VP30*—appeared on stickies in Kosta's copy of *Theogony*."

"Why didn't you tell me this earlier?" I asked.

"Because, there was no reason to suspect Ebola or Marburg viruses as a cause of illness. But when the guinea pigs failed to become ill from *Vibrio parahaemolyticus*, I got to thinking about the word *chimaera* and wondered whether we might be dealing with a strain of *Aeromonas* engineered to contain genetic material from Ebola or Marburg that contributed to bleeding."

"But neither Ebola nor Marburg has anything to do with XK59!"

"One step at a time, Jason!"

I pouted. "Are you thinking our strain of *Aeromonas* could have the *GP* gene in it that escaped detection because of a shortage of testing materials?"

"Precisely."

"And that *GP*, once spliced into *Aeromonas*, somehow elevated levels of XK59 in the victims and guinea pigs?"

"It's a hypothesis," he replied. "And a little algebra will help test it."

"*Algebra?*"

"Pull out Kosta's copy of *Theogony*."

I did.

Brubeck: "Tell me whether the entire text has line numbers."

"It does."

"How many lines of text are there in total?"

I flipped through the pages. "One thousand twenty-six."

"Okay, so here's what I want you to do: Get to the nearest scanner and send me the complete text. Once I get it, we'll do the algebra."

5:16 P.M.

I raced through Annapolis to a copy center where I scanned the text of *Theogony* before sending it to Brubeck. As I returned to my car, my phone rang. It was Frank Grainger.

"Good boy. I received the email you sent to the journal."

"Let's call it even," I replied. "Amends made, so no more threats."

"Not a chance! Your admission doesn't erase the years of pain I suffered."

"I gave you contrition."

"It's a good start. All you have left to do is answer my questions correctly."

"Let's keep our skirmish to ourselves. Others shouldn't pay for my mistake."

"*Mistake?* Did I hear you correctly?"

"I seek resolution."

"Which comes from answering my questions. You've got time."

I glanced at my watch. "Under seven hours!"

"Let me help you, then, by repeating the questions so they're crystal-clear: First, which bacterium was the prime disease-causing agent? And second, why does XK59 cause muscle breakdown when introduced directly by the spider whereas bleeding when ingested or injected via needle? Again, failure to answer each correctly by midnight will result in consequences."

"Be more specific."

Silence, then: "XK59 in municipal water systems."

"*Water*?" I repeated.

While I found the idea reviling that Grainger would seed water with a deadly protein, my studies of XK59 had indicated chlorine in concentrations present in treated water would likely denature the protein. But those were studies conducted in a laboratory under controlled conditions, not in the real world of mega water systems.

"I can hear your doubts," Grainger said. "Chlorine and its byproducts in municipal water will inactivate XK59." He chuckled. "But what if I've employed a system such as activated charcoal filters to remove chlorine first?"

I shuddered. "You mustn't do that," I warned him.

"We shall see what happens."

6:19 P.M.

In the parking lot outside the copy center, I called Brubeck. "Did you get the scanned document?"

"Yes."

I told him about Grainger's threat.

"So let's do the algebra, but let me first tie in Flagstaff! I want him to hear our strategy."

After a brief pause, Brubeck returned: "Randy, Jason, everyone on?"

Affirmatives.

"Okay, check your texts," Brubeck said. "I just sent you something."

Two photos appeared …

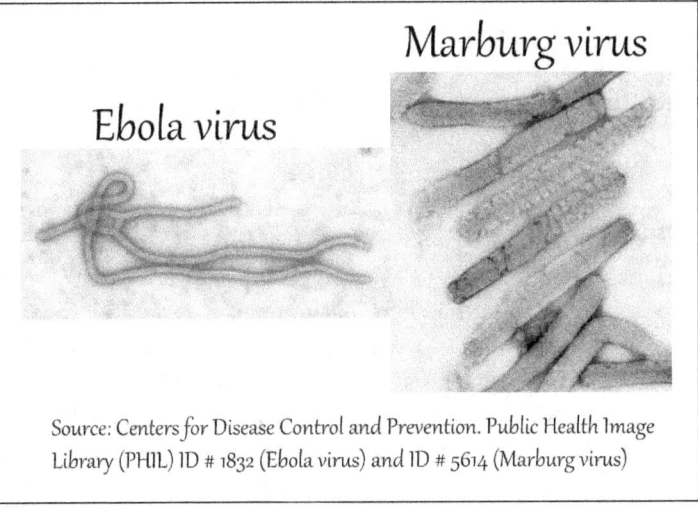

Ebola virus

Marburg virus

Source: Centers for Disease Control and Prevention. Public Health Image
Library (PHIL) ID # 1832 (Ebola virus) and ID # 5614 (Marburg virus)

"Electron micrographs of our two suspects," Brubeck said. "I downloaded them from CDC's website. As you can see, both are tubular viruses that can take on varying shapes. On average, they're about one-seventh the width of a human red blood cell. Each consists of single-stranded RNA and proteins." He paused. "Pull out the diagram of the Filovirus genome for a refresher look."

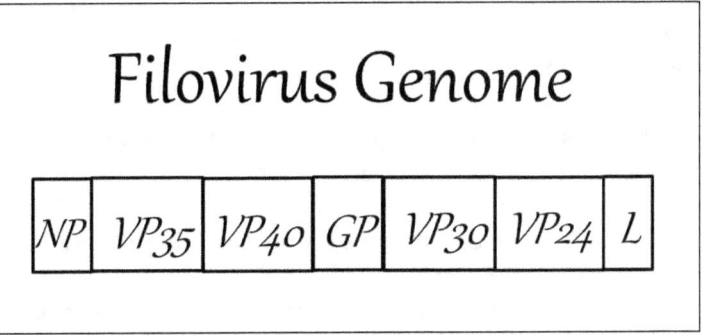

Filovirus Genome

NP	VP35	VP40	GP	VP30	VP24	L

"Surrounding the complex of genes and proteins in the central core of Ebola and Marburg is an envelope bearing spikes."

"Like those on the armor of medieval warriors?" Flagstaff asked. His tone exhibited enthrallment with the concept.

"You can think of it that way," Brubeck replied. "The spikes consist of a sugar-protein mix called 'glycoprotein' encoded by the gene, *GP*. Between the spike-laden envelope and the gene-protein complex is a matrix space where the proteins encoded by *VP40* and *VP24* reside. In a nutshell, that's the anatomy of Filoviruses."

"I'm with you," Flagstaff volunteered.

"Good, so let's move on. As I noted earlier, I suspected we might be dealing with Ebola or Marburg virus in some way because each has four genes that begin with the letters *VP*. When Krispix told me about the line numbers that accompanied the cryptic codes and missives, I wondered whether a mathematical relationship united them in a manner that would reveal which virus was at-play."

He paused, I suspected, to give Flagstaff a respite, but hearing no questions, he continued: "Before we get to the algebra, I should tell you I consulted an online gene bank to see how many RNA nucleotides each virus has."

"Nucleotides," Flagstaff said, "the building blocks of DNA and RNA."

"Right," Brubeck replied, "and the various strains of each virus that exist in nature differ slightly in numbers of nucleotides, but to get the algebra started, we'll use a single strain of Marburg and another Ebola. The Marburg strain we'll consider has 19,112 nucleotides in its genome whereas the Ebola strain has 18,959. My next step was to look up the nucleotide start and stop points for each gene in Marburg and Ebola. So, let's do the algebra."

I readied the calculator on my phone.

Brubeck: "Our starting point is the number of lines of text within *Theogony*. Anyone have that number?"

With midnight less than six hours away, I found Brubeck's professorial style irritating because the running clock allowed time for answers, not questions.

Flagstaff, not to be out done, blurted: "*Theogony* has one thousand twenty-six lines! That's what it says in the email you sent me before this call."

"Correct," I said, hoping to accelerate the pace.

"Okay, so let's turn to Ebola," Brubeck responded. "It has 18,959 nucleotides. Let's assume these two numbers—1,026 lines and 18,959 nucleotides—are intricately connected somehow."

"Why?" Flagstaff asked.

"Just trust me," Brubeck said. "Divide 18,959 by 1,026. What do you get?"

"18.48," I responded, cutting Flagstaff short.

"Right, which rounds to 18.5. So, for every line in *Theogony*, there are 18.5 nucleotides in Ebola's RNA. Before we exploit this relationship, I want you to make some changes to the Filovirus genome diagram. Begin by crossing out the title *Filovirus* and write in its place *Ebola*."

A pause before Brubeck continued: "Okay, now I'm going to give you some numbers that refer to the nucleotide start and stop points for each Ebola gene. Label the top of the bar 'Stop points' and the bottom 'Start points.'"

"Slow down," Flagstaff grumbled. Moments elapsed before he said, "Okay, ready."

Brubeck read a series of numbers I recorded quickly ...

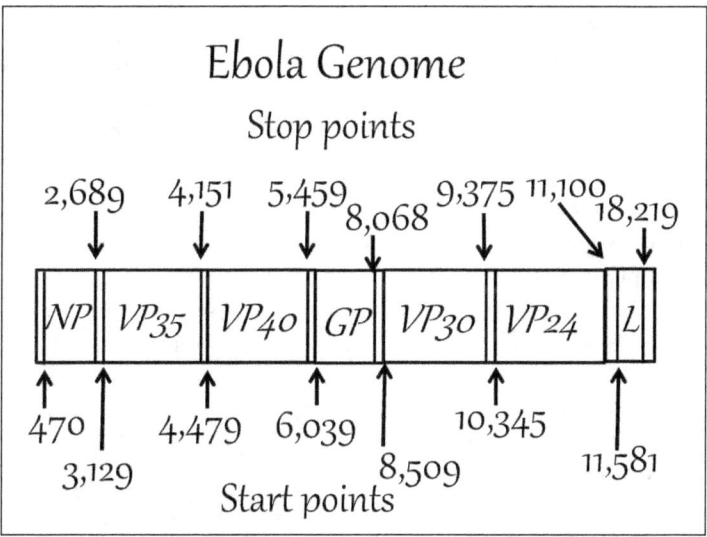

In the silence, I added double lines between each gene and at the beginning and end of the genome to represent "silent" segments of RNA that didn't belong to genes.

"Let's turn now to the missives, line numbers, and cryptic codes," Brubeck said. "Get that list in front of you."

"This is getting complicated," Flagstaff groused.

"Bear with me," Brubeck replied.

I readied the list ...

... your father's cruelty. Line 169. Start VP35—3,129
... of the lovely cheeks, Line 242. Start VP40—4,479
But she, surrendering to ... Line 326. Start GP—6,039
But she, surrendering to ... Line 326. Start GP—6,039
... Power and Strength, Line 385. Stop GP—7,133
... who lives under the earth, Line 460. Start VP30—8,509
... not that rich chimaera.

"Jason, read the first cryptic code," Brubeck said.

"*Start VP35—3,129*," I replied.

"Yes, which accompanies Line 169. The question is: How are line numbers and cryptic codes related? If we turn to the Ebola genome, we see the gene *VP35* begins at nucleotide number 3,129."

"Right," I agreed, checking the diagram with start and stop points .

"Hang on, let me verify that," Flagstaff sputtered. Then: "Okay, I agree."

"So divide 3,129—the start point for *VP35*—by 18.5, the average number of nucleotides in Ebola per line in *Theogony*."

I punched the numbers. "My *Lord*, it's 169!"

"Right, so go to line 169 in *Theogony* and see what it says."

My eyes raced to the site. I read the line aloud ...

Redress for your father's cruelty. After all, he began it by

"The first missive!" Brubeck proclaimed. "What they've done is select a missive from the line number resulting from the division of the nucleotide start point for *VP35* by 18.5."

"How the *hell* did you figure that out?" Flagstaff asked.

"I like to play with numbers."

"Does the pattern hold?" I asked.

"Let's find out, but let me assure you that the algebra for Marburg's *VP35* gene does not bring us to a missive. That appears to sideline Marburg."

I glanced at my watch. "Let's keep moving!"

"Okay, Randy, read the next missive," Brubeck said.

"*... of the lovely cheeks,*"

"And, Jason, the accompanying code?"

I checked my sheet. "*Start VP40—4,479.*" I consulted the diagram of Ebola's genome. "4,479 is the start point for the gene *VP40.*"

I divided 4,479 by 18.5. "The division brings us to line 242," which I read aloud ...

Ceto of the lovely cheeks, and Eurybia, who had a spirit

"Damn, Brubeck, you're a genius," Flagstaff effused.

Brubeck, all business, responded: "Which brings us to the third missive, the only one to repeat itself. What we'll work with here is: *Line 326. Start GP—6,039.*"

I glanced at the diagram. "6,039 is the start point for the *GP* gene."

"Yes, and dividing 6,039 by 18.5 yields line 326, which reads ...'"

Bellerphon with Pegasus. But she, surrendering to

"But why the repeating missive?" I asked.

"Because, we're dealing with a fascinating gene here," Brubeck replied. "Ebola's *GP* gene encodes two different proteins, and while the code for each protein begins at the same start point, the stop points are different."

After whistling softly, Flagstaff muttered, "Holy cow!"

"You see, Ebola's *GP* gene has a built-in editor," Brubeck explained. "On the one hand, it allows the entire gene to express itself to produce a protein 676 amino acids in length called 'glycoprotein' or 'GP.' Alternatively, it can express only the beginning segment of the gene to generate a smaller protein 364 amino acids long called 'secreted glycoprotein' or 'sGP.' The two proteins share a sequence of roughly 280 amino acids yet differ in remaining sequences. This editing ability of *GP* is a feature that clearly distinguishes Ebola from Marburg. Marburg's *GP* gene produces only glycoprotein, not secreted glycoprotein. So, the repeating missive stems from the ability of the *GP* gene in Ebola to produce two different proteins, and it's compelling evidence that we're dealing with Ebola, not Marburg."

"What do the proteins do?" Flagstaff asked.

"sGP, the shorter one, inactivates white blood cells whereas GP helps Ebola invade host cells. It may also attack the lining of blood vessels, contributing to bleeding."

"Give me a moment to sketch something," I said, determined to derive the next missive. I penned a square to represent the *GP* gene and labeled the left-hand border *6,039*, the start point. "What's the stop point for sGP?"

"7,133," Brubeck replied.

"And for the larger protein, GP, the stop point is 8,068, right?" I lifted that number from the stop point for *GP* that Brubeck had given us earlier.

"Correct."

I completed the drawing ...

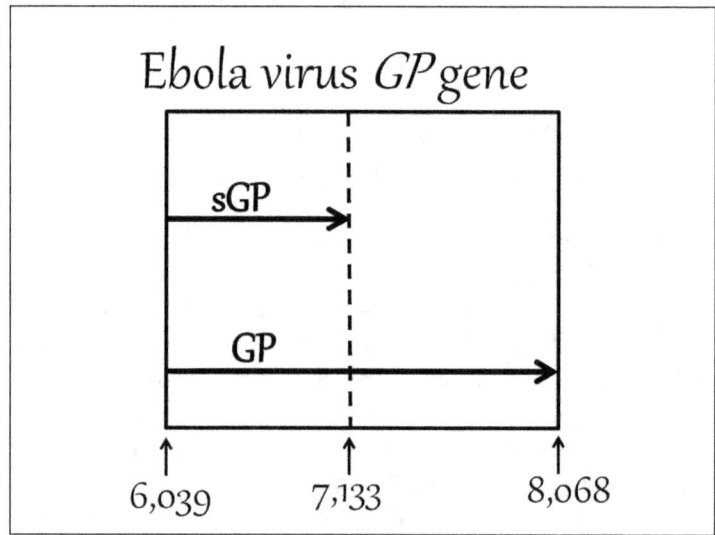

Ebola virus *GP* gene

sGP

GP

6,039   7,133   8,068

"Okay," I continued, "so if we divide 7,133 by 18.5, we get line 385." Once again, I read from the text ...

Power and Strength, outstanding children, who will not...

"That's the next missive," Brubeck observed.

"Which leaves just one more to derive from *Theogony*," Flagstaff said.

From the code, *Start VP30—8,509*, I did the algebra, producing line 460 which read ...

Mighty Hades who lives under the earth,

"Done," Brubeck asserted.

"Done with what?" Flagstaff asked. "None of this tells us how Ebola played a role in the XK59 poisonings."

"I agree," I said.

"You're right, we still need to figure that out, but I doubt the perpetrator of the poisonings would have gone through these machinations if Ebola wasn't involved somehow."

"What we need to do is see if the outbreak strain of *Aeromonas* carries Ebola's *GP* gene," I said. "If it does, perhaps that could explain some of the bleeding the victims experienced."

"We're doing that as we speak," Brubeck replied. "We're sequencing the entire genome of *Aeromonas*."

"When will you have the results?"

Brubeck replied, but the words didn't register because an arm pulled me from the driver's seat of the SUV. A muscular man in a dark suit and sunglasses began dragging me toward a black sedan with tinted windows where a driver waited behind the wheel.

"What are you doing?" I yelled, clutching the cell phone in my hand.

"Shut up and get in!" my captor ordered.

"Jason, Jason, are you there?" I heard Brubeck call through the phone.

7:04 P.M.

What wrestling skills I possess I owe to the farm on which I grew up. At one end of the barn, there was a soupy pit that collected runoff from the stalls where we kept our cows and pigs. It was a collecting pond of the sort one sees in suburban housing divisions, only ours had no cattails or surrounding fence. It held gravy-thick sludge consisting of organic waste—cow excrement, moldy grain, and chicken droppings—that coalesced after storms. My brother built a platform on stilts over the slurry and connected it to dry land with logs. On weekends in summer, we invited friends to the barn for wrestling matches. We played king-of-the-mountain on the platform, a game that honed our balance, agility, and speed. A nearby hose restored our dignity when we fell into the putrid pool.

After my apprehension in Annapolis, I drew on that training to fend off the arms that pushed me toward an open door of the sedan. Spinning, I dug a heel into my assailant's knee, sending him to the ground. With his partner still behind the wheel, I bolted for the SUV knowing that if I reached it, my odds of escape increased for I knew how to drive under duress.

I became intimate with vehicles at the age of eight. Each morning on our farm, I took the wheel of a tractor to haul hay from the silo to the barn. As time passed, I pushed the John Deere to its limits, driving it more like a stock car than a tractor. I set up obstacles around the farm that took me through gullies, over compost heaps, and around sheds. After flipping once, I wore a helmet at my mother's behest, an addition I viewed as a license to drive faster.

I ventured to roadways at the age of fourteen courtesy of a pickup truck my brother bought. Sneaking out at night, I probed its speed and maneuverability. My favorite destination was the high school where I fish-tailed lampposts and dumpsters. Cones borrowed from the football team allowed me to create a course on which I timed myself. At sixteen, of-age finally, I drove in demolition derbies as a hired-hand, using a bait-and-strike strategy to lure opponents before spinning around to demolish them.

I pressed the accelerator now of my car in Annapolis, leaving a cloud of smoke from burning tires. After running a red to enter a thoroughfare, I watched the sedan take pursuit. I wove through cars to distance myself from my adversaries, screeching abruptly at one point into an alley so narrow I barely cleared the fences along each side. Midway through the stretch, I saw the sedan turn after me. Side-swiping a row of garbage cans, I left them littering the pavement. Moments later, as I re-entered city traffic, I looked over my shoulder to see the sedan slamming cans.

The road I joined had four lanes with Victorian homes on each side. Between the lanes, a jogging path coursed along a grassy median which soon widened to host a grove of oak trees. With traffic thickening, I slowed to a crawl. To no avail, I flashed my lights and honked while, behind me, the sedan closed ranks.

Locked in the right lane, I seized an opportunity to move to the left one. Beside me, along the grassy median, I saw a par course with a series of exercise stations. In the distance, beyond the final station, the course ended abruptly at a temporary fence that cordoned off a construction area housing a backhoe, dump truck, and crane.

With the sedan on my tail, I accelerated briefly before jerking the wheel to the left. The move brought me onto the median where I skidded in an arc before striking the final exercise station. The impact dislodged the rear bumper and brought the vehicle to a halt. Behind me, I saw the sedan had made the same turn only to barrel through the fence. A cloud of steam rose from its hood beneath the crane. In the distance, the sound of a siren grew louder by the moment.

I squeezed the wheel and, leaving the bumper behind, muscled my way into traffic going the opposite direction from the one I'd come. At the first intersection, I turned onto a byway that led to Route 50 where I joined a sea of cars that brought me anonymity and solace. It was a short-spanned relief interrupted by a call from the UNIT. I heard Glenn Bird's voice shouting at me.

"You can't escape, Krispix! We're sending another team after you!"

"Your goons will never catch me!" I yelled back.

"The *law's* going to catch you, Krispix. We know about the hundred thousand dollars that was wired to your bank in Bethesda from Antigua. Marcus Calendar traced the transfer."

I moved to the left lane, pressed the pedal, and reached eighty in a fifty-five zone.

"We've nailed the money trail," Bird continued. "Eight months ago, *Starboard* paid *BioVironics* ten million to deal with the seaweed issue but just two days ago Nick Kosta embezzled a million of it into an account in Antigua. It was from Kosta's Antigua account that you received your allotment. Why the payoff?"

I wanted to accelerate beyond eighty but traffic prevented me from doing so.

"Alright, if you won't answer," Bird said, "tell me this: Why did Kosta travel to Ecuador a couple of months ago?"

I said nothing.

"Was it to poison shrimp to highlight the dangers of WAFTA's passage which would promote liberalized trade?"

"Kosta supports WAFTA!" I wailed.

"Why should we believe anything you say, Krispix? You want one thing—money. We know about the cars you're hiding in Vegas: the Lamborghini, Porche, and Corvette. You didn't want the IRS to know about them because you filed for bankruptcy. And then you had the gall to sell XK59 to *Natow* to buy a vintage Mercedes!"

7:38 P.M.

The entry to the UNIT garage was blocked by a hydraulic barrier and retractable barbed wire. I stopped inches from the wire and flashed my badge at the guards. A sentinel emerged from the station and approached me cautiously. "No entry, sir!" he called, maintaining his distance.

I lowered my window and held the badge out to display it more clearly. "Dr. Jason Krispix," I announced. "I'm returning the vehicle."

Eying the damaged rear, he said, "Leave it there, sir. We'll take care of it."

I got out to speak with him. "What's going on? I'm on detail here."

"No longer, sir."

"What do you mean, 'no longer'?"

"Stop there, sir!" the guard said, drawing a gun. "Instructions from Dr. Glenn Bird."

"Are you saying my detail's over?"

"You'd have to ask Dr. Bird."

"How can I, standing here?"

"You could call him, or, if you prefer, I could."

Glancing at the barbed wire, I saw a narrow opening at one end. "Yes, call him."

I waited for the guard to turn before I sprinted to the gap where I hopped over the hydraulic barrier. As I rushed down the driveway into the garage I heard a voice order, "Stop or I'll fire!"

The circular driveway descended steeply, allowing me to escape a bullet that struck the wall behind me. I made several spirals before reaching the level from which I had collected the SUV. After passing a string of vehicles, I swiped my badge in a slot outside the door leading to the Amygdala, but the door remained locked.

Hearing shouts from the driveway, I ducked into a parked SUV and hid on the floor behind the driver's seat. I fumbled for my phone and dialed Flagstaff.

"Jason!" he answered. "Where are you?"

"Closer than you think! Why'd you turn against me?"

"It's complicated."

"I need your help! I've already got enemies *outside* the UNIT!"

I heard muffled voices on the phone before Flagstaff spoke again. "You *broke* into the garage?"

"I had no choice!"

"Stay put!"

He arrived within minutes, joined by Bird and a team of security guards, hands on their guns. I left the car and raised my arms.

"Seize him!" Bird ordered.

The guards approached me.

"Wait!" Flagstaff called. "I think there's been a mistake."

"Randy, what are you saying?" Bird challenged. "We discussed this with Marcus Calendar, remember?"

"I know, but I just talked to Eve Krispix." He turned to me. "What's the name of your bank?"

"Capital National," I replied.

"That's a credit union, right?"

"Yes."

"Located in the District of Columbia?"

"Yes."

"Do you have another bank account?"

"No, only that one."

"He's lying!" Bird shouted.

"I'm not! That's my sole account."

Flagstaff approached me. "That's what Eve said, too, but she received an email from a bank in Bethesda—across the line from D.C. in Maryland—acknowledging the opening of a new account that received a hundred thousand dollar deposit."

"He meant to hide it from Eve!" Bird said.

"If that were true, he wouldn't have opened a *joint* account!" Flagstaff replied. He looked at me. "Did you open the Bethesda account?"

"No!

He addressed Bird: "So, someone opened it for him."

"How could they have gotten Eve's email address to register it on the account?" Bird asked.

"I think I know how," I replied. "It was probably Grainger who did it. He broke into our home in Bethesda shortly after we moved in and stole my diaries. For better or worse, I kept personal details in them."

"But why wouldn't he have wired the funds to your credit union?" Bird asked.

"We opened that account after he broke into our house."

"So, you're saying *Grainger* faked your identity to open a new account?"

"That's my guess."

"That's harder to do than you think!" Bird contested.

He frowned at the chime of his mobile. After studying its

screen, he said, "Shit! McCloskey wants us on Capitol Hill in fifteen."

8:07 P.M.

At the Rayburn Office Building, we went to a lavish suite where Paul DeTrigger met us in the reception area. He nodded at Bird and Flagstaff but offered me a cold glance.

We followed him to a lounge with oak-paneled walls and green-shaded lamps.

"I'll tell Chairman McCloskey you're here," he said.

After we took our seats, I asked Bird, "What about the other Task Force members?"

"McCloskey wanted to see us alone."

I stood to review a series of photos on the wall that portrayed Homer McCloskey's career. The earliest ones showed him standing on the Capitol steps with his freshmen class, delivering speeches, and conducting interviews with the press. Others, further along, featured him with Administration officials, diplomats, and visiting dignitaries, while those at the far end of the wall depicted him as the portly, hunched figure with bushy white hair I had seen on television.

Along an adjacent wall, a collage portrayed his life in Louisiana. In one shot, he stood with a group of smiling children of varied skin colors who held a banner reading, *Support International Adoptions!* At the time the photo was taken, McCloskey had a full head of black hair and a lithe body that allowed him to easily carry a vivacious girl with dark skin and a tilaka on her forehead. From other photos, it was clear he represented a coastal district for in many he stood by the sea. In one, he assisted the crew of a fishing vessel haul in the day's catch, his brawny forearms fairer than those of the men about him. In another, he preened beside a massive marlin hoisted over a dock.

"Like that one?" a gravelly voice asked.

I turned to find McCloskey behind me.

"Quite a catch," I said.

"He was a fighter. I like that quality in fish and men."

He motioned for me to sit, plopping himself into a recliner beside an ornamental fireplace. In spartan style, DeTrigger chose a wooden seat.

"Gentlemen," McCloskey began, "I'm expecting the WAFTA vote to pull me away at any time, so I'll get to the point." He packed his pipe. "It pains me to confirm that one of our own Task Force members—Congressman Nick Kosta—may have betrayed our nation. Thanks to the work of Dr. Krispix here, we learned of the logbook on Kosta's boat that strongly suggests he was the one who mailed the missives. All indications are he had a collaborator by the name of Frank Grainger. I believe Kosta issued the missives while Grainger poisoned the shrimp although I cannot say Kosta is innocent with regard to the poisonings because he traveled to Ecuador two months ago. How and where Kosta and Grainger met, I cannot tell you, but this I assure you: Immediately after the WAFTA vote, we'll interrogate Kosta." To Bird, he ordered: "In the meantime, you're to apprehend Grainger before he carries out his threats, do you hear me?"

"Yes, sir," Bird replied.

"Why not question Kosta now?" I asked.

"I'll grant him these last moments before the WAFTA vote to deal with his constituents. In the meantime, my hope is he will prove himself to be innocent." He shook his head. "It's a tragedy what happened to the man after he divorced his wife of forty years last winter. He hasn't been himself since."

"He's not lacking for company," I said. "Sigrid Bjornstad was with him on his boat in the bay this afternoon."

"Yes, we sent Dr. Bjornstad to be with him. We didn't want him to be alone lest he think about escaping."

"Why did he go to Annapolis on such a busy day?" I asked.

"He finds relaxation at sea."

McCloskey lit his pipe while he examined me.

"When you saw them, was Kosta or Sigrid at the helm?"

"Kosta."

He lifted his brows. "Really? Good for him!"

"Are you surprised?"

He frowned. "Somewhat, because in the past month, he's been acting strange; it's the stress of WAFTA, I trust. Perhaps you noticed the odd way his eyes darted back and forth when we met with the Task Force. It seems to be a new development, as if he were possessed."

"Yes, I noticed those movements," I said. "In medicine, we call them 'nystagmus'—eyes drifting one way before jerking back. It can result from a number of things, including viral infections or taking too much medicine of certain types. It can also affect one's balance, which seems to be the case for Kosta. I trust he's seeing a physician."

"I leave his personal life to him."

The door opened and a wide-eyed staffer poked his head through the crack.

"Mr. McCloskey, the WAFTA vote."

The Congressman stood. To Bird: "Stay close; we may need to regroup tonight."

8:27 P.M.

On the drive from Capitol Hill back to the UNIT with Bird and Flagstaff, I inquired into a matter that had troubled me over the past few days.

"How many Congressmen constitute the Task Force overlooking the UNIT?" I asked.

"Seven, including Chairman Homer McCloskey," Flagstaff replied.

"How evenly are they split by party affiliation?"

"Four are majority members, three minority. Why do you ask?"

"Because, I'm puzzled why only two Congressmen in addition to McCloskey were at the briefing Muñoz and I attended a few days ago and why McCloskey saw us alone tonight."

"It's a hectic time on the Hill," Flagstaff said.

"Perhaps, but did I misinterpret things at that briefing with Muñoz or was Homer McCloskey perturbed with Congressmen Nick Kosta and Peter Shaker?"

"What makes you think he was perturbed with them?"

"You saw McCloskey: He glared at Kosta and Shaker whenever they said anything, turning nice only for Sigrid Bjornstad."

"There's some history between the men."

"What do you mean?" I asked.

"McCloskey, Kosta, and Shaker go back a long way," Flagstaff said.

"In what regard?"

"McCloskey nurtured both Kosta and Shaker through their early years in Congress."

"Fine, but is there something setting them apart now?"

Flagstaff stared ahead in silence.

"Is there?" I asked, pressing Flagstaff.

"Yes," he replied. "WAFTA."

"McCloskey being against it while Shaker and Kosta support it?"

"Correct."

"That's enough,"Bird said, dashing a hand through the air. "Your job, Krispix, is to focus on the XK59 investigation, not on Congressional politics."

8:41 P.M.

Each time I entered the Amygdala, I was reminded of scrub stations outside hospital operating rooms because, as in scrub areas, there were few esthetics in the Amygdala—no photos, paintings, or plants. Dominating the scene were computers, monitors, and screens. Day and night were artificial constructs, a place where circadian rhythms were muted. Without windows, one lost touch with sun and moon, horizon and sky, wind and rain. Data flows controlled the climate: When optic cables set lights aglow signaling new bio-terrorist events, the zone sizzled.

Flagstaff beckoned me to a counter where he handed me a headset. "Put it on and call Grainger."

"Why?"

"We need to track him down. He just eluded a team we sent to capture him."

"Where was he?"

"At his apartment. He leapt from a second-floor balcony to escape. He left behind layouts of water systems in Alexandria, Virginia and Dallas, Texas, although those could have been decoys to mask other sites he intends to poison."

"Poisoning a municipal water system may prove to be difficult if he intends to use the model he deployed with shrimp."

"Why?"

"Because *Aeromonas* and *Vibrio* will die in chlorinated water."

"He could go with XK59 alone."

"True, but to overcome the dilution effect, he would have to dump an enormous amount of XK59 into a water supply, and even if he did, chlorine would likely denature the protein."

"Did you say 'would *likely* denature'?"

"Yes, because no one knows for sure what would happen in a real-life experiment of this nature, especially if he used, as he threatened to do, de-chlorination techniques at the same time he dumped XK59 into the water."

Flagstaff shook his head. "Don't underestimate a guy who managed to poison shrimp with GPS-embedded microchips. From what we can tell, he may have a van full of the protein at his disposal."

"Did your guys get his license plate?"

"Yes, and we've issued an all-points bulletin to snare him. In the meantime, you and I are going to track him down." He pushed a keyboard closer to me. "Dial."

"What if he blocks your tracking program?"

"We'll override the block."

"He could remove the battery from his phone which would make it impossible to track."

"I don't think he would do that because he expects to hear from you before midnight." He donned a headset. "Call him."

I pressed the numbers. The line rang three times before it was picked up but no one spoke.

"Grainger?" I asked.

"Who is this?" the voice replied.

"Jason Krispix."

"Where are you calling from?"

Flagstaff shook his head, circling a hand to keep talking while he worked the keyboard.

"Doesn't matter," I said. "I called to tell you that I'll have the answers shortly."

"They better be correct."

I glanced at Flagstaff. Another circling hand, only more energetic this time.

"I want you to reconsider your threat about poisoning a water system."

"*A* system? *Multiple* systems."

"You're a madman!" I shouted. "Lives are at stake!"

Flagstaff flashed an angry look and swiped a finger across his neck.

I composed myself. "This doesn't need to happen."

"It won't if you meet the deadline."

"How much XK59 do you have?" I drew the words out to buy time.

On the monitor, a flashing "X" appeared on a map of Washington, D.C. and its suburbs. Every few seconds, the map refreshed to show an updated "X." Flagstaff pointed to the mark and mouthed, *That's him.*

"I have what I need," Grainger replied.

"Let's work this problem out together," I said.

"It's *your* problem, not mine; *you* stole the bark."

"And you stole my identity to open a bank account in my name in Bethesda."

"Congratulations, you're rich."

Flagstaff removed his headset and stood, motioning for me to follow suit.

"Gotta go," I said. "I'll have the answers by midnight."

We removed our headsets.

"Did you recognize his location?" Flagstaff asked.

"Yes, he was just across the Potomac River near Reagan National Airport," I replied.

"Yup, heading straight toward a water treatment plant near Alexandria, Virginia."

9:12 P.M.

It might as well have been raining given the humidity outside. As Flagstaff and I left the UNIT, our headlights pierced the night like lighthouse beams. Beside me, Flagstaff pored over a layout of a water treatment plant located just south of the town of Alexandria, Virginia. Before leaving, he nabbed the document from the UNIT library that housed similar constructs for sites deemed to be vulnerable to attack—dams, refineries, chemical depots, and the like. Groaning, he twisted in his seat to hold the plan under the lamp, an awkward position for a man his size. He abruptly set it down to attend his phone.

In the silence, I saw him wince at the device.

"Something wrong?" I asked.

"Text from Glenn Bird. Nick Kosta was hospitalized in critical condition."

"But I saw him on the water just hours ago."

"Perhaps, but Kosta's chief of staff received a call from the Congressman's ex-wife stating Kosta was hospitalized early this evening."

"For what?"

"Terminal brain cancer. It's creeping through his midbrain like a fast-growing vine—vicious and inoperable. He kept the diagnosis secret from all but his ex."

"When was the cancer discovered?"

"About three months ago."

"So that explains it …" I said.

"What?"

"The shifting eyes, the unsteadiness and difficulty climbing stairs; the gauntness; and the sloppy handwritten entries in the log book on his boat."

Flagstaff tucked the phone away and extracted a tiny box of the sort that might hold a ring.

"We found Grainger's weapon of choice," he said, raising the lid. Inside was a transparent sphere the size of a small marble.

"What is that?" I asked.

"XK59."

I grimaced. "Where'd you find it?"

"In Grainger's apartment. It has a starch exterior designed to dissolve in water. We think he has a van full of them." He handed me the sphere. "Be gentle."

I rolled it between my fingers as I drove. Its rubbery exterior reminded me of miniature balls I played with at bath time as a child. I slowed for a moment and held the bead to the control panel. It transmitted light from the speedometer.

"For all we know," Flagstaff said, reclaiming the sphere, "he may have seeded various water plants already."

We passed the Lincoln Memorial and crossed the Potomac River before merging onto a parkway heading south along the waterfront. Above, airplanes in their final descent into Reagan National Airport roared by with landing gear ready to meet the earth.

"How big is this plant we're going to visit?" I asked.

"Big; supplies hundreds of thousands on this side of the river."

"How could he gain access to it? It's gotta be secure."

"Security is relative."

"What part do you think he's going to target?"

"Somewhere near the end of the treatment process where the water leaves the plant." He looked at me. "You can't *taste* XK59, can you?"

"If you're asking whether the public would detect it in the water, the answer is most likely, no, since it's colorless and odorless, and even if it did have a flavor, its concentration would be too low to taste."

"Which raises a question: What would happen to people with wounds that contacted XK59 while bathing or to those with abrasions from shaving?"

"All depends on the concentration of XK59 in the water. If it's high enough, we'd see mass bleeding."

He shook his head. "And hospital overflows."

"You've alerted water plants around the country, I trust?"

"All of them."

After passing the airport, traffic thinned considerably, and I pressed the accelerator. We saw a sailing marina on our left and then a stretch of green with picnic benches along the waterfront. Beyond them, in the river, boat lights bobbed easily in the calm currents of the tranquil night.

We continued through the town of Alexandria before passing the southern loop of the capital beltway. Rather abruptly, the landscape shifted from city to country as the parkway coursed through sylvan lots. After passing signs for *Dyke Marsh Wildlife Preserve* and *Hog Island*, we turned onto a narrow paved road that wound through the woods toward the river. After rounding several bends, I stopped the car suddenly.

"What are you doing?" Flagstaff asked. "We're not there yet."

"I saw a bright light through the woods." I looked over my shoulder. "Down there, by that gravel service road."

Flagstaff leaned across the seat until his face almost touched my shoulder. "Probably moonlight."

I opened my door. "Don't think so. Let's check it out."

We began walking toward the gravel road but stopped short at the sound of a branch breaking. The sound was close enough to make me think someone might jump out at any time.

10:04 P.M.

The light cut through the woods like a blade, forcing us to drop to the ground. Lying in a gully beside the gravel road, we watched the beam probe the space above us. It diced the darkness before melding with the headlights of an oncoming truck. As the vehicle roared past, the ground shook.

Flagstaff inched closer to me. "That truck belonged to the water plant," he whispered.

As we set off again, Flagstaff attended to his phone. "Yes?" he answered softly. He handed it to me. "It's Brubeck."

"Not the best time to talk!" I told Brubeck.

"It's important! I have preliminary results of whole genome sequencing of the outbreak strains of *Vibrio parahaemolyticus* and *Aeromonas hydrophila*. They're intriguing."

"Go on!"

"Nothing unusual about the *Vibrio*—consistent with sequences seen in Bangladesh."

"And *Aeromonas*?"

"Far more DNA than in commonly seen strains. Part of that additional DNA is explained by the presence of a gene for bioluminescence."

"And the rest?" I asked.

"That's where things get interesting. There's extra DNA that we don't recognize, and for that reason I think the outbreak strain is a chimera of some sort."

"Be more specific!"

"I can't yet. We're still trying to figure out what the extra DNA encodes."

"Call me when you get an answer!"

10:12 P.M.

Flagstaff grasped my arm. "Did you hear that?"

I shook my head.

"Clanking!" He looked about. "Follow me."

We crept deeper into the woods, stopping every so often to listen but heard only our breathing and the buzzing of insects. Before long, we came to a clearing where a series of massive pipes ran parallel to the ground before diving underground. Attached to each pipe was a large steel wheel that presumably controlled the flow of water.

"And now?" I whispered, eyeing a sign that read, *Posted: No Trespassing.*

"Let me call the chief engineer. I arranged to meet him at the main entrance up the road, but I'm going to tell him we're here."

As he lifted the phone, I heard a clanking.

"There it is again!" I whispered, pulling his arm.

We went to the end of the clearing, beyond the point where the pipes disappeared underground, and entered an area of tangled vines and shrubs. As we pushed forward, the clanking grew louder, a metal-on-metal sound interrupted every so often by a sullen mechanical hum. After a few cycles, a bright light lit the woods. We dropped to our knees and peered through a bush. Shovelfuls of dirt flew into the air from a ditch. The top of a head popped into sight with each pitch, but not enough to reveal its owner. A grunt accompanied each heave.

From his jacket, Flagstaff produced a pistol. "Moving out," he said.

We slipped around the bush and crossed a short clearing to position ourselves behind a searing bright lamp, a zone impenetrable to the eyes of the man lodged in the ditch. From our vantage, we saw he was of slight build and had dark skin. Beside him, a large pipe had been unearthed for a distance of about ten feet as if it were a prized archeological find. Attached to the top of the pipe was a motorized device and instrument panel from which an electric cord ran to a battery pack that also powered the lamp. A digital display on the panel showed the time and a scale reading *Water Pressure.* Rising from the motorized device was a long transparent cylinder filled with thousands of beads of the sort Flagstaff had shown me in the car. At its lower end, the cylinder tapered to a metal funnel that appeared to have been welded into the pipe.

Flagstaff stepped to the edge of the ditch and took aim at the man.

"*My God,* don't shoot!" the digger cried. He raised his arms. Under the baseball cap were dark eyes that darted anxiously from gun to Flagstaff to me, a nervous triangle carved serially. His skin was smooth and youthful and his teeth immaculate. He looked oddly out of place in his neatly tucked polo shirt, Bermuda shorts, and leather-strap sandals. Sweat rolled from his face to leave his collar damp.

"Who are you?" Flagstaff called.

"Utility worker," he replied. "Fixing a leak."

"My ass!" Flagstaff roared. "Show me your I.D!"

The man lowered a hand to his pocket but his eyes lifted to the lamp. I pivoted to see what had caught his attention but was met with a blow to the back that sent me hurtling into the ditch. I was surprised to see the digger made no attempt to subdue me but, rather, directed his attention to a wrestling match that had begun above us between Flagstaff and a man dressed in black. Flagstaff's pistol lay on the ground beside them.

"Grainger!" I shouted.

He said nothing, sending a flying kick to Flagstaff's groin that dropped the Arizonian to his knees. He fled into the darkness without delay.

Only then did an arm push me aside as a body raced toward a ladder at the end of the ditch. Before the digger reached the second rung, I grasped his shirt and pulled him to the ground, dislodging his cap.

"Minal Chandrapur!" I shrieked. I recognized him from a photo I saw in Bhanjee's condo.

"You're mistaken!" He tried to leap out of the ditch but I restrained him.

"It *is* you! I'm sure of it!" I pushed him against the wall. "You were supposed to be in India dying!"

"According to whom?"

"Giva Bhanjee. She called me to say she was at your bedside in the hospital in Vellore. Because you were so sick, I had her ask you a number of questions to which you supposedly responded by raising one finger for 'yes' or two for 'no.'"

"Bhanjee lied! I left India three years ago and haven't returned since."

"Why would she lie? She's your fiancée!"

"Are you *crazy*? I'd never marry her!"

"You weren't engaged?"

"Of course not! I'd never propose to such a control freak."

"Why would she have said you were to be married, then?"

"Because she messes with people's lives!" He glanced at Flagstaff who kept the gun trained on him. Returning his eyes to me, he added: "She messed with you, too."

"How?"

"She got a hold of some diaries of yours that Grainger had in his possession and read every word of them."

"*Damn*, so that's how she came to know my middle initial was 'E.'" I waited for him to respond, but because he said nothing, I asked: "You are from Vellore, aren't you?"

He nodded. "That's the thing about Bhanjee: sometimes she speaks the truth while at other times she fabricates wildly."

He pointed to my hip. "Check your wallet for your social security card."

I removed it and filed through its contents. "It's *gone!*"

"She told me she pickpocketed you the night you walked the towpath. She took your social security card along with a check in your wallet."

I rifled through the contents again only to find the check I normally carried had vanished. My mind raced to the night I met Bhanjee. I recalled her hugging me twice, once in the parking lot immediately after we met and a second time just before we departed, a duo, I surmised, that allowed her to remove and return the wallet. It explained why the wallet had ended up in a pocket I never carried it in.

"She used your social and check to open a bank account in your name in Bethesda," he added. "She then wired a hundred thousand dollars into it from a bank on the Caribbean island of Antigua."

"If she had a check for my credit union in Washington, D.C., why didn't she wire the funds into it rather than open a new account?

"Because the routing number on the check had worn off in your wallet."

"From what account in Antigua did the hundred thousand originate?" Flagstaff asked.

"One belonging to a Congressman."

"Which one?"

He wrinkled his brow. "A guy with a Greek name. I can't quite recall—"

"Kosta?"

"Yeah, that's it! He used to visit *BioVironics* often a while back with another politician named Homer McCloskey." He puckered his mouth as if he was about to spit. "Damn bitch pilfered Kosta, too."

"What did she take from him?" Flagstaff asked.

"His identity."

"How?"

"She befriended him at a reception *BioVironics* threw to kick off a project to clean some waterway." He frowned. "Don't ask me for details; my job has nothing to do with seaweed."

I waved him on. "How'd she steal Kosta's identity?"

"Following cocktails and dinner at the reception, there was dancing in the lobby beside the aquarium. A band played music with the lights dimmed. After schmoozing Kosta at the open bar, she asked him to dance, and while they did, she stole his credit card and driver's license. She used them to open a bank account in his name in Antigua."

Flagstaff drilled his eyes into Chandrapur. "Why would she have done that?"

"She didn't say, but she claimed she funneled a million dollars into Kosta's account from some funds *BioVironics* received from a group in North Carolina that wanted a waterway cleaned up. I considered everything she told me was nonsense."

"How could she access that kind of money at *BioVironics*?" Flagstaff asked.

"She works all over the firm, including in the accounting office."

"Why is she allowed to float about like that?"

"She's well-connected."

"To whom?"

"To a major investor in the company."

"Who is that person?"

"I don't know, but I believe it's true because she has free rein of the place."

"Why would Bhanjee confide in *you*?"

"I'm not sure it was 'confiding.' She just runs her mouth." He paused. "Okay, perhaps she talks more freely to me than others because of our Indian roots."

I shook my head. "I still don't understand why she would open an account for me and then pad it with a hundred thousand from an account in Antigua."

He said nothing as he peered into my eyes.

With the bright lamp still shining into the ditch, I squinted at him. "Do you have an answer?" I asked.

A look of remorse crossed his face. "Do you gamble?"

I flinched. "What does that have to do with anything?"

"She wanted to create the appearance that you were collecting online gambling profits from Antigua."

"Why?"

"She said your investigation into XK59 was moving too quickly and she wanted to slow you down."

"But *gambling*? How would she know I gambled?"

"The diaries," he replied. His look of remorse deepened. "Do you still gamble?"

It took all I had to restrain myself from charging him. Calming myself, I asked, "What did she mean by the investigation was moving too fast?"

"Your questions were addressing sensitive matters, she said."

"Why would she care?"

"She wouldn't elaborate."

"And what did Frank Grainger have against her?"

The question seemed to surprise him. "What do you mean?"

"He planted spiders in her bed."

"He did?" He chuckled as if amused. "Probably wanted to pay her back for meddling into his affairs."

Flagstaff pointed into the ditch. "Affairs like the one you're involved in down there?"

He nodded. "Among others."

Flagstaff's attention remained on the ditch. "What's in the cylinder?"

"Chlorine beads."

He shot a bullet into the dirt beside Chandrapur.

"Okay, okay! Those beads are filled with XK59. There's a valve set to release them into the water at midnight."

"Dismantle it!" Flagstaff ordered.

Chandrapur removed the cylinder and set it aside.

"Was that Grainger's entire system?" I asked, pointing to the beads.

"No, we inserted an activated charcoal filter at another site upstream to de-chlorinate the water."

"Why did you partner with Grainger?" I asked him.

"Because he helped me become an American citizen. After I filed my application, I was told it was unlikely I'd be successful, but Grainger pulled some strings on Capitol Hill."

"Which strings?" Flagstaff asked.

"He didn't tell me."

"You're a geneticist, aren't you?" I asked.

"Yes."

"So you rewarded Grainger by genetically altering the bacterium, *Aeromonas hydrophila*."

He nodded. "That was easy."

"But Bhanjee told me it was *Vibrio parahaemolyticus* you manipulated."

"She's full of it! That's what pissed Grainger off. She meddled wildly!"

"How did you alter *Aeromonas*?"

"I added genetic material to it."

"What sort of material?"

"Various genes."

"Such as?"

"Ones for bioluminescence."

"What else?"

"A gene Grainger isolated from a specimen he collected in Africa."

"What gene was it?"

"He wouldn't tell me."

A bullet struck the dirt inches from Chandrapur's neck.

"I'm telling the truth! Grainger wouldn't tell me what gene it was. All I know is that it came from a spider."

"You're a geneticist!" I protested. "How could you *not* know what you worked with?"

"I knew only enough to insert the material into *Aeromonas*. Grainger wouldn't divulge anything more, and he warned me not to inquire into it."

"Where did you do the engineering?"

"At a lab Grainger set up outside *BioVironics*."

"Who else knew about what you did?"

"No one."

"Not even Bhanjee?"

"Hell, no!"

Flagstaff leaned over the ditch. "What other water treatment plants has Grainger targeted?"

"I don't know."

Flagstaff lowered himself into the depression. Squeezing past me, he pressed the muzzle to Chandrapur's jaw.

"The metal is cold now but it can turn real hot if I fire this. But, then again, you won't feel it because you'll be dead!"

"Honestly, I don't know!" Chandrapur insisted. "All he said was that he picked another plant, but he didn't tell me which it was."

"Was it in Dallas?" Flagstaff asked.

"Take the gun away! I don't know!"

"How much XK59 does he have?"

Chandrapur pointed to the cylinder. "Multiply that many-fold."

"How could he possibly have produced that much?" I asked.

"That was my job," Chandrapur replied. "He had me producing it for weeks."

I started for the ladder.

"Where are you going?" Flagstaff asked.

"After Grainger."

"The hell you are! He may be armed."

"I don't care." I climbed the ladder.

"Get back here!" Flagstaff ordered.

"I wouldn't go if I were you!" Chandrapur warned. "Grainger's after you!"

10:51 P.M.

In the darkness of the woods, I felt every bush or tree was an ambush point from which Grainger might attack, so I zigzagged to seek the least dense portions. When I reached the gravel road, I sprinted until my throat burned from breathlessness. I felt like vomiting by the time I reached the SUV.

After shutting the door, I saw parking lights appear on a van parked along the paved road ahead. It had a ladder strapped to its roof and a cloud of silver exhaust fumed from its tailpipe. I suspected it was Grainger waiting for me.

I inched forward only to see the van make a U-turn and start down the road. It slowed and then stopped beside me. The driver lowered his window. His cheek was swollen and his nose bloodied. He dabbed a gash on his lip.

"Your buddy is a brute," Grainger said. "He's got the biggest fists I've ever taken."

"I'm surprised you didn't shoot him as you did with Muñoz. Aren't you armed?"

"Should I be?" he asked.

"Not on my account."

"What about you? Did Flagstaff or Bird issue you a weapon?"

I drew back. "You *know* them?"

"I know *of* them, just as I know about that childish *Distamus ab aliis* and *Proprius orbis.*"

"Who's your mole in the UNIT?" I asked.

"*I'll* ask the questions." He glanced into the mirror. "What other water plants do you think I've targeted?"

"Were you concerned we'd abort this one?"

"I've covered my bases." He held up his phone. "I've programmed this to release the beads unless a command is entered to stop them. That way, even if you confiscate my phone, the default is for beads to flow. Unless, of course, you meet the deadline."

"I need more time."

"Not going to happen; I have a schedule to keep." He revved the engine. "And you're coming with me for the first part of it." He nodded over his shoulder. "I'm going to make an about-turn, and then we'll head back up the road together."

"Where to?"

"Somewhere to reflect on things."

I watched Grainger turn and approach from behind. He waved as he passed, and I followed him, close enough to read the bumper stickers on the back of his van …

Global warming—anti-oil conspiracy
Charter schools: keep the government out!

Guns are my civil right

We came to the parkway and followed it away from town before turning onto smaller roads that traversed horse farms and mansions with prim entry gates and white picket fences. The rolling hills gave way to cornfields and wooded lots, and I dropped further back, although never enough to lose sight of the van. After passing a golf course, a field with canvas tents came into view, the domes resembling toadstools in the moonlight. Behind them, a Ferris wheel and roller-coaster stood idle, their frames ghostly white. A billboard announced the complex as a traveling amusement park.

I followed Grainger along a dirt road to a vacant parking lot where the van paused to allow me to catch up. As I approached it, the van took off again, scaling a curb at the end of the lot to enter a field holding the tents. Cautiously, I followed suit, taking care to maneuver between tents, food stands, and trash bins. Here and there, the ground was littered with remnants from the previous day's activities: ticket stubs, spilled food, and empty soda cans. Ahead, the van's brake lights flashed as it stopped before the largest tent in the complex, one with red and white stripes that made me think of a Dr. Seuss book. As with the other tents, it was tethered to the ground, only its ropes were the most massive ones on the facility. A sign before the tent read, *House of Mirrors*.

I shut off the engine, opened the door, and sat still for a moment, dangling a leg from the vehicle. A breeze caught the side of the tent and sent it flapping with the sound of wind whipping a sail. Craning my neck, I peered into the side view mirror of Grainger's van to find the driver's seat empty. Curious to learn where he had gone, I left the SUV but refrained from closing the door to remain as quiet as possible. Although Grainger was nowhere to be seen, I suspected he was watching everything I did.

I walked to his van. A peek through the window confirmed his absence. The interior was cluttered with tools, crumpled news-papers, and empty liquor bottles. Above, on the roof, clumps of mud clung to the rungs of a ladder. I started toward the back to look through the rear window, but before I could do so, my phone vibrated.

"What is it?" I asked Flagstaff.

"Where are you?"

"At an amusement park in the country."

"Oh, the one visiting for the summer. Why are you there?"

"Grainger brought me here. I'm about to meet him in a tent."

"Don't do it! Wait until we send help."

I glanced at my watch—11:09 pm. "No time! Midnight's approaching."

"Then go, but before you do, there's something you need to know: I just heard from Spilbat at the Smithsonian. He shared results from an experiment he ran. He put one of those spiders you collected into a cage with a mouse and watched what happened. It was brutal!"

"What happened?"

"The spider attacked the mouse and then drew back to watch it from a corner. Within a couple hours, the mouse crumpled, at which point the spider began ripping it apart. Before the spider consumed the entire meal, however, Spilbat examined the remnants. He found evidence of massive muscle destruction."

I heard a switch flip, and the tent beside me burst into light. "Gotta go," I said.

"Be careful!"

I approached a curtain at the tent entrance, its fabric wavering in the breeze. Slipping a hand through a gap, I pulled it aside. A small recess came into view with its perimeter lined by rectangular mirrors standing on end like dominos. A mirror omitted directly across the space allowed room for a second curtain to lead deeper into the tent. Above, steel beams held a contingent of lights so bright they warmed the tent.

"Grainger!" I shouted.

"Find me!" he called back.

His voice came from the center of the tent so I started across the recess yet as I walked, I felt cloned by mirrors that multiplied my image. At one point, I swept my arm before me to clear a path but met only air. When I reached the second curtain, I stepped behind the nearest mirror to vanquish the menacing reflections. Reassured I was alone, I pulled the curtain aside to find a space larger than the previous that harbored a strikingly different array of mirrors, ones of varying sizes, shapes, and contours arranged to form tunnels leading in disparate directions. I felt lost as to which to follow.

"Where are you?" I called.

"Over here!"

I entered a tunnel which greeted me with grotesque reflections—a morbidly obese figure; a rail-thin counterpart; and a wiry, waving apparition so distorted I didn't think it could be mine. I stooped to verify the movements belonged to me.

"Are you coming?" Grainger called.

"As I said before, I'm not going to play your games," I answered.

"This isn't a game!"

I passed mirrors that shrank, enlarged, narrowed, and widened me, contorting my form in every conceivable way, even transforming me into folds like the undulating surface of a corrugated tin roof.

"You can't run forever!" I declared.

"Won't need to," he shouted, his voice closer than before.

The tunnel I followed morphed into one lined by tiny mirrors. With lights buried into the floor shining up, hundreds of reflections of my passing form flickered as I moved, making me feel as if I were running rather than walking.

"I kept your bark to advance the field of medicine," I shouted.

"No, you kept it out of greed—to enhance your reputation."

"I wanted to serve the greater good."

"You can't serve by stealing."

Because the tunnel wound back on itself, it seemed to be endless, and I began to feel claustrophobic. I quickened my pace, but as I did, I felt increasingly trapped. I slapped the mirrors and shrieked for a way out. Racing ahead, I saw an opening yet when I reached it, a set of arms threw me to the floor.

11:18 P.M.

"Calm down, Krispix!" the voice said. "And stop hyperventilating."

The beams bore down like tanning salon lights. Glancing at my watch, I realized I had been in the tunnel less than a minute yet it seemed as if years had passed before I reached its exit.

As I clambered to my feet, I found myself surrounded by circular rows of mirrors arranged in amphitheater-style, and from the dome above, I knew I had reached the tent's central arena. A body appeared at my side.

"I threw you down to stop your panic attack," Grainger said. "I want you to be lucid to answer the questions I posed."

I took a deep breath. It served to slow my pounding pulse.

"Follow me," Grainger said.

He led me to a small stage in the center of the tent where, after opening a cardboard box, he removed a model of a tree, a plastic rendition of the sort one sees in architectural designs on public display.

"Show and tell?" I asked.

"Of sorts."

"About what?"

"XK59," he replied.

"I know the story."

"You *don't*." He retrieved a ball of mesh and wrapped it around the trunk. "What do you think this represents?"

"Gift wrap?"

He drew a gun. "Are you going to take this seriously?"

I remained silent.

He tucked the gun into his waist and stroked the mesh. "Imagine this as a spider web on the tree that injured my colleague in Madagascar." He extracted a rubber spider from the suitcase and attached it to the mesh.

"No real ones?" I asked.

"They're available if I need them." He lifted the tree, mesh, and spider. "You see, after you stole my bark, I returned to Madagascar. I went there for two reasons, foremost to retrieve a necklace I'd removed from my colleague after he bled to death in the forest. I'd removed the necklace because I knew it was an heirloom and that his mother would value having it back as a memory of her son. Unfortunately, after removing it, I left it beside a spring where

I stopped to wash myself on the hike back to civilization. So I returned to retrieve it."

"And the second reason?" I asked.

"To get more bark since you stole the piece I loaned you. While there that second time, I discovered the tree that grew the bark had webs encircling its trunk with large spiders on them."

"Of the sort you turned on Zot and Bhanjee?"

"Yes."

"Our expert at the Smithsonian didn't recognize them."

"Because they have never been described before. I discovered them!"

"What do you call them?"

"*Aimofilikos*—Greek for 'bleeders.' "

"Because their venom contains XK59."

"Yes."

"But the venom causes muscle breakdown, not bleeding," I said.

He lifted a hand. "We're getting ahead of ourselves. We have other matters to discuss first."

He set the display down and checked his watch.

"Twenty-nine minutes before XK59 enters a water supply unless you answer my questions correctly," he said. "And I'll accept only one answer for each because I don't want any guessing."

"Very well," I replied, "the first question was, Which of the two bacteria, *Vibrio parahaemolyticus* or *Aeromonas hydrophila*, played the main role in the poisonings?"

"Your answer?"

"*Aeromonas hydrophila.*"

"Why do you say that?"

I told him about the results of the guinea pig studies, adding: "You coerced Chandrapur to insert the XK59 gene into *Aeromonas.*"

"It wasn't coercion! That was a menial task. I would have done it myself had I not been busy with other matters."

"He sought citizenship! You took advantage of him!"

"To the contrary. He needed money and I made it possible for him to earn it by mass-producing XK59." He eyed me intently. "Do you know where the XK59 gene resides?"

"That wasn't one of your questions."

"It is now; answer it."

I glanced at my watch—11:36.

"It's a question that intrigued me," I said, "because I couldn't find the gene in the bark. As a result, I concluded it resided in the pulp and that XK59 seeped from there into the bark."

"Do you still believe that?"

"No, not since I learned the spider's venom is almost pure XK59. I now believe the gene resides in the spider's venom-producing cells."

"But that says nothing about how the bark acquired XK59."

"I think it leaches into the bark from venom-soaked prey. Which leads me to ask *you* a question: Were the webs in Madagascar located on the trunk close to the ground?"

"Yes, but why do you ask?"

"Because, I envision the spider attacking its prey and then pulling it onto the web to tear it apart. With the bleeding that ensues, venom infiltrates the web and bark. All of this takes place near the ground, leaving the rodent's bones and pelt as remnants. I suspect your colleague had the misfortune of falling onto bark that contained XK59 from a recent kill. It made him bleed to death."

"Alright," he said, "since you're willing to entertain additional questions, let's address another one: How did the XK59 gene come to reside in the spider's venom gland?"

A time check: 11:40 p.m.

"No additional questions!" I said. "I'm sticking to our deal!"

From a pocket, he extracted a plastic vial of the sort used to dispense prescription medication and removed a bead similar to the ones that filled the cylinder he and Chandrapur had installed at the water plant.

"Thousands of these are waiting to enter a water supply in another part of the country," he said calmly. "Tell me how the spider acquired the XK59 gene."

We locked eyes.

"From a virus."

"Which one?"

"One related to Ebola," I replied.

A poker face from Grainger.

"You're obsessed with Ebola, aren't you?" I asked. "You littered Kosta's copy of *Theogony* with clues to the virus."

"Clues?"

"Yellow stickies referencing 'VP.' Four of Ebola's seven genes are designated with those letters."

"Name them."

"*VP24*, *VP30*, *VP35*, and *VP40*."

"Go on."

"You used algebra to derive the missives from *Theogony*, first dividing the total number of nucleotides in Ebola virus—18,959—by the number of lines in *Theogony*—1,026—to yield 18.5. You then divided select start and stop points for Ebola genes by 18.5 to identify specific lines within the text of *Theogony* for your missives. The math worked perfectly for Ebola but not for Marburg."

"Sixteen minutes ..." he said.

My mind raced. "And then there were the photos you left in my house of the spider's poison gland. The one showing dots budding from the epithelial cells into the venom sac had to be viruses—a variant of Ebola, I'm guessing."

I stopped short, uneasy with what I had said.

"What's the matter?" he asked.

I shook my head. "I find it untenable that there could be such a thing as an 'Ebola variant,' not to mention that it should reside in a *spider*."

My doubts seemed to energize him. "What if there really is an Ebola variant that differs from Ebola virus as the world knows it?"

"One that produces XK59? Impossible!"

"Nothing's impossible with genetic re-assortment."

"Are you saying you engineered Ebola as well?"

"Fourteen minutes," he observed. "Shall we discuss this further?"

"After I answer your final question!"

"No, let's keep the train of thought." He lit a cigarette and took a long drag. "It's quite simple, really. Nature substituted a gene for *XK59* in place of *GP* to yield the Madagascar variant of Ebola virus."

"How could that have happened?"

"You must consider the extreme environment Madagascar faced eons ago. After the island formed by splitting from Africa, volcanoes erupted for millennia, spewing lava, ash, and gas. Madagascar became a cauldron and in the hellish heat, life forms evolved. My guess is that Ebola virus underwent sequential mutations in *GP* to transform to a gene that encoded XK59."

Another long pull on the cigarette before he asked: "Did your colleagues run tests for the presence of Ebola genes at the envenomation sites on Zot's body?"

"No because his wife aborted the autopsy to have the body cremated."

"But the pathologists could have preserved tissue from the bite sites!"

"Time ran short, allowing them to acquire enough tissue only to test for the presence of the protein, XK59."

He shook his head. "A shame because they would have found all of Ebola's genes there except for *GP*; in its place would have been the gene for XK59."

"If an Ebola variant exists in the spider, how did you avoid becoming infected?"

He grinned. "I can talk about this all night, but eleven minutes remain."

"Explain how you avoided becoming infected!" I demanded.

"I didn't allow the spiders to bite me."

"But with all the work you did on them, how did you avoid inhaling the virus or pricking your skin with contaminated instruments?"

"I took great care after seeing the photo I shared with you—the electron micrograph showing what appeared to be viruses budding from the venom-producing cells. On higher magnification, those dots became multi-shaped tubular viruses suggestive of Ebola. For that reason, I set up a lab of my own to handle such a virus."

"That would have been prohibitively expensive!" I said.

"I got help."

"From whom?"

"That's not the issue right now," he replied. His shoulders slumped. "As it turns out, I don't think all the precautions I took were necessary because I'm convinced this Ebola variant doesn't infect humans since it lacks the *GP* gene, one thought to play a key role in initiating infection."

"But you don't know that for sure."

"True," he agreed, "which is why it will be critical to study the variant in the future. I predict such studies will show the *XK59* gene doesn't have the ability of *GP* to promote infection of mammalian cells. As such, the importance of the variant is its ability to produce XK59, not its potential to infect persons. If that's true, the virus may very well be classified in a group distinct from Ebola."

"But why would the virus take up residence in a spider?"

"Because of a mutually beneficial coexistence. In return for providing nutrients and shelter for the virus, the spider benefits by producing XK59 in its venom which wards off predators such as birds, lizards, shrews, and meerkats."

"But there's no evidence that Ebola resides in invertebrates. Bats have been shown to harbor the virus, but not arthropods!"

"Evolution leads to new bed fellows."

Grainger reached into the box and lifted an alarm clock with French roses on its face and a pair of bells atop it. In addition to having a prominent minute-hand, it displayed a large second-hand embedded in circular form.

"I set its alarm for midnight," he said, placing it on the stage. It showed six minutes remained before day's end.

"And so, the second question," he said. "It's time to answer it."

I looked at the hundreds of reflections coming from the mirrors about us. It was as if a sea of people filled the amphitheater, only they took their identity from Grainger or me. When I turned my head, so did they; when Grainger moved, the sea followed suit. We were two in a multitude of mirror images.

With arms extended, I turned in a circle. "The answer resides in reflections, no different from those about us and the ones produced by the plates on the spider's cephalothorax."

"Ah, yes, the plates!" he beamed. "How glorious they are."

He stepped directly before me to engage my eyes. "It's not unusual for spiders to have distinctive marks on the cephalothorax; consider the brown recluse with its violin-shaped pattern or the black widow with its red hourglass."

He walked to an electrical control box at a corner of the stage. A push of a button triggered a brief buzzing sound before the mirrors about us began moving in circles, alternate rows traveling in opposite directions. The crowd, it seemed, had grown restless.

"Keep talking!" he shouted above the din. "Four minutes, thirty seconds ..."

Through a parched throat, I raised my voice. "Proteins assume three-dimensional conformations that are required for them to perform their functions. If they lose their conformation, they lose their function."

Raising an arm, I asked, "Which hand is this?"

"The left one," he replied.

I approached an oval mirror framed by dark-stained wood that stood on the stage. Placing the same hand before the mirror, I asked: "Now which does it appear to be?"

"The right one."

"Yes," I said, "mirror images."

He pointed to the clock. "Three minutes, fifty seconds ..."

"If you put a left hand into a right-hand glove, would it fit?" I asked.

"Not properly."

"And that applies to XK59. It's fascinating that, in nature, while amino acids exist in mirror-image forms, proteins are built exclusively from amino acids with a leftward orientation—referred to as *levo-* or *l-*. Similarly, DNA and RNA exclusively contain nucleic acids with a rightward—*dextro-* or *d-*—orientation. In contrast, proteins, DNA, and RNA do not exist in mirror-image forms. Except, that is, XK59, which is unique in its ability to take on mirror forms—a leftward and a rightward form. A most phenomenal protein!"

"Less than three minutes!" Grainger bellowed.

"After discovering XK59, I analyzed its spatial orientation and learned it took only one form—a leftward form. But yesterday, in thinking about your second question, I asked the lab at the UNIT to determine the orientation of XK59 recovered from the victims and compare it to XK59 obtained directly from the spider's venom gland."

"What did you find?"

"They were mirror images."

I looked up as the sound of a helicopter became audible, its rotors whirring louder by the moment.

"Ignore it!" Grainger called. "Two minutes, twenty-seven seconds."

He pulled a pair of white gloves from his pocket and, donning them, lifted a pistol from the box, a different weapon from the one still wedged at his hip. Pointing the gun at me, he strolled backwards until he reached a large mirror beside the entryway to the tunnel I had traversed. Tiptoeing, he placed a cell phone on the mirror with its screen displaying the bright red digits of a stopwatch counting down to midnight.

"Two minutes, fifteen seconds," he confirmed.

Heart racing, I continued: "XK59 in the shrimp, *Electric Jolt*, and victims took on an exclusively leftward orientation whereas XK59 in the spider's venom assumed a rightward XK59 orientation."

About us, canvas swayed and lights gyrated from the approaching helicopter. Within moments, the roar tamed to a hum of idling rotors.

"You haven't answered the second question!" Grainger warned, nodding at the phone atop the mirror. "Two minutes left!"

My chest heaved. "In the spider's venom gland, XK59 maintains its rightward orientation but once the protein leaves the gland, it converts to its mirror image, leftward XK59."

Grainger lunged at me and, grasping me by the waist, spun me around. Before I could resist, I felt the gun stab my back.

"Do as I say!" he commanded. "If you disobey, time will expire and the phone will transmit the pre-set command to release hundreds of thousands of XK59 beads into a water supply."

"So let me finish the answer!" I cried.

"No, first extend your arms at waist-level!"

I did.

Pressing himself into my back, he wrapped his arms around mine and inserted the pistol into my hands with his gloved counterparts. "Place your finger on the trigger!"

After I did, he slipped his index finger around mine in a fashion that allowed him to fire the weapon at will. His Rolex glimmered in the light.

"You can see the time remaining on my watch," he said. "One minute, forty seconds."

"Let me talk!" I pleaded.

"Have you fired a gun?"

"Only bee-bees," I replied.

"Okay, so I'll help you. You're going to shoot something."

He aimed at a mirror in a row halfway up the amphitheater. "Pull," he said. When I hesitated, he pressed my finger and a mirror exploded. "That's what's happened to my life," he explained. "It shattered."

"From what?"

"Demands."

"Whose demands?"

He shifted our aim to another mirror. "Shoot!"

This time, I pulled the trigger, causing shards to fly.

"One minute, thirteen seconds!" he announced.

"Grainger, are you there?" a voice called from the tunnel.

It had a familiar cadence, but with the whirring mirrors and idling helicopter, I couldn't place it.

"You want to know who made the demands on me?" Grainger asked, brushing my ear with his lips.

"No, I want to answer—"

"Not yet! I'm going to tell you who placed the demands on me!"

We pivoted toward the tunnel, bringing into my peripheral vision the digits on the cell phone: … *0:57* … *0:56* … *0:55* …

Another swift arc pointed the gun directly at the entry to the tunnel. A figure emerged within it just as a bead of sweat rolled into my eye. As I tried to extract my finger from the trigger, Grainger squeezed it, firing the gun. It sent a man falling to the floor at the tunnel entrance, blood spurting from his temple.

… *0:36* … *0:35* …

"*That's* who placed the demands on me!" Grainger raged. "He forced me to poison the shrimp! It was blackmail—nothing less— and I'm not going to live under his tyranny anymore!"

… *0:29* … *0:28* … *0:27* …

I craned my neck. "That's Congressman Homer McCloskey you killed!"

"No, that *you* killed," he replied, his voice eerily calm. "Your fingerprints are on the gun." He squeezed my arms to keep a lock on me.

... *0:19* ... *0:18* ...

"Let me go!" I shouted, reviled that I'd murdered someone, a Congressman, no less.

"Finish your answer!" Grainger ordered.

I struggled to regain my thoughts. "The mirror forms of XK59 act differently," I began, voice cracking.

... 0:17 ...

"Whereas rightward XK59 in the venom destroys muscles, leftward XK59 blows holes in blood vessels."

... 0:14 ...

"That's the answer!" I shouted.

A jerk of the arms.

"Shoot!" he screamed.

With the phone atop the mirror our target, Grainger squeezed my finger. The bullet missed.

... 0:11 ... 0:10 ...

"Dammit, keep your arms still!" he shrieked.

Another shot, another miss.

... 0:07 ... 0:06 ...

"Give me the gun!" he yelled.

As he tried to transfer it from my hands to his, the weapon fell to the floor.

"*Shit!*" he cried, groping for it.

With his stooped figure beside me, I watched the digits.

... 0:03 ... 0:02 ...

I went limp as the mirrors revolved around us. Lifting my hands, I covered my eyes.

A shot rang out as the bells on the alarm clock rang.

Spreading my fingers, I saw the cell phone had disappeared while, beside me, Grainger knelt with the gun frozen in his hands, its barrel still pointing in the direction of its target.

"Did you get it in time?" I cried.

He nodded and stood. After collecting his box, he started for the tunnel.

"Wait!" I called.

He stopped without looking at me.

"What demands did McCloskey place on you?"

"Too many to count," he replied, stepping forward.

"Tell me this, then: Why did you splice the *XK59* gene into *Aeromonas* when you simply could have stocked shrimp with sufficient XK59 to cause bleeding?"

He faced me. "You're an unfeeling bastard to switch the subject to XK59 after committing cold murder." He motioned to McCloskey's lifeless form.

"*You* squeezed the trigger!"

He let a chuckle run its full course. "Poisoning the shrimp outright wouldn't have allowed me to accomplish my goal."

"Which was?"

"To teach you about XK59. To do so, I devised a lesson plan. The first lesson entailed having you figure out that the level of XK59 in the victims exceeded that in shrimp."

"That was easy."

"Right, which allowed you to progress to lesson number two: deciphering *how* the levels of XK59 came to be much higher in the victims than shrimp. That's why I brought the two bacteria, *Vibrio parahaemolyticus* and *Aeromonas hydrophila* into the picture."

"Because one produced XK59 in the victims."

"Correct, and I suspect you needed the clue I provided to identify the correct bacterium."

"You mean, the glowing *Aeromonas*," I said.

"Right."

"But your references to 'VP' in the cryptic codes didn't help. They made me think *Vibrio parahaemolyticus* was the culprit."

"I couldn't make your lessons too easy!"

"And the algebraic link of the missives to Ebola virus," I added. "I needed help with that, too."

"Which led to the final lessons: The original source of the protein and the dual actions it exerts."

He looked at the corpse. "You should thank me for teaching you because McCloskey wanted me to kill you in Ecuador." He stooped and, inserting the tip of a boot into one of McCloskey's trouser pockets, said: "Take a look. See the ivory?"

I knelt beside him and peered at a handgun with white grip panels.

"I bought that gun in Africa and gave it to McCloskey as a gift. He used it to kill the CEO of *Natow Pharmaceuticals*."

"*McCloskey* shot him?" I blurted. I recalled Bird's revelation in the UNIT the first day I went there that someone had shot the CEO, but to learn now that it was McCloskey who killed him seemed inconceivable.

"Yup, and tossed him into a dumpster after killing him." He wiped his brow. "*I* didn't want to poison the water supply; McCloskey did, and he forced me to do it. All I wanted was contrition from you in the form of an admission to the journal, and I got it."

"Why did McCloskey insist on poisoning the water supply?"

"It was targeted retribution," Grainger replied. "He felt two congressmen betrayed him by switching their stance on WAFTA in recent months. Each had promised him a vote against the bill only to reverse course. He took it personally after years of helping the two through their political careers."

"Which congressmen are you referring to?"

"Peter Shaker and Nick Kosta. That's why he chose the two particular water systems to poison—one in each of their districts."

"So the other plant was in Dallas, Texas?"

"Yes, Kosta's district."

"But horse trading is standard in Congress; votes switch all the time. What was different about WAFTA that led McCloskey to harm fellow citizens?"

"He felt WAFTA threatened his dearest constituents: Louisiana shrimpers. By eliminating tariffs on imported shrimp, he was adamant WAFTA would harm the shrimpers irreparably by making imported shrimp far less expensive than far higher-quality Gulf Coast shrimp. He felt obliged to help the shrimpers, particularly after a crew member from a shrimping vessel lost his life years ago while unsuccessfully trying to save McCloskey's wife in a boating accident. His bond to shrimpers became as strong as steel following those deaths."

He paused as if to regroup his thoughts.

"But let's be clear," he continued. "McCloskey was no angel. He was a mean son of a bitch, often commanding others' lives, including mine."

"What gave him that power over you?"

He looked at me with indecision. "I'm not going to get into that; all I'll say is that I disobeyed him by saving your life. He wanted me to kill you in Ecuador but I refused to because I wanted to confront you face-to-face to teach you about XK59."

"Why was that so important to you?"

"Because, I felt enormous pain after getting rejected from medical school two years in a row. When I contacted some of the schools to ask how I could improve my application, I was met with arrogance on their part. And then you stole my bark as I pursued a PhD, a theft I considered yet another strike from the medical community. The combination of these events made me want to show a physician that I knew something about science and that my degree wasn't inferior to yours. That's why I strove to become your teacher."

"I can understand that, but what did McCloskey have against me?"

"Lots of things, but I'm not going to speak for him." He looked at the dead body. "All I'll say is that he had me bring you here so he could have the pleasure of using that ivory-handled gun to kill you." He grinned. "You see, I've been your teacher *and* savior."

"Hardly a savior; you killed three men—Muñoz, Zot, and McCloskey."

"This one deserved it." He pointed to the Congressman. "He wasn't even man-enough to stick around. Several weeks ago, when he realized the 'ayes' would outnumber the 'nays' on WAFTA, he made plans to flee the country after the vote."

Glowering at McCloskey's body, he said, "We ended that plan, didn't we?"

He kicked McCloskey's head and disappeared through the tunnel.

Day 8.

12:15 A.M.

On the ground beside me, the weapon I used to kill McCloskey lay like a link to a jail cell.

I listened as the helicopter revved its engine. It sent the canvas into a renewed frenzy, testing the integrity of the tent. While my instincts told me to abandon the place before it collapsed, the sight of McCloskey's body beckoned me to remain, not out of reverence but, rather, morbid fascination. During my years as an internal medicine resident, I had seen death often on hospital wards, but in the final three years as a hematology fellow, such encounters had become less common. McCloskey's skin had yet to assume the sallow look of death, and while a pool of blood had clotted beside his head, it still glistened. A dented soda can and a half-spilled bag of popcorn nearby served as a makeshift memorial.

My eyes returned to the gun. Eyeing a stray paper napkin, I wrapped it around the weapon and picked it up. I took it with me as I made my way through the tunnel to the exit. Outside, the moon had painted the earth in a silver sheen, a softer hue than the solitary mechanical light that blipped from a helicopter speeding into the horizon. Silence soon engulfed the land, and I rushed to my car to find it alone now, Grainger's van having disappeared.

It was then I noticed I had missed a call while I was in the tent. A message from Spud informed me that Eve had gone to the hospital in labor. Could I get there as fast as possible?

I sped out of the parking lot with one hand on the wheel and the other working the phone. Anxious to avoid meeting a vehicle from the UNIT, I left the main road at the first opportunity to pursue a narrow country lane. Only when the amusement park was well out of view did I stop to address the hospital operator who answered my call.

"Labor and delivery, please," I said.

"I'm sorry, it's after-hours," she replied.

"My wife, Eve Krispix, is in labor! Can I at least get an update on her?"

"One moment, please."

I waited as the call transferred.

"Dr. Krispix," a voice announced. "Let me get your father-in-law. He's around the corner."

An eternity passed before Spud came on the line. "Jason! Eve's in surgery."

"*Why?*"

"The baby was in distress. Eve's having a caesarean section."

"*My God!* I'm on my way!"

I threw the phone down and pressed the accelerator, following the bucolic lane over hill and dale until I came to a thoroughfare that eventually joined the beltway. My phone rang as I reached 80 miles per hour.

"You're a hard man to reach!" Alistair Brubeck said.

"I've been busy."

"So I've heard."

I let up on the accelerator to take an exit toward Washington, D.C. "What do you want?"

"We found some interesting documents in Grainger's apartment, including a draft manuscript on XK59 Grainger recently wrote. I don't know if he submitted it for publication, but it's fascinating."

"What does it say?"

"It describes the role copper plays in determining the three-dimensional structure of XK59. The spider's hemolymph is rich in the element, which explains the insect's blue-green colors. The highest levels of copper are in the venom glands where an enzyme packs each XK59 molecule with a pair of copper ions. Loading the second atom is a high-energy proposition—kinda like pushing a car uphill—but once it's in place, the second atom switches XK59 to a rightward orientation which, in turn, allows XK59 to destroy muscle fibers. After the venom has been ejected, a copper atom falls out, and without a mechanism to reinsert it, XK59 reverts to a leftward orientation which causes bleeding. That explains why the *XK59* gene in *Aeromonas hydrophila* caused bleeding: without sufficient copper around or an enzyme to push a second atom into place, XK59 remained in the leftward form in humans, shrimp, and *Electric Jolt*."

It also explained why Grainger's colleague in Madagascar bled to death after striking the bark: XK59 deposited there from a spider's previous kill had reverted to the leftward form that caused bleeding.

AFTER HANGING UP with Brubeck, I wound my way through Washington, D.C.'s Virginia suburbs before reaching Chain Bridge. Halfway across the expanse, with no cars in sight, I stopped and rushed outside to a handrail. Below, in the moonlight, I saw a swirling current rush by boulders lining an inhospitable channel of the Potomac River. It was a spot referred to in a recent news clip about a kayaker who lost his life there after capsizing and striking a rock.

Trembling, I lifted an arm and pitched the gun that killed McCloskey into the center of the river. It struck the water without a splash. With a set of headlights appearing behind me, I returned to the car and drove off with arms shaking.

It was less than two miles from the bridge to the hospital, and when I arrived, I rushed to the lobby but before I could reach the elevator, a muscular figure threw an arm around me.

I could say nothing, let alone breathe.

He dragged me to a room around a corner where Flagstaff, Bird, and a bald man with a ruddy face and double chin occupied a table.

"Sit," Bird said. He motioned to ruddy face. "Have you met Dr. Molder?"

"No, I don't believe—"

With a second look, I recognized the man as a partner in the obstetrics practice where Eve received her care. At a visit a month earlier, he had popped his head briefly into an examining room.

"Actually, we have met," I corrected myself.

"Hello, Dr. Krispix," Molder said. He stood to shake my hand. "I did Eve's C-section tonight."

"How is she?" I blurted.

"She's fine, as is your baby girl."

"A *girl!*" I exclaimed. "I want to see her!"

Excitement welled within me for Eve had insisted—old-fashioned as it was—that we learn the baby's gender at birth and not a moment earlier.

"We'll let you see her shortly," Bird interjected. He turned to Molder. "Go on, doctor."

Double-chin: "There's been a small complication, however," he said.

My chest heaved.

"Eve has tuberculosis."

"*What?*"

"Before the surgery, we told her we could biopsy the breast mass after we delivered the baby while she was still under general anesthesia. I just heard from the pathologist that there wasn't a trace of cancer in the biopsy, but it's loaded with *Mycobacterium tuberculosis.*"

"*TB?*"

"Yes, a tuberculous mass; quite unusual these days."

"But, she hasn't had a cough!"

"This isn't the typical form of tuberculosis that involves the lungs. Rather, it's a rare presentation as a solitary breast mass. There are a handful of reports in the literature that describe such presentations, mostly in patients living in developing nations." He looked at me inquisitively. "Has she traveled anywhere interesting recently?"

"Indonesia six months ago; she volunteered there for battered women."

His cheeks lightened. "Oh, so that's where she picked it up!" He stood to leave. "We've consulted an infectious disease specialist to get her treated."

I stood, too, but before I could take a step, Bird reached for my arm. With his free hand, he placed a call.

"What do you want?" I asked him.

Into the phone, he said: "We're ready." Then, to me: "Your detail's over. We need to debrief you."

"No more Latin phrases!"

"Bear with us," Flagstaff said. In the artificial light, his eyes had turned from hazel to coal and the wrinkles across his face deepened, as if a rainstorm had washed the desert, etching arroyos into the earth.

Reluctantly, I sat, and as I crossed my legs, the door flew open to allow a half dozen uniformed men to file in with a civilian at the lead whom I recognized from newspaper photos.

"Jason Krispix," the man said, taking a seat across from me. "Gaylord Williams, Secretary of the Department of Homeland Security."

He looked like a man with a mission, every movement of the eyes decisive and bold. His dark hair was slicked back with nary a wayward strand. He was a warrior through and through, an executive now perhaps, but with roots steeped in combat. Nodding coldly, he said, "Congratulations on becoming a father."

"It's hearsay until I see my child," I replied.

The warrior turned to Bird. "Let's not keep the man long."

Bird shifted to a seat before a laptop and projector. On the wall before us, a grainy video started that depicted the opening of a tunnel framed by mirrors.

"Hey, I was there!" I said.

Two sets of extended arms appeared, one enveloping the other, as a gun pointed toward the tunnel. An older man made an appearance through the tunnel. The image jerked, and then the man fell to the floor.

Bird froze the frame. "Why'd you kill McCloskey?"

"*I* didn't kill him! Frank Grainger forced my finger to pull the trigger!" I pointed to the image. "How'd you get that?"

"Your shirt," Bird said. "Left collar ... "

I removed a small bead from it. "What is this?"

"Mini-cam. We saw everything live."

"I planted it," Flagstaff explained.

"When?"

"In the woods near the water treatment plant; we had to know where you were at all times in case we separated."

"Well, it was Grainger who pulled the trigger," I huffed.

"We believe you, son," Williams said from across the table. "McCloskey had it coming, anyway. He'd become a pain in the ass ever since WAFTA heated up. Now we know he was a traitor as well." He shook his head. "I *told* the President not to give him the UNIT but McCloskey prevailed."

I felt like a guest on a Sunday politics hour of the sort McCloskey had attended routinely. "Where would you have placed the UNIT?" I asked Williams.

"Under my department, of course! *We* do security; Congress does politics."

"A Washington turf battle …"

"*Everything's* turf in this town, son," he snapped. "One grabs what one can."

"Is that what this has been—a turf grab?"

"If it turns out that way, so be it."

"Another notch for you—having the UNIT transferred to Homeland Security."

He smiled.

"A costly way to get turf," I added. "Fifteen ill throughout the U.S., including three deaths, not to mention my colleague, Muñoz, and the owner of the shrimp farm in Ecuador."

His face reddened. "Don't give me that shit, Krispix! All of this happened because McCloskey orchestrated the poisonings with the help of a pervert, Frank Grainger. It's a damn good thing my folks kept an eye on them because things could've been worse."

My voice cracked. "Why didn't you stop them?"

"We didn't know McCloskey's plan of attack, only that he had an ill-defined intent to use your protein to inflict harm somehow."

"Or was it you *wanted* him to commit a heinous act in order to claim his turf?"

He moved his head side-to-side as if to say, maybe yes, maybe no.

"My *God*!" I whispered. "Sick!"

"Welcome to Washington, son."

"*You're* responsible for putting me through this hell! It wouldn't have happened had you acted preemptively! I'm just a pawn!"

He snickered. "You're being far too generous with yourself: You're no pawn; you're a speck of dust on a Washington chess board."

"Save the quote for a journalist," I said.

Williams turned to Bird who, in response, displayed a slide on the wall. It was a photo showing the remains of a sedan totaled from a front-end collision. Through the broken windshield, one could see a man's head propped atop the steering wheel, forehead dented, face bloodied, hair bedraggled. "Who do you think that is?" Bird asked me.

"No idea."

"He was a former recruit, a guy like you who we brought to the UNIT on detail. He was a radiation engineer. Unfortunately, he made the mistake of contacting a reporter after he completed the detail to talk about what he did at the UNIT—this despite instructions not to do so. The day after the reporter called the UNIT to corroborate the story, a Mack truck ran into the engineer's car. Poor soul's looking up from his grave now."

"And the reporter?"

"He's alive, although he'll be living in a nursing home the rest of his life." The next slide showed a middle-age man in a hospital gown slumped in a wheel chair. He had a vacuous look as drool ran from his mouth.

"Reporter?" I asked.

Bird nodded.

"What did you do to him?"

"Let's just say he sustained a brain injury."

"You guys design Hallmark cards on the side?"

"Yeah, here's one of them." The next slide depicted a man whose face had been ripped from its head and dangled below the chin by a pedicle of skin. With the front of the skull severed, glistening frontal lobes were visible while beneath them, two eye balls hung limply over the back of the throat, one of the eyes bloodied. Incredibly, the faceless figure sat upright, conscious, it seemed.

"Wanna hear the story?" Bird asked.

"No," I replied.

"Note the crimson-colored eye. Ironically, crimson has symbolized fire and power for centuries. This guy abused his power." He paused. "Another recruit with loose lips."

"So you blew off his face?"

"A bomb did; somehow found its way into the dashboard of his car and exploded." Bird turned off the projector. "You'll avoid such mishaps with silence."

I shook my head. "Which President was it who said, *America is a shining city upon a hill whose beacon light guides freedom-loving people everywhere?*"

Williams beamed. "That was Ronald Reagan, but, don't kid yourself, boy. Nine-eleven changed everything. Freedom's second to security now." He stood. "A pleasure, son." His delegation prepared to depart.

"Wait, what about Grainger?" I asked him.

"He's dead." He rubbed a lapel. "We shot his bird down over Pennsylvania after he refused to ground it. You'll see stories about mechanical failure felling a copter over the Poconos."

"*Grainger* flew the helicopter?"

"Yup, I'll give him this: he was an excellent pilot—fixed- and rotary-wing aircraft. He commandeered McCloskey's helicopter at gunpoint outside the tent and sent the pilot fleeing in that decrepit van."

I WAITED FOR Williams to leave, but he planted himself before the door with his sentinels sandwiching him. Odd, I thought, that a man as busy as he should remain, especially given the hour. I tested his resolve.

"When did McCloskey and Grainger meet?"

"About a decade ago," he replied.

I probed further.

"Where?"

"Here in town."

"How?"

"It's a long story."

"Fine, another time." I pushed my chair back.

"Sit!" Williams ordered, pointing to my chair.

He waited until I'd taken my place. "They met after Grainger committed crimes against humanity in Africa."

I drew back.

"Yup, with Interpol on his back, he snuck into the U.S. over the Canadian border."

"What did he do in Africa?"

"He went there initially to work as a mercenary pilot after earning his wings in the Serbian military. Ferried arms merchants about and then sold his soul by dropping a barrel bomb on Nigerian villagers battling the rebel group, Boko Haram."

Flagstaff stirred. "Not entirely proven, sir, that Grainger piloted the aircraft."

Williams lanced the Arizonian with his glare. "There's video showing Grainger entering the cockpit on the day the bomb was dropped and testimony from a worker in a hangar who saw Grainger load the bomb and pilot the aircraft solo."

"He may have been framed," Flagstaff said. "Someone may have spliced the video and purchased the witness."

Williams dismissed the rebuttal. "One thing's indisputable: With authorities on his back, he slipped into the U.S. His first stop was Fargo, North Dakota where he purchased a new identity."

" As 'Frank Grainger,' I presume."

"Affirmative. He also had plastic surgery there."

"As he seems to do," I huffed. "The guy's a chameleon."

"A calculating chameleon: He kept the tattoo of the pistol in his sternal notch to see whether you'd recognize it."

"Yes, he wanted us to meet eye-to-eye," I acknowledged.

"In any case, from Fargo, he went to Louisiana because he liked the idea of Mardi Gras. He matriculated in a small college in New Orleans where, during his senior year, he won a private sitting with McCloskey after raising a thousand dollars from campus donations. He was a master at separating people from their money."

"McCloskey offered him a job after college," Bird interjected.

Williams waved him off. "Right, which Grainger accepted."

"Doing what?"

"Raising money, what else? But not in the usual way: He sold weapons on the international market. And he was phenomenally successful at it."

"Why did he leave Washington?"

"Because, while working for McCloskey, an uncle of his in Serbia died from a snake bite. The death prompted Grainger to apply to medical school, but he couldn't get in because his grades and test scores were too low."

"And McCloskey couldn't throw his weight around to get him in?" I asked.

"Apparently not, so Grainger pursued a PhD in biochemistry. He focused his research on venomous invertebrates."

I stood again. "Look, I really want to see my wife. I've heard enough about—"

Williams snapped his fingers at me. "You've heard *nothing* yet, Krispix!"

Reluctantly, I sat.

Williams: "As you know, during grad school, Grainger was arrested for breaking into an apartment to reclaim a laptop someone allegedly stole from him. The university withdrew his financial aid, forcing Grainger to turn to McCloskey for help. The Congressman complied by paying for Grainger's room, board, and tuition. He also funded a second trip to Madagascar so Grainger could collect an heirloom he'd left there that belonged to his colleague who bled to death there."

"And to get more bark," I added.

"Right, because you stole his first piece."

I scowled at him.

"McCloskey even paid for Grainger's prosthetic leg."

"So, what turned the two against each other?" I asked.

"WAFTA, principally."

He waited to see whether I might connect the dots.

I couldn't.

"McCloskey was a master at reading tea leaves, son, and when he saw the leaves pointing to passage of WAFTA, he devised a strategy to defeat it."

"By poisoning shrimp with Grainger's help."

"Thatta boy!" he beamed.

"Did Grainger demur?"

"Big word, son … *demur.*"

"Did he?"

"Very much so, which led McCloskey to play his trump card: He threatened to turn Grainger in to Interpol if he didn't carry out the poisonings."

"Why did Grainger reveal his past to McCloskey in the first place?"

"The Congressman was his insurance policy in case anyone exposed him by some means; doesn't hurt to have a powerful man on your side."

"So, McCloskey had a noose around Grainger's neck."

"One that became even tighter when he brought the Swedish psychiatrist, Sigrid Bjornstad, onto the Task Force: He wanted Grainger to know that he had a direct link to the International Criminal Court if he needed one."

"But Grainger complied; he poisoned the shrimp. So, what set the two apart?"

He pointed at me. "*You* did!"

I frowned.

"You published your paper on XK59!" His face reddened. "Which we told you not to do!"

"What does my paper have to do with anything?"

"It cost McCloskey a fortune, or so he thought."

"How?"

"As Grainger neared the end of his studies, McCloskey loaned him several hundred thousand to set up a lab to turn XK59 into a pharmaceutical drug. He made the loan on the condition that Grainger repay it in-full along with a share of royalties from XK59 sales. But you pulled the rug out from under them by publishing your paper, leaving Grainger hopelessly in debt. That's why he made Grainger take a job at *BioVironics*—to begin repaying him."

"Why *BioVironics*?"

"Because McCloskey was a principal investor there and held sway over the place."

"*He* got Grainger the job?"

"Yup, because he wanted to keep Grainger on a tight leash to carry out orders like poisoning your friend, Danny Rogers."

"Son of a bitch!" I hissed.

"I feel for your loss."

"No, the only thing you feel is the amount of political turf under your feet. The more the turf, the better you feel."

"Look, I'm sharing facts, one of which was McCloskey's connections to *BioVironics*. It was a connection so close he convinced Kosta to earmark a bill that funneled ten million dollars from *Starboard* to *BioVironics* to clean up the waterway."

"Yeah," I harped, "a million of which Giva Bhanjee embezzled into an account she opened in Antigua under Kosta's name. Grainger told me about that."

Williams' face turned red. "She embezzled more than that! She cleaned out everything left in the waterway account! And that was McCloskey's plan all along."

"Huh?"

"McCloskey adopted Bhanjee when she was a little girl. He did that shortly after his wife died in a boating accident in the Gulf of Mexico. He raised his little girl alone. They worked hand-in-glove since."

I turned to Bird. "Did you know Bhanjee was McCloskey's daughter?"

"You think we're stupid?" he scoffed.

"Why didn't you tell me?"

"It was confidential."

"But I risked my life by meeting her alone a few nights back!"

"You published your paper," Bird replied. "You're a loose cannon. We couldn't tell you everything."

"Had you heeded our advice not to publish it," Williams added, "McCloskey may not have gone off the deep end. Instead, you stroked your ego and McCloskey poisoned shrimp."

"Wait!" I said. "Are you telling me you knew about McCloskey's dealings with Grainger and XK59 way back when I submitted my manuscript to the journal?"

"No, not that far back; a lot of what we've learned came to our attention more recently. The point is, we knew no good would come from your paper."

I moped.

"You're not alone, son," Williams said. "McCloskey screwed others with his XK59 folly. Take Dudley Zot, for example, the shrimp farm owner. He had Grainger infest Zot's bed with those deadly spiders because Zot began asking tough questions about the glowing pond. And another poor soul: the former CEO of *Natow Pharmaceuticals*. McCloskey hired the guy solely to acquire XK59 from you so he could poison shrimp."

"And then there's Kosta," Bird interjected. "McCloskey screwed him for supporting WAFTA by picking a Greek theme for the missives and then framing Kosta as the missives' sender."

"But the logbook on Kosta's boat," I protested. "It showed Kosta motored along the waterway on the dates the missives were mailed."

"That was McCloskey's doing," Williams said. "He used Kosta's boat to dispatch the missives to make it look as if Kosta had done it."

"McCloskey mailed the missives?"

"Every one of them. He accessed the victims' addresses from UNIT records."

"Unfortunately, that's true," Flagstaff added. "We received the names and addresses of the victims as part of our surveillance system."

"So much for microchips in shrimp being the mechanism of identification of the locations of victims," I said.

"Yup, but McCloskey was clever," Williams noted. "He suspected the presence of the microchips would deflect attention from the possibility of an insider being involved."

"How did he get Kosta's boat?"

"He told Kosta they could mend their differences on WAFTA if Kosta lent him the vessel. The two shared a passion for the sea."

"So Kosta wasn't the algebra whiz who derived the missives?"

"Nope, that was Grainger."

"But wasn't McCloskey worried about being gone from Congress during the lead-up to the WAFTA vote?"

"Grainger flew him back and forth from the Waterway as needed. The guy was an amazing pilot. He flew to Ecuador twice, first to taint the shrimp and to plant microchips in them through a special feed, and then to meet you and Muñoz there."

"What about Kosta? Why did he go to Ecuador two months ago?"

Williams frowned. "Poor guy was desperate; he was seeking alternative treatments for his cancer after his doctors here told him they'd run out of options."

"How did you learn all of this?" I asked.

He pointed to the bead on the table I removed earlier from my collar. "Mr. Flagstaff, care to comment?"

Flagstaff leaned forward to collect the bead. "Looks like an engorged tick, doesn't it?" He paused to examine it. "We planted a bunch of these on Bhanjee's clothes after our security team saw her leave Charles E. Oxford's business card on your doormat a few days ago. We thought it strange that she should do that."

"We also bugged the hell out of her condo," Bird added. "Phones, computers, even the walls. And believe me, the babe was a talker. We learned more about her than we cared to, including who she slept with."

"Minal Chandrapur?"

"Among others, although he was only a convenience-sleep. All she wanted was his money."

"Did she have a true lover?"

Williams smiled. "Wouldn't you like to know?"

I glanced about the room. "I'm sure you know; you have all the other answers."

Williams' smile morphed to a grimace. "Not all of them; we're missing one."

"Which one?"

"Where Bhanjee is right now; she got away, dammit!"

"Can't her lover help you with that?"

"Possibly," Williams replied. "Every man has his Achilles, including Charles E. Oxford."

"Oxford was her lover—the CEO of *BioVironics?*"

"Correctomundo, although it's been an on-again off-again tryst. She's tempestuous. Like Flagstaff said, she left Oxford's business card on your doormat."

"That makes her 'tempestuous'?"

"In this case, yes; she did it because the two had a spat. She didn't think Oxford was spending enough time with her."

"How would leaving a business card on my doormat punish him?"

"It raised the profile of his company at an awkward time," Flagstaff said, "just when *BioVironics* had popped onto the radar in the form of *Electric Jolt*."

Williams flashed a look of disdain. "She had the guy wrapped around her finger. Although he's married and has three kids, she expected him to be at her beck and call. But I'll tell you this: We're gonna skewer the guy until he tells us where Bhanjee went."

I stared at a wall as I processed what I'd learned, not just there, but during the previous week. I envisioned a game where balls dropped through a maze of pins to find the bins below. Each event of my detail bounced frenetically before grounding in my psyche. The mental pings made me oblivious to the sounds of moving chairs and shuffling feet.

By the time I came to, I was alone in the room.

IN THE SILENCE, I rubbed my eyes. Through the haze of fatigue, I looked about to find the chairs pushed back helter-skelter in an otherwise abandoned room.

I took my exit and went to the lobby to catch an elevator but stopped short when I saw the up button had been inked into a crimson eyeball. A pair of markers lay on the floor beneath the buttons, one black and the other crimson. They rested on an envelope with my name printed across it.

I lifted the envelope and opened it. Inside was a single sheet with the following words …

> *Sorry for falsely charging you about hiding the Lamborghini, Porche, and Corvette from the IRS. I just learned you surrendered them to the U.S. Government.*

Pivoting, I expected to find Glenn Bird behind me, but no one was there.

I forsook the elevator for the stairs and began trekking to the fourth floor. When I reached the maternity ward, I found it quiet save for monitor beeps and subdued chatter from a mother and father being transferred from a delivery suite to their room. I felt remorse for missing the birth of my own child and a key week in Eve's life, a time during which I had hoped to accompany her in the sojourn from couple to parenthood.

I strolled along the hallway looking for the room number Spud had given me, using the moments to assuage my trepidation about becoming a father. Could I—would I—be the loving, caring, doting man I wanted to be? Could I—would I—release the past seven days for the promise of a new life?

I stopped before the shut door to Eve's room.

Gingerly, and with a wobble in the legs, I took a deep breath and pushed it open.

The answer to the questions, I assured myself, was an affirmed, *yes*.